# SEA BABIES

Tracey Scott-Townsend

Wild Pressed Books

First Edition

This is a work of fiction. Name, characters and events are the product of the author's imagination. Any resemblance to actual events or persons, living or dead, is entirely coincidental.
The publisher has no control over, and is not responsible for, any third party websites or their contents.
Sea Babies © 2019 by Tracey Scott-Townsend.

Contact the author through their website:
www.traceyscotttownsend.com
Twitter: @authortrace
Cover Design by Jane Dixon-Smith

ISBN: 9781916489639
Published by Wild Pressed Books: 2019
Wild Pressed Books, UK Business Reg. No. 09550738
http://www.wildpressedbooks.com
All Rights Reserved.

No part of this publication may be reproduced or transmitted in any form by any means electronic, mechanical, photocopying, recording or otherwise, without the prior permission of the copyright owner.

*In memory of Dad,
and the Alexander Wilsons of historical Glasgow.*

# SEA BABIES

# PART ONE

The heating broke in our flat and we
didn't leave the bed for longer than five
unfed minutes. Have you ever used a hairdryer
under billow-sheets for warmth?

**From *Love in the Cold* by Nick Conroy**

# 1

*Edinburgh, April 1983*

NEIL INCHES FORWARD blindly. His eyes are covered by the scarf – tied perhaps too tightly around his head. Lauren's painfully sensitive to every change of his expression. And the fact he put his trust in her.

'It pinches,' Neil says. He reminds her of Jesus. When she first laid eyes on him in the university canteen he looked just like Ted Neeley in her favourite film: brown shoulder-length hair with a hint of gold – intense blue eyes and tanned skin. He was even wearing a cream linen grandad shirt. Biblical. And leather sandals, in *March* (although, admittedly, it was a warm spring). She saw his friends as his disciples.

Lauren wants to be Mary Magdalene – the one in the film. She pulls him by the hand up Granny's Green Steps, both of them slightly out of breath. Grasping his warm fingers in hers she's corporeally aware of the slight tremor in Neil's hand. His pulse tipper-taps into her palm.

The slope below the castle is bathed in yellow light. Underneath, in the shadows of Kings Stables Road and Grassmarket, an evening chill descends but up here it's still warm. Squeezing her eyes shut she experiences a flickering aura from the warm sun on her face. Tendrils of hair lift off her forehead in the calm breeze. Above, in the castle grounds, bagpipe music whirls upwards. All the surrounding sounds had mingled together when she could see, now each is distinct and separate: the pipes, the rush and blare of traffic from the road below, the chatter of local accents and unintelligible tourist babble. Footsteps, bumps and nudges from passers-by on both sides, moving up and down the steps. Lauren and Neil are stranded in the middle of it all.

Seagulls cry in the air between the castle and the streets below the hill. She forgets to open her eyes and stumbles, feels a sharp pain as her shin catches on the next step. Neil flips her round to face him. He's not wearing the scarf anymore. Without warning he covers her mouth with his and she can't breathe. *There couldn't be a better way to die.* She doesn't struggle, allows their lips to meld. When he peels away he glances as if surprised at his hands, falling from her shoulders. Lauren gasps for air. Neil's arms hang at his sides now. Her scarf lies on the ground at his feet.

'Sorry.' It's the first time they've kissed.

Her cheeks flare hot, she's been waiting for weeks for this, and yet, already, the responsibility's terrifying. It was only a game. And she was supposed to be in control.

'You took the blindfold off.' She blinks.

'Good job I did, someone had to be there to catch you.'

The intensity's too much. She turns and indicates across the slope of grass, out beyond the furthest picnicking couple. A lone reader at the far edge is surrounded by a pile of books. Dips her hand repeatedly into a bag of crisps, inserts each into her mouth as though into a slot machine.

'Look.' Lauren forces words from her closed throat. 'Rabbits. Hopping about everywhere. They're not bothered by the people at all.'

'Hopping *aboot*. Aye, they're *no* bothered, are they?'

'Ach, shu' up,' Lauren gives him a slap with the flat of her hand, tension released. 'I canna help how Ah speak, any more than you can, Mr *Caenada*. Mibbe we should both take elocution lessons, eh?'

'No' a chance,' Neil mimics again. 'Dinnae ye dare, Ah love you just the way ye are.' She slaps him again. 'Okay,' he says, 'I'll stop now. Anyway, I'm actually Scottish too, you know, on *both* sides. My mother came from around here. My father's grandpa was called Donald MacDonald. He emigrated from the Highlands. Or maybe it was the Western Isles? Anyway it was in the eighteen-forties.'

He's babbling. And she's paying scant attention to his heritage. She bends instead to snatch the blue scarf from the ground, holding the end of it between the tip of her finger and her thumb. She watches it reach into the breeze like a flag. *I surrender.* Neil takes her other hand and presses it between his. She senses trembling in his whole body. He *is* human. The moment catches and breaks, along with his voice. 'Come on.'

She lets go of the scarf and the wind snatches it. They watch it fly above the serrated-edged turrets and rooftops. He holds her hand while they climb over the rail and then he pulls her down onto the grass beside him. They balance on the edge of a slope above the city and he fits his arm around her, as if she's the missing piece of his puzzle.

# 2

## *Ferry to Stornoway, September 2016*

THE LEADEN FEELING in my belly isn't worth the brief pleasure of the chips I've just eaten. I tug the sprigged A-line top down again, feeling self-conscious. Sheena came shopping with me and helped me choose it for my leaving do at the Centre. *Ye look awright in it, Miss W.* she said. That was what she called me in public, or just *Miss*, even though the rest of the kids called me Lauren (or Loz). *Honest, ye do.* I don't think she really believed I would leave and now I can't believe I meant to leave her behind, either.

As I smooth down the top again I notice a prominent stain, baked beans. Picking at it with my thumbnail only grinds it in further. I sorely miss Sheena – she would have told me. I now see other splashes of alien colour on the pale cotton, some dating back to breakfast. My eyesight's getting worse. How long have I been walking around decorated in my own meals?

I push the plate aside and stare at the muted light reflecting off the rough surface of the sea. When I turn away from it my vision's blurred. With my eyes closed momentarily, the jumble of sounds from the cafeteria separate into distinct parts. Voices speaking different languages, the muffled bark of a dog from the dog-lounge behind me – the resonant thrum of the ferry's engine. When I open my eyes again the sounds mingle back together.

Salt seeps in through the loose sealing at the edges of the window, crystalizing on the glass. I put on my reading glasses then remove them again and wipe them with a clean corner of my lunch napkin. Searching for my Kindle I have to swallow hard when my fingers meet the textured surface of the cover. Sheena made it for me as a leaving present. Buttons and a string of tiny embroidered flowers from the scrap box, sewn on with her careful hand.

'Why do ye have tae leave, Miss?' She'd reluctantly handed me the gift at a poke in the back from Angel Wilde, her social worker-in-training. 'Do ye really ha' tae go? Disnae bloody leave me wiv *that* Mincey heid.' She frowned over her shoulder at poor Angel, still in her probationary year. The trainee's cheeks flooded red.

It wasn't like Sheena to show how upset she was. When I said yes, again, Sheena asked me once more if I could take her with me. Tried the tactic that had worked well when she was younger – did I not like her anymore? I promised I did and explained that it was time for me to move on. She was one of the reasons. It's unprofessional to get too involved. She continued to pester, trying to keep her swag, but I could see the panic in her fluttering eyes. 'Ah fucking hate it here, Miss, ye know Ah do. You wiz the only reason Ah kept on coming here and now you're leaving. It's not fair.'

But I'd already made my decision. I thought she was grown-up enough, should have seen that her panic was genuine.

I wish I hadn't been so stubborn. Everybody leaves those kids. When they're old enough to have babies the whole vicious cycle will begin again.

I picture a slightly older Sheena with a toddler in her arms, the little girl's skin the colour of toffee just like in the photos of Sheena before she messed up her face with piercings, and her neck with a foster-brother's attempt at a home-made tattoo.

The ends of my fingers go numb from pressing so hard into

Sheena's handiwork.

I'll lose myself in my book. I wish I could revisit my young self and give her some helpful advice like Henry in *The Time Traveler's Wife*. He also visits his future wife when she's only six years old, and gently eases her into the difficulties to come. If I could go back in time there are several things I'd put right. One would be rectifying the biggest regret of my life. Another would be to stick with Sheena – see her through her troubled adolescence. If I could only pay her a visit when she was six, take her away before things got too bad. In the end I gave Sheena five years, which is more than I gave the other special girl in my life.

The ferry lurches. My fingers tighten on the Kindle and I concentrate on breathing steadily in, out. It feels cold in my head. But I read doggedly on and before long I've re-immersed myself in the story of Henry and Claire. I'm at the part where Claire sees Henry in the present for the first time when she's visiting the –

*What the...?*

Some *bawheid* is sliding into the seat opposite me. Plonking a couple of mugs of tea down, both of which overspill slightly when a galumphing foot nudges one of the metal poles that hold up the table. For God's sake, it's not as if there are no empty tables around. I deliberately came in late for this reason. *I just wannae be alone.* So I keep my head down to avoid acknowledging whoever's squeezed himself (I catch a glimpse of a hairy hand) into the bench opposite me and is now, I notice from the corner of my eye, pushing one of the mugs towards me.

*The cheek o' it!*

Despite my struggles to avoid looking, something about the hand nudges my consciousness.

The thing that's familiar. A scar, running across the back of it from the bottom knuckle of the forefinger to just below the wrist bones.

*It's Neil's scar, the one I gave him with the vegetable knife shortly before we split up.*

# 3

## *Edinburgh, August 1983*

LAUREN DOESN'T GO home for the summer – Christmas was enough. She needs to accept she'll never fit in with that family. Her maw wouldnae notice whether she was there or not, and her da calls her a 'dosser'. The sense of freedom, having made her decision, is exhilarating but coupled with guilt. It's the first summer ever that she hasn't visited Granny Mary in Ireland. And there's Meg to think about – six years between them, but Meg's the sister she's closest to. Lauren had a letter from her asking where she was. And hasn't Bridie become so appallingly thin? But Bridie would never talk to Lauren, it's Pepe she looks up to. Pepe's probably encouraging her not to eat. It ought to be Maw worrying about them, not Lauren. Maw's face has slackened from the pills. Nothing bothers her anymore. *They wouldn't thank me for interfering.*

She's known she was different ever since Michael once let on that Da wasn't really Lauren's da. Said it was only fair Lauren knew that Da set Maw up with the *heid bummer* at McLeod's in some dodgy deal. To rid himself of a debt. And with Brendan a baby in his cradle at the time. But Kathy came and shushed him before Lauren could get any more out of him. Kathy isn't the eldest but everyone calls her their second maw.

Lauren calls Edinburgh home now. She lives in a squat, works evenings at a busy pub in Grassmarket and lunchtimes in a pizza place on the Royal Mile, even busier than usual because of the festival. The money she earns doesn't last long – she spends it mostly on vintage dresses. Her expanding record collection. And books.

Neil's stayed in Edinburgh for the holidays, too. His relationship with his da is strained. He works at the hospital pharmacy and rents a room in a third-year flat from an older student who's backpacking – funnily enough, in Nova Scotia.

'Come 'n live at the squat with me.' Lauren urges. 'Plenty of room.'

'I'm fine where I am, thanks.' Neil's frown deepens. 'I don't mind paying for hot water and a comfortable bed. I'm surprised you've stuck in that place as long as you have. I mean, I know *you* take proper care of your personal hygiene and all that, but you've got to admit some of them are a bit whiffy, Lauren.' He strokes her hair to counter the insult but she can't help feeling tainted. She smells of wood smoke – to save on bottled gas they cook on a campfire in a cleared patch of garden and heat water on it. They wash themselves and launder their clothes in a tin washtub Markus found half-buried by the vegetable patch. There's an outdoor shower made from a bucket with holes in the bottom, filled from another bucket that hangs on a pulley. The shower enclosure is built from pallets. Neil doesn't trust Lauren's housemates not to spy on her. She wishes he wasn't so guarded – Ted Neeley's Jesus wouldn't have worried about things like that.

He untangles his hand from her hair, fishes a note from his wallet to pay for their coffees. When he lets her go she can't help catching one of her chin-length curls and taking a sniff. The scents of earth and fresh air. There are worse things, but Neil's accustomed to antiseptic and latex gloves.

Something's bothering him. Maybe another letter from his brother.

'Come on then.' Neil has no idea what she's been thinking about. Sometimes it confuses her that they can be so separate, each within their own mind. He bends to kiss the side of her forehead and reaches under the chair for the hessian satchel with a faded *I Love Canada* stamped on the rough fabric. The first thing his mother bought when she emigrated as a teenager. The bag's all sharp corners, bulging with medical textbooks and notebooks. Lauren's brought a novel out with her but she probably won't read it. She has her Walkman, loaded with a Paul Young cassette (*No Parlez*) and with Genesis' *And Then There Were Three* as a spare. But she may just go to sleep on the grass of the Meadows, her favourite place in Edinburgh. She pulls an elastic band from the pocket of her circular skirt, blooming with huge white flowers on a navy background, bunches unruly curls up at the back of her head and welcomes air onto her neck. She stands, looking up at Neil. The sun blazes behind his head, painting him a halo. Music from *Jesus Christ, Superstar* drifts through her mind and she shivers. He tilts his head with an enquiring expression. 'You're blocking the sun,' she says, rubbing her arms.

'Sorry,' he steps aside. They hold hands, waiting to cross the road. *I have been promised...* 'Watch out,' Neil pulls her back from the curb, from a near-miss with a car turning from a side road. *A land of my own. Superstar* came out when she was hitting adolescence. The sexiness of *that* Jesus, so physical. The sultriness of the actress's version of Mary Magdalene – all opposites to the teachings she'd grown up with. *Close your eyes and relax, think about nothing.* Neil stirs up those feelings, a new religion to fill the hole left by the other one. Neil carries his pain inside and she wants to soothe him as she'd once wanted to soothe Jesus in the film, wanted to *be* Yvonne Elliman.

Obviously, Neil isn't Jesus. But the halo's stuck now.

# 4

## *Ferry to Stornoway, September 2016*

I CAN'T PULL my gaze away from the scar. A cough jams my throat. One of the mugs of tea approaches me, driven across the table by a finger of the hand that bears the scar.

The liquid in the cup rocks from side to side with the sudden cessation of its forward trajectory, in tandem with the boat, rocking on the grey waves.

A moment of dizziness. *The sea alive with the screams of people adrift, drowned children washing up on beaches.* I move my head to dislodge the thoughts but they don't go. If chance had placed me in a different life, it could have been me in a flimsy dinghy with nowhere to land. *It's not my grief to bear but I feel it, along with the guilt of privilege.*

*Sheena, my Sheena...* She's my own grief to bear. I could have called her my daughter if I'd only had the guts to go through with the fostering. *I didn't think I was good enough to become her mother.*

An eon has passed. And yet I know that it's no time at all. I've come awake again and watch as the scar on the hand ripples and tightens over the skin. The fingers curl into themselves, dissociating from the mug of tea. Hairs rise on the backs of the fingers, I don't remember those hairs. Maybe hairiness is an age-related thing. Definitely the skin on the hand has become looser and there are extra freckles, too. I sigh, remembering how we exposed ourselves to the harmful rays of the sun before we'd ever heard of sun cream or skin cancer. Lying on our backs on the grass at the top of Granny's Green Steps when Neil was a medical student and I studied Sociology and Anthropology. *You had your shirt off and I pulled the skirt of my dress up to my thighs.*

I acknowledge that the hand belongs to *you.* Ah yes, you. I won't be able to avoid you forever.

The scar's still raw and pink, as if weeks old, not years. Not decades. It seems baby-new – younger even than that. An *embryo* of a wound that goes much deeper than skin. It was supposed to. That. Was. What. It. Was. For.

My eyes prickle, I blink rapidly. 'Don't go startin with yer bubblin again, Miss,' Sheena would have said if she were here. As she did on the occasion I cried because she made me a 'Not-Mother' card for Mothers' Day. But I won't cry now and I refuse to daydream about how our first Mothers' Day together would have been if I'd had the courage to fully give my heart to her.

The hand twitches. I sit transfixed. After a moment it seems to make up its mind and fingers still curled in, begins a retreat back across the table.

# 5

## *Edinburgh, 1983*

SHE WORRIES ABOUT not going to Granny Mary's that summer. The Wilsons have always visited in summer, sometimes all together if there's a family gathering in Dublin or Howth or one the villages in between, sometimes in pairs or in threes or fours. 'You and I could go together, Neil,' she says. 'In autumn mibby, when the others have left. Before term starts, eh? What do ye think? Granny'll love you coz ye look just like the Sacred Heart picture on her sitting room wall.'

'I look like a heart?'

'Ach, I forgot, you're a non-Catholic. Probably never seen him then, oor blue-eyed Jesus on wanny them wee prayer cards. Holding his chest open so we can worship his bleeding, shining heart. We all got one for oor First Communion.'

'You mean like, glistening with blood? Anyway, Jesus was Jewish and lived in a hot country, why would he be blue-eyed?'

'Yer very literal, Neil. Shining with rays of light, Ah mean. His heart has its very own halo, you know. *Sweet heart of Jesus, fount of love and mercy...*' she hums the rest of the tune.

'Are you *very* Catholic? I've never seen any sign of it.' Neil shifts his feet in the grass, stretching his toes out over the ends of his sandals.

'I was once.'

Lauren can't explain the confusion of feelings brought on by all that worshipping and imploring. She would've shaved her head, worn a hair shirt under her habit – lashed herself with a whip if need be. Neil frowns as if he can read her thoughts. The song in her head changes to *I don't know how to love him.*

A breeze rustles through the cherry trees lining the path through the centre of the Meadows. Lauren pulls out her cardigan and slips her arms into it.

'My father brought us up Methodist,' Neil says abruptly. His fingers ravish the grass, plucking buttercups. He tilts Lauren's chin with a yellow-stained forefinger, holds a delicate flower beneath it. 'You definitely like butter.'

Lauren pauses a beat. 'You hardly ever talk about your dad. You say he brought you up Methodist; was your mam a Methodist, too?'

'She tried to be whatever he wanted her to be. We all did.' He meets her eyes from under heavy eyelids.

'I'm sorry,' Lauren must kiss him now, must stroke both sides of his face with her two hands. Must become closer and closer to this elusive soul. *I don't know how to love him.*

---

A letter arrives for Lauren. It had gone to her friend Ruth's houseboat, where her mail's directed. The postman's afraid of delivering to the squat because of Squonk. Lauren doesn't blame the postman, she's rather afraid of Markus's dog, too. Granny Mary reprimands Lauren for not visiting her. The other Wilsons have all returned to Scotland now, Granny says, and she wishes Lauren to come and spend a few days with her. *You can bring your friend,* she writes. How does she know about Neil?

Granny Mary has a sing-song voice, old as the rocks that line the beach where she collects seaweed to add to her stews. She's actually Lauren's great-granny, but nobody calls her that. Lauren knows she would have spoken the words aloud as she scratched them onto the paper with the ink pen she was given by her father when she graduated from school – an unusual thing for a girl to do back in her day. Her leaking tears – she has an eye disorder – tinted brown from the Guinness she drinks. Brackish water pouring down her face, like the brook that runs through her village. She's so old, Granny, that she seems at one with the sea and the hills. Her face is carved like the cliffs her cottage perches upon. When Granny Mary dies she will fold effortlessly into the landscape she's inhabited her whole life and Lauren will make sure to religiously tread the ground her bones are fused into. Granny talks a lot about the land being in her blood.

# 6

## *Howth, Dublin, 1972*

THE YEAR SHE turned nine, Lauren and her siblings spent the whole summer in Ireland. Maw had stayed in Glasgow, about to have Ardal. She couldn't cope with them all. Granny sent them out for a walk one day and they followed the road up to the cliffs, the younger ones complaining about sore feet and the ache in their calves. Lauren dragged Meg by the hand – she cried for her mammy but refused to be carried by a sister – and Kathy lugged Bridie on her hip. At four, Bridie was more than a year older than Meg but always remained slightly smaller. Michael was fourteen and bossed the others around something awful. Between the sharp bursts of Meg's wails they heard shouts and whoops far below. The hillside was covered in tall ferns and grasses that went high over Meg's head and at first they couldn't see anything. Butterflies and bees fluttered and buzzed in the plethora of wild flowers and dog-roses, the scents so strong they made Lauren dizzy.

Michael ordered them all to move over to the wall and stand still. Pepe was stung by a nettle and let out a squeal. A few moments later a snaking line of boys swam into view in the transparent sea below. Hovering above the dark green seaweed and the white sand on the sea bed. They could see the boys' shadows beneath them. Lauren and her brothers and sisters stood at the wall, watching. There was a rocky pillar, plonked right there in the bay, sticking up like a sore finger as Granny once remarked. One of the boys spotted them high above and swam in a circle, waving and calling for Lauren's brothers to go down and join him.

Lauren leant over the wall to watch the boys in the water scrabble for handholds on the chalky rocks. One after another they scrambled up onto the high shelf at the top of the pillar, daring each other to jump. Their voices rang out, echoed by the curving arms of the bay. Each white-fleshed body formed an arc before it straightened and plunged into the water, causing a white cascade to spray into the air. Declan was raring to have a go. 'Michael, come wi' me. C'mon, man. Come on, Michael!' Declan danced with excitement by the gate, already barefoot, his plimsolls in his hand. But Michael held back.

'I canna, I have this lot to mind.'

'Aw, c'mon, Kathy can dae it, she's twelve. Ye disna want to, do ye? Ye're a wee chicken, man.' Colour flooded the back of Michael's neck. His hand gripped Colin's shoulder. He was scared of water – whenever they swam he stayed in the shallows with the younger ones.

'I'll come wit ye.' Brendan shouted. 'Wait fer me, man.'

'I will as well,' Pepe cried, not to be left out.

'Ye will not, neither of ye.' Michael let go of seven-year-old Colin and transferred his hands to Brendan who had just turned ten. 'It'll be me who gets it frae Granny if she found out I let ye.'

Lauren giggled as Brendan spewed swearwords, while Declan tore off his outer clothes. Goose pimples rose on her brother's skin, though it was hot and the sky an intense blue. His t-shirt and shorts lay abandoned on the grass. Perpetua was quick to pounce on them, folding the scant collection into a neat pile. Lauren pretended not to notice, though when Pepe turned away Lauren saw that her sister had placed Declan's plimsolls with their soles upwards on top of his clothes. The hole in the bottom of one of them looked hungry. Declan was hopping about in his grey-white underwear.

Lauren watched him pick his way down the path to the cove, yelping at the sharpness of stones. He soon disappeared out of sight. The boys on the rock whooped and waved ahead of Declan's reappearance in his siblings' view. Lauren got a prickly feeling in her chest. She watched her favourite brother swim out to the rocks with strong strokes, and climb confidently up the face of the cliff. She imagined his trembling anticipation before the jump.

By the time it was Declan's turn to dive, even Meg had stopped whimpering. She allowed Lauren to pick her up and balance her on a flat part of the wall, keeping an arm around her tummy. They all cheered as Declan pumped his fists into the air before leaping. Perhaps that was what caused him to slip.

You could hear the crack of his forehead on rock before the rest of his body hit the water. Years later, Lauren sometimes dreamed of the way his white skin contrasted with the red blood and the turquoise water. He could have died. Her chest dropped into her stomach. She tried to stop the sick rising but she threw it all up at the base of the wall, still holding onto Meg. Pepe's, Bridie's and Meg's screams mingled into a thin, high siren. Kathy was white and shaking. She gathered the girls together and shouted at Colin and Dominic not to follow their older brothers, as Brendan and Michael scrambled for the gate and went crashing down the path to the cove.

The boys in the sea brought Declan in to shore. Michael yelled up to Granny from the beach. She heard him and hobbled down to the telephone box at the end of her road to call for an ambulance.

Declan needed seven stitches in his head. Granny tucked him up on the uncomfortable sofa in her tiny parlour when he was brought home. She fed him soup from a spoon, like a baby. She cackled at Declan, telling him he was linked to the rocks and the sea by blood now, making him more Irish than Scottish. Pepe fussed around the sofa with blankets and pillows like the 'little mother' Maw used to tell her she was, and Lauren saw Declan give her one of his crooked grins. It made Lauren go hot inside.

# 7

*Ferry to Stornoway, September 2016*

COME BACK, HAND. You're far across the table from me now. I want you back now that you've gone. When you first approached, hiding behind the mug of tea, my own hands couldn't help stiffening. They were unsure of what action to take when they sensed you coming. So they gripped the Kindle harder as if to hide, perhaps inside the millions of electronic words within the machine.

In the past our hands spoke so much more eloquently than words. In fact it was often words that got us into trouble. We had passionate and sometimes frightening arguments: your passion drove you to bear down on me and I felt threatened, though you never hurt me. But you were taller than me and my hands sometimes flew out and hit you when you loomed over me. I scratched your cheek so badly once that you went to A&E to check whether it needed a stitch (you did *fuss*), and you were embarrassed in case anyone you knew was on duty. *Ditch the mad girlfriend*, they would have advised. Nobody who didn't know you intimately could ever have guessed at the fire beneath your reserved exterior. I imagine you still have that hairline scar on your face as well as the deep one on your hand, though I can't bring myself to look at your face. Not yet.

During our arguments one or other of us often threw

something. We'd both turn and watch the item break against the wall, cringing from the rebounding shards of glass or china. So much fragmented matter to sweep away afterward, so many unsightly stains that could never quite be removed from the walls or the carpet. Friends learned not to buy us anything breakable and Ruth took back the soup tureen she had wanted us to keep. Remember that plastic water jug Fiona bought us for our third anniversary of being together? It was cleverly designed to look like china. When we held dinner parties we served the food on melamine plates.

Could Jesus have had such a temper? The one in the film did, if the scene in the temple is anything to go by.

When we gave our notice on that flat the landlord refused to return our deposit. We each threw blame at the other, along with a final few items of pottery. Just one more bitterness to cope with at our parting.

But, hand, observing you now, folded away from me beside your own mug of tea, nudging against it, fingers reddening – how long will it be before the heat becomes unbearable? I miss you. I miss you so much. The wordless comfort you gave me during those long Edinburgh nights. Particularly when I was exhausted from the conference calls with various family members at the time Da was ill, trying to work out what to do about his wilful descent into a permanent alcoholic fugue.

Perhaps I only miss that feeling now because I'm about to begin a new stage of my life and I'm clinging to the past. Nostalgia has hit me hard. I've given up everything I was familiar with and right now I'm numb to the future. I'll just continue to stare at you, hand. A familiar beacon in my darkness.

I went back to Edinburgh you know, eventually. I always wondered whether I'd bump into you there. Could it be possible that you'd ever again stroke hair away from my face while kissing me good morning? Would my hand hold yours as we strode side-by-side, matching our footsteps up Market Street on a Saturday? Or touch each other at a concert in that church in New Town – you know, the one on George Street? Or did you have a new girlfriend's hand to hold by then – or maybe a wife? Colin told me you phoned a few times after I first left but I didn't stay in Glasgow long.

It's so unexpected, hand-of-Neil, to find you here in such close proximity on a ferry to the Outer Hebrides, after twenty-nine years apart. I suppose this means you'll be getting off at my stop – there's only one stop, after all. What will this mean to us, Neil's hand? How will it shape our futures?

Perhaps... perhaps you will reach out to one of my hands as the funnel blasts our approach to land. Will you then offer a stroking caress to the back of my hand? Tracing it all the way down from between the bones of my wrist to the tip of my middle finger as you did in the past? You will find my skin moves more readily now, no longer the tight sheath over muscle and bone that it was in my twenties, so don't be shocked by the change. Or maybe, just maybe, you'll take my breath away by performing that funny tickling motion against my palm. *That one.* I once described to you how that particular movement of your finger was a hotline to my secret places. So what did you do? You incited me to fire, in plain sight, in the National Library. And also in that very church I mentioned in the New Town. Simply by stroking my wrist in a particular way. How you enjoyed watching me squirm with the hammer of that wanting. Your hand, Neil, was an artist's tool in those days. Mibby still is. On whose body have you painted colourscapes of emotion since me? Actually, don't tell me. I don't want to know.

Shh, now. I meant to talk to your hand only. When you have touched me, hand, at the end of this journey, will you then pass over a note covered in generic doctor-style handwriting while people gather their coats and bags and queue in the doorways to leave? If you do this, what will the note you've written say? Will Neil's eyes and mine ever look into each other at all, or will there only be written words and the memory of the one brief touch between us? The touch that hasn't happened yet. And if it does, will it be enough for us both to take away?

---

## Edinburgh, 1980s.

We had no central heating in our tenement flat above the shops on Cowgatehead. *A hoose o' wur ain* at last. We both had to take on extra shifts at our part-time jobs to afford the rent and the bills – keep the gas fire burning over that first winter. I don't know how we got our university work done, let alone finished our degrees. What I remember most about that place is the smell of joss sticks (they covered the smell of damp at least). And the record player constantly revolving with progressive rock and folk music. We piled quilts and blankets on the bed and spent a disproportionate amount of time under the covers, touching and stroking, taking it in turns to jump out and turn the record over. Or change the channel on that miniature black and white TV Kathy gave us when she bought her first colour one.

At the beginning of my third year of Uni (you'd just begun your fourth) our landlord installed central heating in the whole tenement building. What a mess our hoose was with all the plaster-dust, not to mention the stairwells and back close. We threw off some of our bedcovers once it became warmer in there and from that point on our hands often found more important things to do, or so we justified our less-frequent touching. To be fair, we were having fewer arguments by then as well. But I don't want to think about the beginning of our separation. Not yet.

Hand, I feel my cheeks reddening at the thought of you, at what you did to me in those early days. In particular the way you encompassed my hip-bone when Neil and I were lying together naked under that pile of blankets. Your fingers digging gently into my stomach. I would wriggle when you touched the ticklish bit. You pulled me towards you and then pushed us apart again so you could slide between us and circle my belly in languorous, stroking laps until I could hardly bear the intensity. Then your fingers tracked a lower pathway until your palm covered the part of me you'd named *Mount Agatha*. You moved still lower until you fitted perfectly between my legs and then you held the moment, while I expanded with pleasure. You watched my face, the features of Neil melting too. Then I squeezed my eyes tight shut and finally, finally your fingers spread out as I leaned onto them and they slid inside me and I came...

# 8

*Edinburgh, 1983*

IT'S WASHDAY AT the squat. Lauren's wrestling with her clothes in the tin bath over the fire. The garden's a sun trap and she can feel the back of her neck burning. Tonight her skin will begin to itch and in a few days flakes of her will drop off onto her seldom-washed bedding.

Fiona's clothes have already been through the sudsy water Lauren's using now, and Andrea is waiting to use it after her. They take it in turns to have first go. There's a rota for rinsing as well. All the water needs to be carried from the tap at the back of the building and it takes an age to heat up, but none of the girls is prepared to share their washing water with the boys.

An annoying curl keeps escaping from the scarf tied around Lauren's head. She ought to loosen it and cover her neck instead but that would involve a delay in the proceedings and a possible end to Andrea's patience. While she pummels the clothes a final time Andrea waits by the back door, her favourite dungarees clutched in her arms. Her mouth makes a thin line.

Neil reaches forward to tuck the curl gently back beneath the scarf. 'I'm interested in everything about you. Your history is part of what you are.' He's been asking her – again – about her Catholic childhood. 'What was it like?'

'I dunno what you mean.'

'You seem so *anti* anything religious, I don't understand how you can go from one set of beliefs to another like that.'

'Religion isn't about *belief* for a Catholic, Neil, any more than taking a bath every night was. Gaun in the water after ma older sisters, or, like, having cornflakes for breakfast. It must be the same for a child brought up in any other faith. It's just what you know. You just gae along with it. When I left home I finally got my head straight. I saw that there wiz more to life than the narrowness of religion. It was up tae *me* to make whatever choices ma conscience told me to, not up tae Father Patrick or Sister Anne.'

'Did it upset your mum, though, you turning against it?'

'It's no really any of her business, is it? And to be honest, nothing much upsets her.' A mother, to Neil, is someone who pays attention. 'Anyway, I don't know why you're so bothered.'

'It's just that you had something. You were an integral part of something bigger than yourself, bigger than your whole family. Chapel wasn't like that for me. It was negative. I could tell my mother hated it but Dad insisted we all went.'

Lauren hauls the wet clothes out of the tub and dumps them on a plastic tablecloth spread out on the scrubby lawn. Fiona's pile is already half-drying in the sun. A siren blares by on Lothian Road, temporarily drowning out the other traffic. Somewhere far off is the snatched sound of bagpipes. It sets Lauren's nerves on edge. Andrea marches across the lawn and dumps her dungarees into what's left of the water in the tub. The fire is still burning underneath it.

'Ouch,' she says. 'It's bloody hot. Took your time, didn't you? I'm gonna be late by the time I get round to my turn to rinse.'

'Sorry, hen. Dinnae worry, I'll do your rinse for you. You can get aff noo.'

Andrea grins. 'Ta, mate. I'll just give these another dunk and they should be all right. I can't risk being late again or I'll get the sack.'

'You go on,' says Lauren. 'You can owe me one.'

Andrea gives her dripping dungarees a perfunctory squeeze and dumps them on the plastic sheeting next to Lauren's stuff. 'See ya later.' She takes off towards the back door.

'That's not very fair,' Neil remarks after she's gone.

Lauren takes a deep breath. 'What isn't?'

'Well. Fiona's nowhere to be seen and Andrea's just dumped her washing on you as well. What are you, the local charlady?'

Lauren doesn't know whether to be amused or offended. It's not as if he couldn't have offered to help.

'It's called communal living, we help each other out. Another time they can do my washing for me. Now, lug this tub over tae the tap and fill it up with cauld water will ye? I'll do the rinsing by the tap, it'll be easier than hauling the tub back over here.'

Gathering the edges of the plastic sheeting she drags the wet laundry to the other end of the garden. Neil remains in place with his arms hanging by his sides, looking zoned-out. At a glance from Lauren he bends to lift the almost empty tub from the embers of the fire.

'Use the rags,' Lauren instructs. 'The handles'll be hot.'

Neil rubs a hand over his face. He's exhausted, the summer café and pharmacy shifts wear him out as much as the ones at the hospital in term-time. He frowns at the scraps of an old t-shirt, lip curled. 'I might catch something.'

Nothing about her life in the squat impresses him, whereas she feels like a pioneer. Still, Neil wraps the grey-looking rags around the handles of the metal tub before consenting to lift it, holding the blackened metal as far away as possible from his pristine clothes.

Lauren straightens her back and water from the washing dribbles refreshingly down her front.

'Thanks, hen. If you're good I'll let you paddle in the water when we've finished the rinsing. Or you could sit on our lovely auld broken chair over there and I'll give you a footbath.'

Like Mary Magdalene in the film. If only her hair were longer.

Neil's also been doing nightshifts as a porter. He should be sleeping but he chose to be with her instead – the least she can do is humour him. She'll get him lying down on a blanket under a tree in the shade when her tasks are finished, massage his feet after he's soaked them in the tub. *Sleep and I shall soothe you.*

# 9

## *Ferry to Stornoway, September 2016*

NEIL. I TALK to your hand, here at the table in the restaurant on the ferry. I study it as it lies curled like a mouse on the smooth vinyl, the backs of its knuckles red from the steam of the tea. Ah, now. *Other* hand, there you are at last. Lifting the mug off the table and rising out of my line of vision, no doubt to meet a pair of lips... But I mustn't raise my chin to find that out. Not yet. To see those lips again; fitting around the rim of the mug. I'm not ready. I'll keep my gaze on you instead, hand-with-the-scar, examine the bitten nails on the perfectly clean fingers – you never got into gardening then, Neil? It was one of the hobbies you were keen to take up. It was why you chose that particular house we were going to buy – the one you may have bought after we separated, for all I know.

Wait. You started biting your *nails*? You chided me for that. You said it was an off-putting habit. Fastidious you. I hate that you've gone back on your convictions, Neil. Whoops, I almost lifted my head to look into your eyes and tell you that. But not yet. *Focus, Lauren. Focus on the hand.*

You used to keep your nails more manicured than a woman's (not me). I teased you about it. *Certainly better than yours*, you agreed. But not anymore – look at my nails now. Sheena gave me a manicure. It was her second leaving present to me and while she was busy, with her eyes downcast, she kept asking me to promise I would email as soon as I got settled. That she'd be allowed to come and visit me sometimes. In case you're interested her third present was a poem, tucked into the pocket on the front of the Kindle cover.

But she didn't tell me about the poem. I only found it afterward. I hadn't realised she'd been studying Yeats in English – she used to get mad with me for probing into her private business, as she called it. Why couldn't I see what a poetic soul my young charge had until it was too late? *'For I would we were changed to white birds on the wandering foam: I and you.'*

I scour the foam of the sea now, searching for white birds but there are none. A movement brings my gaze back to the table. Your finger tapping very gently on the surface. Be patient, hand. An eon has passed and yet I know in reality it has been no time at all.

Sheena gave me an opportunity to do a good thing. I mean a proper good thing, not just to do with my job. For once in my life I behaved in a completely altruistic manner. Yeah, me. I put someone else first.

Oops, I nearly looked again. This thing I did, it might somehow have made up for the bad thing I let happen when I was with you. Not the scarring of your hand, which was justly deserved.

It's like being in a time machine, *hand of Neil*, sitting at this table with Neil's body stretching away from you, only a section of it in my view. I allow my gaze to lead me up beyond Neil's hand for the first time since his body sat down.

*Oh.*

I linger a few moments on the wrist. Neil, I'm guessing you haven't turned to fat like me as your wrist looks more or less as I remember it, apart from the loosening of the skin and those extra freckles. A painful pound of my heartbeat causes me to stop breathing a moment. I inwardly intone the relaxation mantras I learned after my health scare five years ago – the one that turned out to be only panic attacks. There, it's gone back to normal, my heart. Well, almost.

I was turned on by the bones of your wrists, Neil, back in the day. Brittle and vulnerable as they suggested you were. I inserted my thumbs between those bones, traced patterns on the undersides of your wrists with my fingertips until you couldn't help moaning softly, your eyes fixed on mine as if I were your lifebuoy.  Your pupils widened, their outlines blurred. *No*, I still haven't looked into his eyes, I want to remember him piece by piece, take my time on the journey upwards towards what must be our mutual gaze.

The wrist-encircling always ended with you and the other hand swivelling to grasp mine.  You couldn't help pushing mine down onto Neil's body. Other hand would let go of mine and drag Neil's zip open and guide mine into the gap. *Remember?* I do.

Ach. What have you done to me, all these years on? Yes, Neil, your hand and your wrist have taught me that I'm still all woman as you used to call me. My body wants to react in all those old ways. It gives me prickly heat, contemplating your wrist in such detail. As a medic, you might be interested to know I've had some gynaecological problems. Nothing to do with what happened...

At appointments, the first thing I'm asked is when my periods stopped. Well, they haven't stopped, Neil. Do you think my body is trying to tell me something? Especially in light of meeting you again. Not that we can say we've actually *met*, as yet. Perhaps they will *never* stop. Possibly my body has unfinished business.

So here we both are, arrested in this moment of proximity a full twenty-nine years later, and we've yet to look into each other's eyes. *I can't.* I can't do it. Not yet. I'll move my eyes further up your arm instead, study the fold inside your elbow where I can see that the skin is papery, loose. Flaky. That was always a sign of stress with you. What could have caused it? I wonder.

# 10

## Edinburgh, 1983

**13th January**

*TUTORIAL: SOCIOLOGICAL ANALYSIS – (Margaret Stone) Means of Production. Serfdom – Feudal Society. In return for land owned by Lord, serf worked for him several days a week & fought wars etc. for him.*

'Wars etc.' How on earth is she supposed to write an essay based on that? Are these really the only notes she took during the whole tutorial? She remembers some discussion about the Highland Clearances, the greater importance to the landowners of land for grazing sheep on over their less-profitable human tenants – who existed by subsistence farming, but not much more. Mags (their tutor) should have noticed the way Lauren's eyes had glazed over. She should have asked her some questions to check she was listening.

She must have been daydreaming. *About Neil.* The tall Canadian medical student. *Neil MacDonald.* Ach. Stop it, Lauren. *You have tae concentrate on this essay, you've handed the last two in late as it is.* At the squat she works by the light of a tilly-lamp on a plank balanced on bricks, her legs crossed, sitting on a cushion on the floor. But she can't blame her lack of concentration on that. Or the fact that Markus mistakenly used her first set of notes to start a fire in the communal room grate. He said it was a mistake, anyway. No, it's the constant parade of fantasies about when and where she might next clap eyes on Neil. Will it be in the university library or the Student Union?

What can have come over her? Not since she fell in love with Ted Neely in *Superstar* has she felt like this. Her personal tutor has already issued her with a verbal warning. Apparently the promise Lauren showed in the first term has been broken already. Like it was a promise she actually *made*. But in a way it was, to herself and to Da's attitude problem. She will make something of herself. She can't be sucked back into life in the Glasgow tenement.

*The smell of curry from the shop on the ground floor. Ma comatose with tranquilizers on the settee and Da slaughtered, his eyes sewn with red thread. Having to descend the ladder from her closet bunk and slip on the pair of tights Pepe will swear she accidentally left draped over the rung. Where Kathy'll be crying in the bathroom because Da made her feel guilty about leaving. Her brothers' pungent feet and masculine legs stretched out along every square foot of rucked-up rug. The younger kids bickering. The smell of teenage girls' hormonal sweat in the crowded rooms.* The thought of returning's enough to make her boke.

---

*Four weeks previously.*

'You shouldae gone into nursing like your sisters. Kathy and Pepe ae daein' fine weel. Putting their bit into the hoosekeepin' an all. You could a done that instead a wastin' yer time being a student. Relying on handoots, ma foot! A daugh'er o' mine. Ah never thought Ah'd see the day. Ah expect ye'll be tapping yer da fer handoots a'weel, when you run oot o' money? Weel, ah'll telt ye noo, there's nae danger o' that.' His hand goes to his diaphragm and his face creases into a series of wincing expressions until he forces out a burp.

The living room floor is covered with glitter and children. The clock ticks loudly on the mantelpiece. Da wipes his palms after stirring himself tae haul Christmas decorations from the back of the lobby press, leaving a smear of oily dust on the festive tank top Pepe knitted him. Steps over Meg and Dominic on his way to his beloved, beer-dispensing fridge. The cross-legged kids on the carpet are untangling threadbare strands of tinsel for the tree. Ardal clamours to be the one tae place the angel on top. 'It's no' time yet,' says Pepe. 'Ye have to wait until the tinsel's on.' Declan puts his finger to his lips and winks at Ardal, gives the youngest a lift up and nearly knocks the tree over. Pepe flounces off in a huff. Lauren tries to rise above the smirk that threatens.

Brendan and Colin began their job of decorating the lobby conscientiously enough but they've now started popping the balloons they're supposed to be attaching to the dark wood coving. Both of them tangled in swathes of Sellotape – they take turns to climb up on the heavy wooden sideboard in the central hallway. Bridie creeps stealthily out of the bathroom. There's something off about her and it's not simply the perm Pepe's given her. She's unnaturally thin.

Lauren's like a ghost, hovering on the edges of everything. Or a non-participatory observer. Her family's a video in a sociology tutorial.

The chaos continues. Maw sneaks into the kitchen for an extra pill from the box she hides at the back of the drop-down cupboard where the coal used to be kept. Lauren watches Maw's head jerk from side to side to check if anyone's noticed, knowing it would set Kathy off on a preach.

Michael hasn't been seen for days and no one knows where he's gone. (He doesn't come home that whole Christmas.)

Lauren closes the front door behind her, braves the cold of the stairhead and retreats to the ancient communal toilet in the back close. *Five minutes' peace.* She wouldn't mind a Valium herself, but Maw counts the pills obsessively.

She longs to go back to Edinburgh but Neil is in Canada for three weeks and her room at the squat's being loaned out to friends of Fiona's. Leaning with her arms on the sofa back, ready to duck any further missiles from Da, she places her face close to Maw's ear and tries something. 'Are *you* proud of your daughter at University?'

Despite the noise of the film all the ears in the room pick up her whispered words. Several pairs of eyes shift over Lauren and then over Maw, slumped at one end of the sofa. Ardal lays half on her body, her hand rests heavily on his mass of blond curls. Her blue-eyed boy. Maw's eyes keep staring in the vicinity of the TV, similar to those of the wally-dogs flanking the clock on the mantelpiece. 'Maw?' *I should just leave it.* But Lauren has a burning desire to hear Maw say she's proud of her. Be Maw's ain girl again. Maw swallows. Lauren tenses, seeing the muscles in her neck moving but nothing else happens. The stuffy room releases its held breath. Maw isn't going to speak.

'Leave her alone, for fuck's sake,' Declan shouts. Everyone except Pepe stares back at the screen. 'Always so attention-seeking, Lauren, aren't ye? Layin it aff aboot gaun tae Uni. Just because you were Maw's favourite.'

As if Maw's no longer here. Pepe turns her glittering eyes back to the screen, where Mrs Brown is giving Paddington a bath because he has marmalade in his fur.

'Yeah, you were always her *favourite*,' Bridie parrots. Her eyes are hungry. She follows Pepe around like a poodle – looks like one, too, with that perm. Her face is narrow between the curls.

Tears sting Lauren's eyes but they don't fall.

# 11

*Ferry to Stornoway, September 2016*

MY FOCUS TRAVELS higher up your arm. I see the cuff of a ribbed t-shirt sleeve, good quality. The lightest shade of blue that went fine well with your goldie-hair and blue eyes.

Oh, Neil, I remember now. The first time I saw you, it wasn't at university at all. You were shadowing a junior doctor in A&E the time my friend Ruth helped me in with a sprained ankle. I'd tripped on the gangplank of her houseboat. Okay, I was a little worse for wear. I would've fallen over the edge if it wasn't for the heavy chain on either side. I had two welts on my arm as well as a bruised and grazed knee. My ankle had swelled and my foot hurt like hell. There was a bloody-edged hole at the knee of my patterned tights, sealing the fabric to my weeping flesh. The hem of my flowered dress was badly torn. So was the sleeve of my long knitted jumper but that was nothing to do with the accident.

Your eyes ran over me, from the fat purple foot protruding from the now-footless leg of my tights, up over my bleeding knee. Upwards from my torn skirt and grubby jumper to my tear-streaked face. I had mascara running down my cheeks and my lipstick had smudged all over the handkerchief Ruth had passed me to blow my nose on. Ruth was like my second mother. Behaved like a real one. Your gaze, when the supervising medic asked you to assess me – I had to laugh.

Your eyes rested uncertainly on my birds' nest of hair. All brown tangles. Back-combing was in at the time – a good job since I rarely brushed it anyway. I don't think you knew what to do with me but I suspect you would have begun with a full makeover if you'd had the choice.

You cleared your throat. 'Does it hurt?'

I mistook your accent for American. 'Of course it crapping does.' I winced when you grasped my foot and turned it the wrong way, maybe thinking you could set it straight with brute force. Possibly another swear word slipped out of my mouth, but only the mild kind. Looking at your face, anyone would have thought I'd used the kind of language I was familiar with from home. At least I didn't call you a cunt or a twat. Perhaps my Glaswegian was a bit much for your sensitive ears. Ruth giggled. The supervising doctor brushed you aside and took your place at my ankle. You stood behind him in your blue shirt, shoulders sagging, nervously fiddling with a loose tag of skin at the corner of your nail.

I think that's when I fell in love with you, right then. You looked so vulnerable.

Your bicep gives the impression of being firm, Neil. You'd just begun lifting weights when I parted with you. You'd taken up the hobby as if you were trying to compensate for something. When I first met you, the tone of your upper arms was soft. You were soft all over, though thin. Your mother had died earlier that year. You'd been in hospital with an infection the first few weeks of your residence in Scotland. Even had to miss the start of your course. And you had *nobody*. I wish I'd known you when you first arrived. I could have been a hospital visitor. I would have written you letters and compiled a tape of your favourite songs for you to listen to on your Walkman.

There's no denying I was blown away by your good looks. By your Canadian accent. But it was definitely compassion in my chest the first time we really talked. In the Student Union a week after you twisted my foot the wrong way. We recognised each other but what you didn't know was that I'd already begun looking out for you in the canteen, in the library, in the square by then. Walking across the meadows or in that mysterious dark club on Cowgate. And then to see you at Rock Night in the Student Union, find myself wedged shoulder-to-shoulder with you at the bar. I still had a bandage around my foot but nothing could make me miss my monthly dose of Led Zep and Pink Floyd and Free. I loved swinging my hair to *Alright Now*. Standing crammed so close I realised it was you I'd spotted watching me on the dance floor. You'd been standing next to that Indian guy, Ed from Architecture, while you sipped a pint. And yet here you were ordering another immediately after the song had finished. My chest tingled, like something had come alive in there.

You gave me a shy smile. Even under the lurid lights your tan made you stand out from the pasty-faced English and Scottish boys.

'Do you want a drink?' you said. The barman was waiting for your order.

'Ach, go on then. I'll have a cider with a shot a Pernod and a wee squirt a blackcurrant.'

'Seriously?'

'Aye.'

You repeated my order to the barman. We crossed the heaving dance floor and found a couple of seats at the back of the room. You were drinking *BrewDog*. I gulped my Pernod/cider concoction and it went straight to my head. Long after the music had quietened we sat there, still talking. You said you never normally opened up like that but you thought I seemed different from the other girls you'd met.

# 12

## Edinburgh, 1983

**14th February**

*TUTORIAL, MODERN INDUSTRIAL Society. The Decay of the Inner City. Is it inevitable?*

*Different situation for working class and middle class. Working class, decline of fishing industry. Before – rehousing people from inner city to outskirts and trying to encourage industry to expand out there to provide jobs.*

Again, the sum of Lauren's notes doesn't amount to much. Thank God for the handouts at every tutorial (*ye wiz right, Da, ahm getting handoots after aw*). She digs around in her brain for memories of the tutorial. Phuong Nguyen, she recalls, raised the contemporary context of refugee resettlement in rural areas of high unemployment, a topic close to her heart. She spoke of being one of the luckier ones with her father a doctor and her mother speaking five languages. Phuong doesn't waste her time daydreaming.

*What else?* Sheep were probably also mentioned by hill farmer's son Malcolm MacPherson, they usually were. *Where can I fit sheep and land usage into this topic?*

Lauren managed a 'C' for her essay on the Feudal System. Had to sit in Mags' stuffy office while she was given a stern glare over said tutor's glasses. Mags, or someone else maybe, had drawn a stick-figure in the layer of dust on her white-painted bookshelf. It kept beckoning to Lauren while the tutor insisted on going over practically every word of the essay, telling her she was lucky to scrape through.

*I met Neil in the refectory today. My hands were shaking so much I nearly dropped the tray. I was in front of him at the counter so at least I didn't have to make the decision whether to sit with him or not. And thankfully he followed me to where I was lowering my rattling tray onto the table and sitting next to Andrea. She looked at me like, what the hell's wrong with you? Until she saw Neil. She made goggle-eyes at me then and I raised my eyebrows back as if to say 'I know!'*

Needless to say, Lauren's diary is more conscientiously written than her tutorial notebook. She's hardly seen Neil since another party they were both at near the end of January, when she'd bumped into him at the makeshift bar, spilling her drink down the front of his t-shirt. He'd turned a deeper shade of red under the red glow of the bulb, muttered something about borrowing the host's hair drier and disappeared. She'd expected him to come back but he didn't reappear. About a week after that her ears picked up a rumour that he was going out with a Philosophy student, the one with masses of Pre-Raphaelite hair. *Sexy Sarah*, according to Geordie Willis in Sociology.

At lunch in the canteen Andrea fishes in Neil's unfathomable silence with comments about Sarah. In the end Neil stops chewing. He sits quietly, holding his knife and fork in front of his face, until her chatter putters to a stop.

'I don't know who you're talking about,' he says into the pause. 'So please shut up.'

After that he asks Lauren if she's planning to attend the CND protest at the end of the month. Lauren panics for a second, scanning the refectory walls for a poster she noticed earlier. There it is: an anti-nuclear demonstration. She tugs her eyes back through Andrea's questioning gaze to Neil's and nods briskly. 'Yeah, of course we are. We were just talking aboot that earlier. Weren't we, Andrea?'

# 13

*Ferry to Stornoway, September 2016*

WE LURCH OVER waves. I swallow down the threat that my chips will resurface and concentrate on the table-top – watch the torn salt and pepper sachets sliding from side to side. See your fingers twitching on the mug handle. My hand goes out to catch the stray packets and weigh them down with the knife and fork on my plate. *Now.* I allow my eyes to rove up as far as your right shoulder, and a new burst of tingling fires off inside me. I can't help thinking of the times my head rested there, in the hollow between your collarbone and your chin. Grey hairs peep over the neckline of your t-shirt, remind me that we're both getting old. I picture us as a pair of time-lapse videos in a gallery, on separate monitors. The sort of thing Ruth used to drag us along to. Age befalling us to the extent that we crumble intae dust. I want to turn away before the end of the video.

Sheena and her friends reminded me of my age often enough, of course. I wish I could see Sheena curl her lip at me one more time as I sing along to the music on her phone. 'You're embarrassing yourself, Miss.'

The other girls take the piss out of me and she pretends – pretended – to go along with them. Privately, afterward, she apologised for shaming me in public. 'It's awkward. We canna be mates, Lauren. Ah'll tell ya what tae do, pretend tae be snooty like Miss Jessop. That way they won't think you're worth bothering.'

I don't feel any different in my head to when I was seventeen. It's a shock to find myself in an older body, especially sitting here with you, Neil. I'm sure when Sheena's fifty-two she'll feel the same as she does now.

Oh. I can't believe that for a moment I forgot.

---

Which takes me back to another time I walked out on my life. Remember the patchwork bedspread I made, Neil? I created it about two years after we got together, using scraps of clothes we didn't want any more and those curtains we had in our flat for a while, before we replaced them with the ones from the charity shop. You even went a bit mad and allowed me to shorten the strap of your mother's hessian satchel so I could stitch a piece onto the bedspread, along with the silk rose from the garter Maw wore on her wedding day. She randomly gave it to me when I left home to go to university. That bedspread was like a map of our lives. I left it at the flat for you. I hope you looked after it.

We had a hand-drawn map of Canada on the wall, made for us by your brother for Christmas. Ewan was doing so well at Art College in Toronto, and planned to apply to Glasgow in the future. I wonder if he ever did.

You had a photo of your mother, Barbara, sitting on a metal chair beside your father at the family barbecue where they first met. And a later one of her standing alone wearing the headscarf you bought her just before her hair started falling out. Because you knew it was happening even before she did, you said. You told me it was your mother's cancer that made you want to become a doctor.

I had one photo of Maw when she was a girl in Ireland, with all those brunette curls like mine. She's smiling, despite having her problems even then, like the fact that her mother was locked up in an asylum. And one of Da working on a building site, taken a week before they met each other at an Irish wedding she'd travelled to in Glasgow. I still have the photo of Dad but not the one of Maw. It must have got lost in transit, or maybe Perpetua really did take it, as I suspected, that time she invited herself to the flat I had in Edinburgh after I was back from Reykjavik. I don't want to think about Reykjavik right now, about the things you don't know. All right, I'll admit it, I got married. But it was only for a while. No-one has ever been able to replace you, Neil, I promise you that.

Maw died a few months ago. It's not as if she and I were close but it's not as if I didn't want us to be, either. You remember how embarrassed I was for getting upset when you first told me about your mother dying? You said you'd shared everything with her. It hurt to hear that. I'm ashamed to say you ended up comforting me, when I should have been comforting you.

*Anyway.* The picture in our bedroom that I loved the most was the one of Colin and Ewan together. Our brothers, linked. And yes, I took the photo with me when I moved out, in case you were wondering. Remember when Ewan came to visit us? It was in 1984, just before I went to Greenham Common to stay with Ruth in her bender. Your brother couldn't abide my older brothers, he took their banter too seriously. He might have liked young Dominic but he'd gone off travelling by then and Ewan never got to meet him. Colin though, he was fascinated by Ewan's stories of backpacking in the Alaskan wilderness.

My youngest brother was only twelve at the time. I don't know if you were aware of this but Ardal idolised you, Neil. So did my younger sisters. Bridie even allowed you to give her some dietary advice. I promise you she did keep on trying to eat – for a long while.

No. I refuse to allow myself any tears for Bridie right now. Let's just say Maw had one of her girls waiting for her when she got to the other side. *Christ, I sound like Granny Mary.*

I liked your Ewan. Sad that when you split up with someone you also lose their family. He never answered any of my letters and when Facebook happened he rejected my friend request. I hope he's well. Alive at least.

So many funerals over the past couple of years. The worst was Ruth's. *My second Maw.* I met up with a group of our University friends at the funeral. We spent an evening in the garden of her favourite pub down by the river. We smoked joints for old times' sake and drank a lot of cider. I did kind of wonder if you might be there, if you were still around. But it wasn't really your sort of thing anyway.

You liked Ruth. You were fascinated by her alternative lifestyle and my interest in it but you made it clear you would never be prepared to live on a boat when I got it into my head that we could. Ruth died last year. It was an accelerated form of Parkinson's disease. What a thing.

I can feel that my eyes are wet. I'll take myself back to our bed while I continue to gaze at your shoulder. We'd go to bed early and usually begin by reading. I was more of an avid reader than you. When you'd had enough of reading you'd start breathing in an exasperated way, throwing yourself from one side to the other. I knew you wanted me, but my book might be too engaging to put aside just yet. So I warded off the moment as long as possible, caught in the printed world, but I always gave in. It was always worth it.

I nestled with my head on your shoulder. You kissed the top of my head. Your hands roved my hair and my neck, my back and bottom, as if you had more than two. Then my hands began a slow trail across your body. I liked to twist my fingers in your chest hair. I liked to kiss the hollow at your throat and move up over your chin to draw your lips into mine. We could kiss for hours, it felt like. A portal into a deeper consciousness, we seemed to fuse into one being. Your finger stroked the air half a millimetre from the bones of my pelvis, winding downwards – setting off a rogue pulse between my legs. It felt especially intense if we'd had an argument that day. Every probe of your tongue between my teeth, every feather-light touch from your fingertip, the way you cupped me in the palm of your hand, sent the inner me spiralling so far away I feared I might never come back.

It was love, Neil, not only sex. Love so deep it was painful. You were like Ted Neely's Jesus when I was a budding teenager. Love that made my heart flare so fiercely I wanted to rip my chest open – certain that a white dove would flutter out.

How could it ever have lasted, love like that?

# 14

*Reflections on scarring, while on a ferry to Stornoway*

THE LAST TIME I saw you, Neil, was a month after another of those hospital visits we participated in together. The second-to-worst hospital visit. Travelling the familiar route to A&E, we drove – I drove – in stunned silence as you sat shaking and white in the passenger seat next to me. *White*, Neil, as if your nut-brown skin had shed a layer. It was amazing. What was underneath seemed unbearably new, simply too pure.

You were wearing a white t-shirt and cut-off jeans, faded and patched. Glancing down while we waited at the traffic lights, I noticed your clenched toes, your feet arching in the brown leather sandals you wore every summer. *Jesus* sandals. You grasped your right wrist tightly with your left hand, holding the right hand upright but not still enough because of how violently your body was shaking. And though I'd applied a makeshift bandage from a folded tea towel with a long stripy sock tied around it (which for some reason had been in the kitchen drawer, wrapped around a bar of soap), blood still poured down your arm and into your lap.

I never found the partner of that sock.

I remember how an hysterical urge to shriek with laughter seized me in the car, also that I gripped the wheel tightly as I watched the growing spread of red in your normally pristine lap. You hated wearing stained clothes. I stifled those giggles, my stomach hurting with the effort. I tried not to picture the look that might appear on the receptionist's face when we arrived, perhaps thinking I had cut off your penis.

*Don't think it hadn't occurred to me.*

I stuck like a limpet to your side as we were shown into a cubicle, though a helpful auxiliary pointed me towards the vending machine. My teeth chattered when I refused to buy tea, a rigor-mortis attempt at a smile on my face. By this time I'm sure I had turned as white as you. Maybe it was shock setting in. And I expected the police to come and arrest me. I thought the hospital staff would take one look at your hand and know it was me who caused your injury. But you didn't give me away did you, Neil? You didn't explain that I'd gone mad while holding a sharp knife, just because you'd remarked that I ought to be *recovering* by now and that it was *time to move on with our lives*. You didn't mention to them that you had tried to reclaim my sore, bleeding body without asking me first.

No. Instead of grassing on me you concocted a lie about how it had happened, a convoluted tale of the guinea-pig having escaped from its indoor hutch and getting trapped beneath a kitchen cabinet. You said you'd inserted your hand underneath, and caught the back of it on a protruding nail as you withdrew the guinea-pig, clutched (triumphantly – you even added an embellishment) in your fist. You made it sound so real it became easy to picture our Squeaker, fat, lazy creature that he was, taking himself off to explore. When in fact we'd always had to tip him out of the hutch for his exercise.

I wonder what made you come up with that story.

Perhaps you wanted to have rescued something.

A doctor whipped the curtain back and light flashed into my eyes like an interrogation lamp. They'll separate us and ask me some more questions, I thought. I rushed to assemble the pieces of my story. But instead the nurse related your account of the guinea-pig's adventures to the doctor and he merely muttered something about Tetanus and pulled the flaps of your skin apart with scientific disinterest. You'd been given some kind of anaesthetic by then and only slightly flinched at the probe of his latex-covered finger. 'This is quite impressive,' the doctor said. He looked as though he meant it. You glanced at me and I couldn't help feeling a tiny bit proud. Your legs dangled forlornly from the bed. When he looked at your face the doctor suddenly recognised you from your placement in the department and you both started discussing Doctor X who he was sure you used to know, and Nurse Y who had now left to help out in a Romanian orphanage. It made me feel shallow and unworthy. After several minutes of this namedropping exchange the doctor left, having called someone in to stitch the flaps of skin back together.

'You are a brave boy,' the red-headed nurse said in a stupid, nannyish tone – at odds with her childlike appearance. When she turned to walk away, carrying one of those cardboard trays full of bloodstained cotton wool, I swear she winked at you. I noticed your good hand lifting as if to reach towards her and beg her to stay. But you were left alone with the subdued madwoman that was me.

We didn't speak. Then an older nurse with a thicker waist appeared beside the bed, now paint-spattered with your blood. An image slammed into my mind of the sheet between my legs when I was in hospital and you'd run away because you couldn't bear to see me in pain. I swayed at the memory, clutched at the blanket on the end of the bed, but neither you nor the nurse noticed. Both intent on the dressing of your stitched-up wound. When she'd finished she handed us a spare pack of lint and bandages to take home with us, instructing us (me) to change them every other day. Then they said you could leave, with some strong painkillers and an almost-wife who could have killed you, either before or after the hospital visit. I'm sorry to say I felt little if any remorse at what I'd done. Only shock. I lived in a state of shock around that time. It was as if a hole had opened up inside me and all the emotion I used to have had poured away through it. I doubted I'd ever be able to feel things properly again.

That night you lay on your side with your back to me, breathing so quietly I feared you were dead. It was me who rocked the mattress with my crying. It was definitely time to admit our relationship was beyond fixing, even though we'd already put the deposit on a new house.

*Your scar is nothing, Neil, compared to the internal one I've carried for the almost three decades since we split up. It may be invisible, my scar, it doesn't advertise itself like yours does. But it's the scar you gave me. It changed my life. Can you say that about the one on your hand?*

# 15

## *Edinburgh, August 1987*

AT THE LAST minute Lauren picks up the framed photo of Ewan and Colin from Neil's side of the bed. Stuffs it into her rucksack between a bundle of socks and her angora jumper. The soft blue wool induces a strong compulsion to take one of Neil's shirts as well – the colour that most reminds her of him. But she mustn't. She doesn't even know why she wants the photograph: maybe because it reminds her of the time when everything was perfect. When she was certain she and Neil would become a family.

*Oh no, more tears.* A wave of nausea rises with the flood.

She sinks onto the bed and releases the waterfall. Not just tears, more a feeling like Martina Navratilova has hit a tennis ball into her stomach, knocked all the breath out of her chest. She can't cope, *I can't live with the pain.* But just as she's about to die, the shuddering ebbs.

She pulls the drawstrings tight at the neck of the rucksack, drags the flap over the top and manages to fasten the buckles.

The rucksack is closed, life with Neil packed and ready to be dispatched. Standing on shaking legs, about to hoist the heavy burden onto her back, a long, low moan doubles her over again. Lauren wraps her arms around her waist, pats her sides as though she's someone else. A lost child who needs comforting. But Maw's currently in full-time psychiatric care. Lauren's youngest siblings are farmed out between the married oldest ones. (Poor Ardal and poor Meg; having to live with Pepe.) As for Da... catch him on the telephone before noon and he *might* just remember he has a daughter named Lauren. Catch him after twelve and he'll either be maudlin or loudly repent his many sins. Or he'll be pure nasty, call Lauren a slag or a bastard. Which she may be. Da's been told he'll die if he carries on drinking but it doesn't seem to bother him.

Woes tumble over rocks in Lauren's throat and she struggles not to choke.

The telephone rings. She's still crying when she picks it up. 'Come on, Lauren,' says a firm voice. It's Andrea, in the telephone box on the corner of Cowgate. 'I'll be given a ticket if I stay in that parking space any longer. Get yourself down here, now. Anyway,' she adds when Lauren doesn't manage to answer (Andrea's learned over the past few days to ignore her friend's sobs and deal with her brusquely). 'Neil will be back soon, you don't want to end up having another row, do you?' That gets Lauren moving. She truly believes she'll die if this grief is exacerbated by any more of Neil's apologies. His pleas to give them one more try and the false promises that they can replace what he's caused her to lose.

Kathy has put her in touch with the cousin of one of her nursing friends who has a room to sublet in a Glasgow tenement. Lauren's going back to the town of her birth. Packing away her degree in Sociology and Anthropology and the work she enjoys in the youth resettlement centre to take up the promise of a job in a *Bargain Basement*. It will just about pay her new rent. Her supervisor on the social work course can't believe she's throwing away her potential. 'You've shown such promise, Lauren, you've a natural affinity with disadvantaged kids.'

*That's because I was one – my younger brothers and sisters still are.* 'Why don't you move to another flat in Edinburgh and carry on working with us here?' her supervisor asks. But she doesn't understand, Lauren can't risk the possibility of bumping into Neil. What if she needs to go back to A&E? Neil's bound to be there. The owner of the new shop in Grassmarket also thinks she's mad to give up a coveted part-time job in fossils in favour of plastic cutlery and party-poppers in the rougher end of Partick.

Andrea kisses Lauren goodbye at the Market Street entrance to Waverley Station. 'It's not that far, Glasgow. I can easily pop over and see you. You'll give me my tea, won't you?' But Lauren doesn't even smile at the Glasgow versus Edinburgh joke. "You'll have had your tea already?" is how an Edinburgh householder would supposedly greet a visitor. Their student life together flashes before Lauren's eyes as Andrea's Lancashire accent washes over her. They shared a room in Halls before finding their future home together in the abandoned tenement building.

*The two of them had taken to going out at all hours whilst their contemporaries sat in the Student Union getting drunk (neither Andrea nor Lauren could afford the regular binges) or studying (they thought they had all the time in the world for that). One night, after descending one of the many stone wynds leading from one level of the city to another, they spotted two kids with dreadlocks pulling aside a sheet of corrugated iron, inexpertly nailed over a doorway across the road. Curiosity led the girls closer and they dared each other to follow the pair inside.*

*They followed a thread of music coming from deep within the dark, musty building, felt their way towards a flickering light and the sounds of voices and music. At an internal doorway they met each other's eyes in the dimness. Excitement welled in Lauren's throat, a taste she tested for fear but found lacking. Before them was a gaping room. A meagre fire burned in a grate at one end and at the other a paraffin heater breathed warming fumes. Several candles were arranged on the mantle of a tall, stone fireplace. She smelt onions. A glance around revealed a pan of soup on a portable stove near the door. Lauren realised she was hungry. The thick smell of weed also hung in the air. Andrea and Lauren hesitated in the doorway, eyes still getting used to the dimness. Involuntarily, Lauren's fingers crept towards her friend's and they held hands.*

*A huddle of bodies breathed steam into the candlelit dimness. A bearded boy wearing an army greatcoat and a thick woollen hat noticed them only when Andrea sneezed from the dust. Slowly, other heads turned towards the two girls. The scene before them had an unreal, filmic quality that shortened Lauren's breath – anything can happen in a film. It was possible that Andrea and she would be hunted by this pack of feral kids, through the corridors, up the winding staircase of the derelict building, into a tower-room, perhaps, that they might not get out of alive. But it didn't feel as though they would.*

*A girl wearing a similar woolly hat to the bearded boy clambered to her feet, steadying herself with her hand on his shoulder. She stomped over to the girls, boots heavy on the bare floor. Her face was almost in silhouette with the candlelight behind her. Lauren held what little breath was left in her lungs, causing her heart to pump uncomfortably hard. These outlaws probably hated students; would consider them privileged, however misguidedly in hers and Andrea's case.*

*'Got any money?' the girl said gruffly. Lauren watched her breath dissipate on the air before them, then she glanced nervously at Andrea. Both of them felt in their pockets and each pulled out a few coins, tipping what there was into the girl's hands.*

*'It's all I have.' Lauren's voice shook. What would she want next?*

*"S okay.' The girl's blonde hair escaped in candle-lit wisps from her hat. She counted the coins into her other hand. 'Should be enough. We get our giros themorra. Markus,' – glancing over her shoulder at the boy in the greatcoat –'your turn tae go out. More baccie, man. I'm Fiona,' she said to*

*Lauren and Andrea.*

*Lauren and Andrea arrived back in halls stoned. Lauren attempted to open the wrong room door and Andrea knocked the fire-extinguisher off the wall after lurching against it. They laughed too loudly and while attempting to manipulate the extinguisher back into place they heard the fumbling of a lock. A skinny wee bunty burst into the corridor, shouting at them to* shut the fook up *in his Brummy accent.*

*The squat residents' held a meeting and a few days later, on their invitation, Lauren and Andrea dragged their few belongings through the streets and alleyways to the tall stone building off Lothian Road. Lauren lived there for seven months until she moved in with Neil. It meant she could work fewer hours at her part-time jobs. There was a weekly contribution towards communal utilities. Food was a continuous pan of soup that lived on the portable stove, a few extra potatoes thrown in every day from the large paper sack in the corner of the makeshift kitchen.*

Andrea is now married to an accountant. She is the mammy of Lauren's two-year-old goddaughter, Elspeth. Fresh tears sprout from Lauren's eyes. She waves and blows a kiss to the baby in the back seat of Andrea's car before walking quickly away along busy Market Street into Waverley station. Over the footbridge to Platform 11. She waits for the train, lodged into a corner, making herself invisible. A grey woman pressed against yellow-grey bricks, rucksack upright between her knees. Tears stream down her cheeks.

By the time the train comes into the platform, Lauren's managed to keep her face dry for five whole minutes. She's determined not to arrive in Glasgow crying. *What's done is done*, as Granny Mary often says. *Time to move on.*

# 16

*Edinburgh, five months earlier*

'EH, LAUREN, HEN.' Ruth gives her a gentle push on the shoulder. 'Yer awfy peely-wally lookin' the day. Tell Ruthie all aboot it?'

Lauren frequently finds herself crying into a mug of tea on Ruth's boat, or into an empty mug in this case. Usually after an argument with Neil. Ruth's a cross between a mother (one whose medication works) and a sister, (Kathy). It helps that she's a fellow Weegie, too. 'I've missed two periods.'

There, now it can't be unsaid. She's pregnant. Best admit it. *But it could still be a mistake of some kind, couldn't it?* Perhaps she hasn't been eating properly, maybe that's it. Hasn't had much appetite lately. Now she comes to think about it, she once read that poor nutrition can cause periods to stop, maybe that's the reason. But she knows in her heart it isn't.

Water laps the sides of the boat and also her cheeks. She wipes them dry and raises her face to Ruth's before letting her gaze slide over the familiar objects in this home-from-home.

Books cram the shelves in every available nook. There's a miniature wood-burning stove and a compact kitchen worktop. Lauren sits in an undersized armchair facing Ruth on the neat, wooden-armed sofa. On the flyleaf table a stretched-legs distance away a pile of workbooks and papers leans precariously to one side. Ruth must be the coolest teacher in school for living on a boat and dressing like a gypsy. Or the most laughed-at, but she takes it in good grace.

A kettle steams on the flat top of the stove. Ruth leans forward again and detaches the mug from Lauren's hands. She places it on a cleared corner of table. After pouring a fresh stream of hot water into the teapot she opens the door to the tiny bathroom and retrieves a roll of toilet paper, which she hands to Lauren.

'Cam on noo. Stop your greetin'. It'll make no difference to what's already done. Question is, what are you gonnae do aboot it? I was wonderin when you were gonnae tell me, hen.'

Lauren blows her nose.

'Ah guessed a couple a weeks ago, you have a peely look. And you went aff coffee. You used to love coffee. So, two months, eh? Best be making some decisions. I'm guessin' you havenae told Neil?'

'No. He's too busy. And he's so tired.' Lauren catches a glimpse of her face in the shell-framed mirror above the tiny kitchen sink. She's tired, too. And she can't go home until the rawness of her eyes has faded. She can't face telling Neil today.

'He needs a calm environment. They're making him take on more and more responsibility at the hospital. He wouldnae cope with this, I just know it.'

'What aboot you, hen?'

'What about me?'

'How would you feel aboot a wee barra?'

A pain stabs Lauren's heart. *A wee barra of ma ain.* Someone to cuddle during Neil's long hours at the hospital. A baby! Boy or girl, it wouldn't matter... names float through her head. Now she's admitted it, they come. Syllables that have been waiting behind a locked door.

*Kathy has two girls, three-year-old twins, and Michael has a trio of boys aged between one and four. Pepe is getting married soon and Declan's young wife – too young, some say – is pregnant. Mibby I would finally feel I belong in ma ain family.*

But she hasn't belonged since she went off to study Sociology instead of nursing. Or refused Mass shortly after her love-affair with Superstar began. Or was never Da's in the first place.

'I can't.'

'What can't you?'

'Have a baby. Neil's only in his foundation year. We're supposed to be planning our wedding, but not until he goes into Practice. A baby now would ruin everything. He'll freak out.'

'Hen, its' no' just about him. What do you wannae do? In your heart? Be honest, now.'

Coral light breaks through the dark bank of clouds hovering over the boat.

'I. . . I want to keep it.' Unconsciously, Lauren lays a hand on her belly. 'I do. I want a baby. I never realised how much until now.'

Telling Ruth makes it real. The parade of released names trips and dances through her head, *Delphine or Zane. Aaron or Alice. Sebastian, Guinevere. . .* Not Irish names, tributes to Catholicism like Kathy's girls, Siobhan and Sinead, or bog-standard ones like John, Andrew and James – Michael's sons. Hers will be different – special. Maybe Phoenix – the English form of Phuong, Lauren's Vietnamese friend from Uni who lost three members of her family at sea. The first poem Phuong learned in English was Yeats: *I am haunted by numberless islands, and many a Danaan shore. . . I would that we were changed to white birds. . .*

Or Tira, after *Tir na nOg*, an imaginary island in the poem. Lauren could raise her baby there. Maybe the only place she could truly belong. She shivers.

Years in the future, a girl of whom she is very fond will copy the same poem out for Lauren as a leaving present.

'Here, hawd that, warm ya cockles.' Ruth hands her a second mug of tea and Lauren takes the handle, cups her other hand above the steam. 'Weel.' Ruth clears her throat. 'You'd best get it over with as soon as you get hame, tell Neil. Give him time to take everything in afore the wee barra starts to show.' Ruth leans forward and presses the back of her hand to Lauren's cheek. 'It'll work out fine, hen. He loves the ground you walk on, you know he does. I think you forget that, sometimes.'

The setting sun reflects orange back from the river into the boat's cosy interior. Lauren hears the sudden flurry and quackle of ducks in the reeds at the water's edge, followed by the tramp of footsteps on the bank above. The clear ring of children's voices. Ruth's Italian friend Clara has arrived at the boat with her son and daughter for the English tuition Ruth gives them. The children always bring bread for the ducks before their lesson. Lauren dabs her eyes. She'll drink her tea, say a quick hello and leave them to it.

# 17

### *Ferry to Stornoway, September 2016*

I MOVE MY gaze a few inches to one side. Your Adam's apple seems to have grown since I last saw it. I watch the lump bob up and down as you swallow a deep gulp of tea. It must be hot, the tea. You used to drink it almost straight from the kettle, I joked that your mouth was made of asbestos. You were always in a hurry, Neil, busy and important. Hot tea no less easy to swallow than the daily sorrows you had to deal with at the hospital.

The rocking of the boat makes me nervous. I snatch a sideways glance out of the window at the rolling waves – I feel threatened. I never used to be nervous of water, but I am now. The fear makes me glad of your presence, so tangible and comforting. Doctor-like. Can you sense my relief?

I turn away from the water, refuse to let the fear engulf my lungs, blind me to the reality of the present. I'm safe on this boat. But water's haunted my dreams recently – stories I've heard about drowning. Useless lifejackets, broken boats. Dead babies. The world sorrowing, and as quickly forgetting. *No room for refugees*. Waves of history, ever-repeated. How can we...?

Back to you, Neil. Every atom of me recognises every atom of you. The pores on your surface are still as familiar as my own skin. Tiny hairs on your neck reach out to me. A breathing silence between us. I like this, I don't want it to change. Your presence has always been with me, I see that now. Sometimes, during the years since we were last together, I've woken in the night and believed you were by my side. On these white-tipped waves, on this steel-grey sea, I understand how much my being has been permeated by yours.

In the past I always had more friends than you. You've probably imagined me as married and with several children by now, but the opposite is true. You, on the other hand, it's easy to imagine that you've stayed single. My guess is that you spend your evenings listening to Radio 3, reading non-fiction. Or perhaps watching a documentary on the latest fancy TV, which you're bound to own. Wall-mounted, for tidiness's sake. Look at you, here on your own, just as I am. Or perhaps you do have a wife somewhere, one who is a doctor like you – no, I see her as a tenured lecturer at a university. A self-contained woman who doesn't mind you travelling. But *children*... you never wanted them. Whereas I did, so much.

I risk another glance out the window. The sea has turned a darker grey, white horses, white birds ride the waves. Threatening clouds gather in tighter knots. I feel myself curling inwards. Thunder and lightning might be on the way. We're so exposed, here on the ocean. The hairs on the backs of my wrists are raised.

In my early twenties I used to dream I was adrift at sea. Crowded with fellow refugees into a rickety wooden boat. I'd heard of the terror first-hand from Phuong. It haunted me to listen, but she needed to speak. Stories need to be told. I've always had a fear of drowning.

Sheena flits back into my mind, never far away.

I tried to save her Neil, I really tried.

Phuong married an English student, the eventual headmaster of a private boarding school in Kent. Last I heard, they'd recently become grandparents. I was invited to the christening party in their English country garden and I was planning to go but at the last minute I couldn't face it. Phuong had let go of her past, was so anglicised, I don't know why it made me so uncomfortable. *If only I could let go of my ghosts.*

I lost touch with most of our university friends when I left Scotland. Caught up with one or two on my return to Edinburgh and a few more since Facebook. Andrea and I had nothing left in common.

*I wonder if Phuong still dreams of the dark waters that stole some of her family. Perhaps, like me, she's unable to sleep at night for the images that crowd her mind of toddlers washed up on beaches. The thousands of individual stories forming a single cry of helplessness.*

*On the foam of the sea.*

*Water-babies.*

*Do as you would be done by.*

I tried, Neil, to save Sheena.

I lift my eyes higher and allow my gaze to rest on your lips, damp from the hot tea. I won't look at your eyes. Not yet.

# 18

## Edinburgh, June 1987

THE FIRST TIME Lauren felt bubbles popping in her lower abdomen she put it down to wind. Now she realises it's her unborn child, making herself known. Wriggling like a fish. *There, it happened again.* Lauren holds her breath. She's fourteen weeks pregnant and had been told she wouldn't be able to feel the baby move until at least fifteen weeks. *My child is an early-developer.*

Neil refuses to refer to the baby as a baby. 'It's a *foetus*, Lauren. It wouldn't be capable of survival if it was born at this point and therefore it's only a foetus, not a baby.'

His haggard expression grows more defined with the advancement of Lauren's pregnancy. She now has a small bump. Soon he won't be able to deny his child. He's trapped. She has the power to release him – he implores her with his eyes every time he can bring himself to look at her.

*But I feel it moving, Neil.*

*I want her.*

A female foetus, she's certain of it. *Alicia, Sarah, Hannah, Eliza, Genevieve, Cecily, Allegra...*

'You do realise, don't you, that I won't be able to have anything to do with it, even if you do insist on going ahead with the pregnancy? You'll have to look after the baby completely by yourself.' He tries everything. 'And you'll have to make sure it doesn't disturb my sleep. I'm struggling to cope with my workload and this crippling exhaustion as it is.' Does he actually believe they could continue living together with a baby he refuses to acknowledge?

Neil looks like death. A decision will have to be made soon. *I love my baby.* But does she want to be a single mother if he forces her to choose? *I couldn't afford the rent on my own.*

*This is my body, this is my blood.* But what about Neil's health? Bruises blossom under his sore eyes, he's developed a cough he can't seem to shake off. *I don't know how to love him.*

She's a set of scales. Weighing her need, her baby's need, against Neil's despair.

Neil sleeps on the sofa in the sitting room. He says it's not because he's angry with her – his broiling feelings are blatantly deeper than anger: panic, sadness, confusion. He says it's because he sleeps restlessly. At night she can hear his fitful breathing from the other room. Lauren remembers how he once described her as his shelter in a storm.

'Please, Lauren,' he's tried begging. 'I understand it will be hard for you, not to go ahead with the pregnancy. The feelings will pass, though, I promise.' *How can you promise me that? You're not carrying our daughter in your belly.*

And on another occasion: 'We can't have a baby yet – I can't, I just couldn't cope.'

Finally he tries: 'One more year and then I'll be more in control of my own life. I'll join a practice, we'll be settled in our new home with a garden and then we can have a baby. Just not yet. See sense, Lauren, please?'

When Neil's working at the hospital, Lauren takes out the fine woollen shawl Ruth knitted for the baby. A talisman to fortune. She bundles it into a baby-like shape and cuddles it against her cheek, rocking in front of the mirror. She can't possibly go through with an abortion now, it's too late – she already loves her daughter.

At the Centre the girls flick her with appraising eyes,

continue to chew gum while they mutter behind their hands. Playing table tennis, Megan's elbow knocks into Lauren's ribs and Kirsty, across the table, calls, 'Watch out for Loz, she's up tha spout. It's obvious, mate,' she says to Lauren. Lauren bends over, out of breath. 'I heard ye cowkin' in the bogs earlier. Aab'dy knows, anyway.'

Lauren's supervisor beckons her into the office. Assures her that the pregnancy won't pose a problem. 'As you know, we have a créche here, and there's also one at the college.' She speaks as though it's a celebration. As though producing a child will not change *everything* in Lauren's life.

---

Lauren lies dreaming on the sofa. The windows of the flat are open to the sounds of traffic on Cowgate and the hot air smells of summer. Dust and traffic and dandelion clocks. In her dream Neil had been happy about the baby, throwing it up in the air and catching it, making it shriek with laughter. They'd been picnicking in Greyfriars Kirkyard and strangers had paused to smile at their chortling daughter in the safety of her father's arms. *Such a pretty child.*

Lauren wakes up sobbing.

*It will never happen.* Dread lodges in her gut. She can't keep both Neil and the baby.

*Olivia, Maura, Grace, Aisling, Juliet...* Neil walks in the door as Lauren murmurs the name Barbara, that of his mother. It means foreign, or strange. Or protectress against fire and lightning. She knows the baby name dictionary off by heart. She's tried out Karina and Mhairi as well, variations on her mother's and granny's names. But Barbara is the name he walks in on. Neil stops dead and his bag slides down his arm to the floor. His eyes are stark. She looks up at him. Great, hoarse sobs explode from his chest. He becomes bowed, like an old man. The deep-set *Superstar* feelings return. Neil's vulnerability when he told her about his mother. She pushes herself up from the sofa and hops on pins-and-needle feet towards him – wraps her arms around his shaking body. *Neil is here, Neil is now.* She cares for him so deeply. How can she be the one to cause him such pain?

When Neil's sobs subside, they sit down and talk. Properly, for the first time. She sees him as if he's new to her again. He looks deep into her eyes while he explains his feelings. Discussions go on all evening, they order a takeout for supper.

Neil can't get past his dread and fear of the baby. He reveals that he's had a warning from his boss and will have to repeat his foundation year if his standards don't improve.

'Patients have complained.' More tears spring to Neil's eyes. Lauren hasn't seen him cry before. She feels unstable. Pins and needles stab her hands, gripped by Neil's.

Maybe he should never have tried to become a doctor, he says. 'I'm not kind enough. Do I even like people?' He can't make sense of anything right now and he believes he's suffering from depression. 'I just can't see a way out, Lauren.'

The ground laps around Lauren's feet, tries to suck her in.

Having a baby will destroy him.

*Neil was here first.*

She pulls her hands out of his and grips the edge of the table, her head spinning.

'You're breaking out in a sweat,' Neil says. Snot blocks his nostrils but he's ever the doctor. 'Are you all right? Come and sit down on the sofa.'

Strands of hair plaster themselves to Lauren's cheeks. He sits her down, brings her a glass of water and settles himself into the cushions beside her.

'It's much harder than I thought it would be, Lauren.' He lifts the cold flannel off her forehead and lays it to one side. He strokes her hand, lying inert on her lap. She notices the flaking skin on the inside of his elbow as she traces the veins up his arm with her other hand. Layers of him peeling away – the physicality of his stress. She runs her fingers up his bicep, across his shoulder, rests them in the hollow of his collarbone.

*I know every inch of you.*

The complete surface of his skin.

'I never realised,' he says softly. 'I mean I never properly empathised before. It was all science. But now I see that patients are real people, they depend on me.' He checks her eyes for a response. She blinks away saturating tears. 'There's this woman – a girl really – who keeps swallowing safety-pins. She's been blocked from three hospitals already and this is her third admission with us. She's perforated her bowel. They operated on her. I watched the operation and I was the one who had to talk to her afterwards. She knows *exactly* what she's doing and for that reason they can't section her. She'll just keep doing it again and again.'

His compassion is palpable. He drags a trembling hand over his eyes. 'I honestly don't think I can cope with all the work and the pressure of it, and then have even less sleep and more worry with a baby in the flat.'

*He said he would worry about the baby.* The secret code behind his message – he would be forced to love her (or possibly him) and it might break him.

*Your baby, Neil. Your daughter (or son).* A gulf between them, her desire to love their child, his not to. How can it be breached?

'I'm so sorry to feel this way,' he says. 'I know how hard all this has been on you. Oh, darling.'

'Oh, Neil.'

'Lauren, you do know how much I love you? I can't imagine life without you. I'm sorry to make you cry. Come here, lay your head on my shoulder.'

The first place she's ever belonged. She falls asleep with his hand stroking her hair. And later, he rouses her gently and leads her to their bed. He helps her undress and they make love slowly, so deeply she feels he's bathing their baby in renewal. Lauren drowns in Neil, and she can't imagine life without him, either.

# 19

## *Ferry to Stornoway, September 2016*

YOUR LIPS, NEIL. Reddened from the steam. Your teeth appear between them as they break into a smile. 29-years-older lips. Grey stubble now shadows the top lip and the outline of your jaw, but still it's the same mouth, the same chin I knew. The full lower lip, the perfect V in the upper, both flatten into a straight line when you smile. I feel my lips stretch in response. Our two mouths greet each other again, across space and time. I wish to remain here, gazing at your lips forever.

*A night at the squat off Lothian Road, the same evening that you first kissed me on Granny's Green Steps. Andrea tactfully made herself scarce from the tiny, littered room she and I shared, giving me a thumbs-up on her way out. You and I lay wrapped in blankets on the thin mattress, kissing for hours. Just kissing, kissing and kissing. Kissing and kissing and kissing, with all our clothes still in place. For the whole night. Perfect bonding – we were sea-anemones on rocks, swept by a warm, recurrent tide.*

The mouth that I once kissed begins to speak, emits throat-clearing sounds before forming words. 'Hello, Lauren.'

Now... do it now, I think. *Do it.*

Am I ready yet?

Do it now. *Lift mine eyes to thine.*

I swear it happens in slow motion. My gaze combs the whole of your face. I see the slopes of your cheeks, your strong, straight nose with the same slightly flaring nostrils I remember. Moisture gathers at the lower edges of your eyes, at the opening of your nostrils, at the corners of your mouth. Your face the way it was when I last saw you, as if your features are about to disintegrate.

The skin hangs looser on your face than before. Dark shadows in violet and blue beneath your eyes. Delicate skin, like crinkled tissue paper.

Am I ready, yet?

My eyes fill with water, as yours will have done. My vision of you will be through mist. There's a wavering veil, with you on the other side. In the place we've always both remained.

*Where time would surely forget us, and sorrow come near us no more.*

On our magical island of dreams. Me, you and Barbara.

Nobody was never able to replace you, Neil. I shouldn't have got married to Ellis.

I must have made some involuntary movement of my hands. I hear something solid slide to the floor, probably my kindle, but I can't drag my eyes away from the plane they are fixed on. Your eyes, distant through the mist. I press the heels of my hands into my mine. Then, as my vision returns I see your eyes crinkle at the corners. You're still far away. Your smile is glazed with a film of your own tears. You use the back of your wrist to disperse them. My mouth mimics your smile and it makes me ache. We continue to smile at each other. Our smiling could go on, and on and on like the kissing of that first entwined night. Sometimes touch isn't even needed.

Am I ready to break the silence of the smile with words?

Not yet.

# 20

## Edinburgh, July 1987

LAUREN ENDURES THE labour of childbirth for fifteen hours. She observes the young woman from a distance, a girl with dark chestnut curls escaping the ponytail at the back of her head, strands sticking to her neck. The young woman who walks haltingly up and down the smooth-floored corridor outside all the rooms in which women moan. A young woman dragging a drip-stand on wheels. A young man walks by her side, his hand slipping under her elbow. He strongly resembles Neil.

Lauren jolts back into her body. It *is* Neil, and the girl beside him is herself. She immediately feels the dragging ache in her back again.

When she pauses to lean against the wall, Neil tries to rub her back as the nurse has advised, but Lauren pushes him away. She's been lied to, deceived – nobody told her it would be this bad. From rooms on either side of the corridor the low moans and high-pitched screams increase in volume.

*I am in Hell.*

The pain worsens. She reaches out for Neil's hand but the space beside her is empty. He's gone. She's on all fours on a narrow bed, twisting her face into the pillow.

'I'm sure he'll be back, pet. In the meantime, let us give you an epidural?' When Lauren hefts herself back over, the midwife's wearing a trained expression of neutrality. 'No point going through all this pain for nothing.' Her tone never wavers.

*But that's what happens in Hell. Pain, pain.*

'No.'

She deserves to suffer for her sins.

---

Neil reappears when it's all over, his face green-tinged. He presents her with flowers and attempts to make a fuss of her but too late. She can't forgive him for opting out. *We were supposed to be in this together.*

He mumbles explanations, excuses. 'I'm sorry, I couldn't bear to see you suffer. I have to watch patients in pain every day. It hurt too much when it was you.'

And, 'I knew you'd be stronger on your own, I was only getting in the way.'

And, 'You didn't seem to need me, so I left.'

Lauren turns her face away, announces to the wall beside the bed – 'It was a girl. I knew she was.'

A scuffle, a chair knocked over. She turns her head back to see Neil make it to the sink only just in time.

'Barbara.' Lauren dishes out cruelty with her sorrow. Neil retches again. *Barbara Mhairi*, Lauren thinks. Her daughter's name seals her lips and eyes closed – perhaps forever. A granddaughter for Neil's dead mother. *At least the baby won't be alone. But I am.*

Remembering his daughter every time he thinks his mother's name. Neil's punishment for what he's made Lauren do.

---

At what point did her baby's small life end? Was it when the first contractions squeezed her in the womb, startling the foetus into awareness of her too-early birth? Or was it later, when she was catapulted into the unviable light of an alien world? Or at some point in between.

Lauren can't help wondering if Barbara was scared. Born unto death. No dust, no ashes, no funeral. Forever a shameful secret.

---

*One last push*, says the midwife. A tearing pain as the clip attached to the catheter scrapes Lauren's raw vaginal flesh. *Push one more time.* And one time more. And then another. There's burning pressure. With a sickening vacuum sensation something rubbery is expulsed onto the sheet between Lauren's trembling legs. She strains to catch a glimpse. Sees a doll-sized figure encased in a cloudy, translucent sheath. Skinny arms and drawn-up knees, oversized head. Chin tucked onto chest.

The seconds of Lauren's viewing expand into forever. Is it possible the foetus moved? Is it possible to put her back where she belongs? The midwife is busy sorting out some kind of business down there, probing and pulling. Lauren still holds a flicker of hope. *Maybe, maybe, maybe, I'll have you for me.* The midwife quickly tucks the tiny pink limbs and face out of sight, whisks away a bundle that could fit in the palm of Neil's hand. Bustles it away from Lauren's line of vision. Folding extra cloths around it while Lauren leans sideways in the bed. She begs, 'Let me see properly?'

'Best no',' the midwife is brusque. She drapes a sheet over the trolley. 'We'll make you presentable and then you can have a wee sleep, you must be tired out.' She turns her back on the trolley and moves over to Lauren again, still blocking her view.

'At least tell me then, is it a girl?'

'Aye, she was, hen.' Tenderness finally breaks the midwife's professional detachment. 'Best no' think aboot it any more. What's done is done.'

Lauren wakes in the early hours of the morning. Burning in a fever of regret and grief. Crying in her sleep. *My baby is dead, my baby is dead.*

Her whole body weeps – milk seeps from her aching breasts. *There's been a mistake, I want her back.*

Later she dreams of an older woman, who floats towards her, swimming serenely through a watery dark. She sees that the older woman resembles herself. The older one reaches to take baby Barbara, awake in the bed beside Lauren and carries her away in her arms. When Lauren wakes up again in the morning, she feels completely empty.

Later Neil arrives, subdued and remorseful, to take her home.

# 21

*Ferry to Stornoway, September 2016*

OUR ENCOUNTER FEELS unreal, as if I've dreamed you. But you're really here, smiling at me over the table. I glance at the glisten of tears on your forearm, running down towards the scar. And before I can catch myself my hand creeps out and smooths the wetness away. I'm actually touching you. But it's not like we're strangers, since I've just relived our history. Your tears soak my skin. I leave my hand in place, my palm over your knuckles. My finger runs along the puckered skin of your scar. I think Barbara's name and I wonder if you hear my inner voice.

My eyes find yours again, while my finger acts of its own accord. It slides under your wrist and feels your pulse, steady and calm. I wish we didn't have to speak but my voice wants to act independently of me as well.

Shall I speak?

I speak.

'Neil.'

'Lauren.'

You never wanted me to leave, you loved me – I know that. You thought everything could be okay afterwards. I loved you, too, but my love was as tainted by the crime as yours for me had been while I was pregnant. Your aim was to carry on with our original plans once the trauma was over. It wouldn't last long, you believed. Then we would go ahead – move into a house of our own and take up where we left off.

You understood, in theory at least, that I would need time to grieve. And I'm certain that in your heart you must have grieved as well. *But you never showed it, Neil.* All I saw was relief and I couldn't stand it.

We had a house picked out. But walking into the two spare rooms I thought of her – I only saw the space she should have inhabited.

'How have you been?' your voice comes out croaky. 'You look well.'

'I am, thank you. What about you?'

We sound like acquaintances, chatting on a ferry. Do I want to get into a deeper relationship with you – do you with me? I can tell you're struggling to gauge my intentions as much as I am yours. I slide my hand off yours, fold it around the mug of tea and bring it to my lips. Never mind that I don't usually drink tea anymore. Perhaps I'll begin again.

'I'm well, too, thanks,' you answer. 'Recently returned from Canada.'

'Canada, you went back there?'

I've pictured you settling into a GP practice in Edinburgh and remaining in your adopted town. I've thought you were there all along. Now I'll have to re-imagine the story of your life.

'I went back for my dad's funeral and decided to stay on. It was good to reconnect with my brother and there was work there. I still had my Canadian passport. No reason to return to Scotland. You know. Stuff. A fresh start.'

Re-imagining takes place in my head. You finish the remains of your tea while I'm taking the first sips of mine.

'Thanks for the tea.'

What I mean to say is, *when did he die, your father? How is Ewan? Did you meet anyone special in Canada?*

'You're welcome. I saw you sitting there, and...'

'I'm glad you came over to say hello. It's good to catch up again.' I take another sip.

Good to relive my life, it surprises me to learn.

You hated your father when we first got together but your relationship with him had improved by the time we split up. He visited Edinburgh with Ewan to attend your graduation. And you were upset that I struggled to equate the rather affable man I met with the cold-hearted tyrant you'd conveyed to me. But you finally admitted that he seemed to have mellowed. He was visibly proud of you for becoming a doctor and in the awkward moment of your long-overdue bonding, he told you your mother would have been proud, too.

'Whereabouts are you headed? Stornoway, obviously. But are you staying on Lewis or going island-hopping?'

Perhaps you're taking a holiday, simply a break on the islands before returning to Canada. Or maybe you'll settle back in Edinburgh, you always had a fondness for it because of your mother. But I'm not expecting the answer you give me.

'I'm taking up a position as a GP – based in Stornoway but I'll be working all over the island. The position came up when I was looking for work back in Scotland, so. . .'

'Oh. . .'

There's a weight on my chest. I draw breath carefully and struggle out from underneath it. Of all the places in Scotland, you end up in the same one as me.

My life has swung full-circle, a new start has led back to the beginning. I keep breathing.

'And you?' You trace a pattern in spilt salt on the table.

I take another swallow of tea. 'Youth and family services, specifically drugs.'

'Ah. You continued in social work, then. I'm glad.'

Annoyance bubbles in my chest now – what business is it of yours to be glad about the path I took? There's so much more to me than you know. I didn't stay in Scotland my whole life, either, but I'm guessing you assume I did.

*Stop being so defensive, Lauren.*

'Where are you based?' you ask next. 'In Stornoway as well?'

Do I notice the pulse at your throat quickening, or have I imagined it? Perhaps it's simply that it pleases me to think your heart has speeded up because we'll be working in close proximity. I want to deflect your questions, I need more time to take you in. So I keep my answer vague.

'Around the island. All of the Western Isles, in fact.'

My home will be in a district called Uig, although the office is indeed in Stornoway. I wanted an isolated location. I won't need to go into the office every day anyway.

Your eyes smile at me.

'You haven't changed, Lauren. I recognised you straight away.'

I understand how you can see the past in me. I too feel comfortable sitting here with you. The same you, despite the grey stubble on your cheeks and the delicate pouching around your eyes, the enlarged freckles on the backs of your hands. To my eyes you haven't changed, either.

I want to ask so many things about the past; what you did after I left. Whether you missed me and for how long. I want to tell you about Dublin and Reykjavik and my return to Edinburgh, about the stint I did working with young people at the refugee camp in Calais, how it made me want to move on from Edinburgh because there are young people living in so many different kinds of situations in different places, and I want to know all about them.

Most of all I want to tell you about Sheena. I would describe one of the many funny things about her, like how she could do a perfect impersonation of the First Minister.

But I don't. A klaxon blares, startling both of us and making me put my hands over my ears.

'You never liked loud noises.'

'I still don't.'

'Bonfire nights were the worst. And the Edinburgh Tattoo, the *very* worst.'

'Not to mention the beginning of the festivals. *Ocht.* Those fireworks. One year you gave me a mild sedative, remember?'

'Ya wee sook,' creeps from your throat. Tears threaten me again and I blink hard. *Silly old woman.* A wee sook, indeed.

You nod, smile, open your mouth to speak again but an announcer's voice breaks in with a report that the ferry will shortly arrive in Stornoway.

After that there's too much to say. And not enough. We both fidget, you stack the cups and I jam things into my bag and find my Kindle and check that my car keys are in the correct zip-up pocket. My heart beats somewhat irregularly. *What do we do now?* Apart from make our way down to the car decks as we've been instructed by the tannoy. The engine noise increases, too loud to talk over. Throbbing indecently.

My cheeks flare. Is it panic I feel, at the thought of separation? I offer you my hand and close my eyes momentarily, the better to savour your grip.

'It was nice to meet you again,' is all I can think of to say once the noise dies down. People push past in a stream towards the staircases.

'What deck are you on, Lauren?'

'Two. The forward staircase.'

We fit ourselves side-by-side into the queue of shuffling car-owners, swelling at the entrances to the steps.

'I'm on the lower deck – the opposite direction to you, I'm afraid. We're going to have to say goodbye for now.'

*For now.*

Still we hold back, stare at each other. You take my arm gently and steer me to one side and the expectation comes into my head that you're going to kiss me. But in your courteous manner you're only helping make space for others to pass. Nevertheless, it's crowded in the lobby. A woman knocks into me with the corner of a large, wheeled bag she drags down from a storage shelf, gives me a dirty look when a swearword escapes my mouth. You catch my eye, the corners of your mouth turn up in a smile and we both laugh.

I wish we could spend more time together.

The chugging engine changes tone again as the boat nudges land. The churning motion goes through me. Another announcement blares through the tannoy.

'Goodbye, then,' I'm still rubbing my leg where the suitcase bumped it.

'Hang on, Lauren,' you say at the last moment, just as I turn away. 'Let me write down my number for you.'

You pull a notebook from the jacket draped over your arm and flip it open to an empty page. The sheets have a perforated edge, the pages a gold trim. It's satisfying to see your taste in stationary remains the same. Tapping your other pockets, lines of panic etch your face.

'A pen?' I open my handbag.

'Thanks.' You scribble something, tear the sheet off. 'Here you are, just in case you want to meet up in Stornoway. It would be nice to talk some more. Give me a call once you've settled in.'

Your hand trembles as you pass the paper over. Lean towards me. Our faces hesitate in the gap and we both take a step forward. Our cheeks brush, an action that passes for a kiss.

*I want to hold you.*

A sob rises in my throat, disguised within a hurried cough.

'Are you all right?'

The flurry of people has thinned and the openings to both staircases are accessible. We really ought to leave.

'Goodbye, then,' I repeat. I feel the way I used to when you were on nights and I wouldn't see you properly for two or more days.

'Goodbye, Lauren, let's meet up soon.'

'Yes, let's. . . '

'Wait. . . would you scribble your number on here for me?'

I hesitate, but who am I kidding? I scrawl my number in a child's handwriting on the notebook you hold in front of me. I'm not sure whose hands are shaking most. Now.

One of us has to make the first move. I turn my back on you, place my hands on the stair rails either side of me. But I change my mind, step back and allow a couple of stray people to pass. I want to see you a final time, offer you a wave, a meaningful smile, but I've left it too late. *Neil.* I can only just see the back of your head as you disappear down the opposite set of stairs, my vision of you already occluded by a hurrying couple coaxing a Golden Retriever down the steps behind you.

# PART TWO

One day in May
she was my deepest breath,
and she sounded like afternoon maple.
I sounded like tartan damp and hour-old
gristle before I could even catch up.

**From *Love in the Cold* By Nick Conroy**

# 22

*Stornoway, Isle of Lewis, September 2016*

EVERYONE I LOOK at reminds me of Neil. All the men in the bright yellow jackets directing the vehicles off the ferry. My hands tremble on the steering wheel. *I need time to think!* A hi-vis arm waves at me and I have to move. It's only when I drive right up to the steward that I can convince myself he's not Neil because his face is different. I feel goose bumps all the way up my arms. It's my turn to drive down the unfolded metal ramp onto land but I hesitate until I can see that the car in front is on solid ground. The hi-vis man looks like Neil again now I can only see him in my rear view mirror. He's frowning. I'm holding up the queue. *Go, do it now.* concentrate on driving a straight line between the low metal edges, the only thing protecting me from the sea. The potential misjudgement of my steering above dark waters, my old life with all its mistakes, it's all glaringly clear in these few seconds.

I only realise how tightly my hands have been gripping the wheel once I've made it safely onto my new homeland. I'd like to stop the car and get my bearings but I'm trapped in the line of vehicles. My hairline's damp with perspiration. I encourage the fingers of my left hand to unhook from the wheel so I can wipe the sweat from my forehead. Blink away these tears. In the rear view mirror I see the last of the Neil-clones disappear from my view and I feel like I've lost him all over again.

As I drive away from the ferry port the views from my side windows go by in a blur, caught up in the crawl of traffic. I'm tormented by a fresh flood of pictures of my encounter with Neil. *He wasn't meant to be a part of my new start.* Or was he?

This must be Stornoway's version of the rush hour. Traffic blurs by and I try to remember the instructions from the estate agent. *Follow the road around the edge of the harbour.* Almost hyperventilating, I secure a parking space by the harbour wall, sideways on both to the road and the water. I switch off the engine. Hold my shaking hands in front of my face. *This is me, I'm real.* After... after Sheena's accident I was told to expect recurrences of shock. Flashbacks. But adrenaline's flooding my body again after the shock of Neil. I'm disintegrating. Banging my wrist on the steering wheel re-solidifies me.

*Did I really touch you? Where are you now?* Somewhere on this road Neil must be sitting in his car. I don't even know what colour it is so it's pretty pointless searching for it amongst the rumbling, tooting traffic. A cold knot lodges in my stomach. *This can't be happening.* Still, the hair-roots on my arm tingle as if the scar-bearing hand I'm sure I studied so thoroughly on the boat has touched me again.

The woman in the estate agents tells me I'll find a note from the owner at the house, with instructions for operating the heating. She also says I should expect to find basic provisions in the cupboards so not to worry if I forget any essentials. 'That's very kind,' I say, concentrating hard on being normal. 'I'm not used to landlords being so considerate.'

She smiles. 'You'll soon get used to it here on the islands. Now, do pop back in and see us, let us know how you're getting on, won't you? Uig is such a lovely area, I'm sure you'll be very happy there.'

I come out of the shop carrying a gift bag containing chocolates and a bottle of wine. Before returning to the car I make myself visit the Co-op for some basic shopping. *Now time to go home.* Oh God, I have an hour's drive ahead of me.

It takes me a while to segue into the steady flow of traffic around the harbour, but the slow pace gives me time to glance into the shops and galleries and look at the boats in the harbour. Moving out of town I break free from the clogged lanes of vehicles.

I keep up a steady fifty miles per hour until I reach a single track road, then I need to drive more slowly. I breathe carefully, play musical passing places with camper vans, cars and even the occasional foreign coach. The road is too narrow! *Concentrate.* The sky is impenetrably blue, reflecting in the many lochs which nestle into the curves of the twisting road – sapphire beads threaded through the green, sculpted landscape. I breathe high up in my chest. From the corner of my eye I keep thinking someone is sitting in the passenger seat beside me. I fight the urge to stretch out my fingers. *I touched your arm. I wiped away your tears.* I make myself concentrate again on the landscape.

Look. A heron perched on a rock. There's another, flying in a straight line towards the opposite bank, legs streaming out behind. I pull into a passing place and breathe into my hands. Did it really happen, my encounter with Neil on the ferry? *Stop, Lauren. Pay attention to your surroundings.* I never knew water could consist of so many colours. The wide-open loch seems alive, jumping with salmon, contained in a grid of enclosures. When I close my eyes for what I think is the briefest moment, the inside of my eyelids ripple with those same water-colours, interwoven with aspects of Neil. *You. Your fingers, the scar on your hand, the hairs on your arm.*

I make a noise in my throat. Start up again and drive through a long, narrow valley. The road seems insignificant in this wonder. A peaty burn bubbles alongside the road – a landscape from a folk tale. I begin to take in that it could – perhaps – be possible for me to be happy.     Neil notwithstanding. I've been on my own for years, I'm self-contained – I want to be useful. *But Neil.* I never took into account that I might ever see him again, let alone *here*, on the island. Or rather, on the ferry. *If it was true.* But the visceral memory of his hands as they were on the table convinces me it was. The feeling of his presence expands in the car. I open the windows and allow air to tickle my scalp. Fill myself with oxygen.

Within the space another presence haunts me. *My girl.* It was the right decision to leave Edinburgh, despite the emotional costs. It wasn't my fault, what happened to Sheena. I wish I could pour it all out to Neil, right here, now, in the car. I need to connect together everything that means anything.

*I did my best to save her, Neil. Truly I did.*

# 23

*Uig, Isle of Lewis, September 2016*

THE SINGLE-TRACK ROAD swoops in a downward curve towards the sea. I hold the wheel tightly. There don't appear to be any street names, and the houses each bear a plaque showing their number and the name of the township. Two cottages share a tiny side-road and one of those houses is mine. The one furthest along, closest to the sea. Tingles shoot up my arms as I steer down the track at crawling pace, feeling like an imposter. I glimpse a face in the window of the first house. Blood roars in my ears.

The cottage is built on a hillock. I have to take a sharp turn into the drive and the gap between the gate posts is narrow. I switch the engine off, double-check the handbrake. Sit in the car a moment, play with the car key in my hand. Smile to myself. *I've done it.* At the same time there's a constriction in my throat. I feel full of unshed tears. *Imagine if you and I had been coming here together, Neil. . .* But if I had a choice it would be the Lauren and Neil from the past, not the two of us now. We could have come here with our daughter, she would have loved it.

As I open the car door a fierce breeze tugs at my hair and at my breath. I gulp, taste salt. Stand upright and stretch out my arms. Feel the rush of that same salted air through the sparse scattering of trees that grow close to the cottage. A more insistent roar threads through the intermittent gusts of wind – the voice of the sea.

*. . . Are you sure I can't come with you?* Was that Sheena's voice, or could it have been Barbara? My girls, my girls. Stop it, Lauren. Neil's opened up a portal and I don't know how to close it. *What's done is done.* Breathe, breathe again – close my eyes. For now, I don't want to think of who has been and gone. I don't want to think about my new job, which starts next week. Or about Neil. I mustn't think about anything but this landscape, this house, my new home. Definitely not about Neil. *You came back too late.*

It doesn't stop my imagination placing him beside me as I gaze out at the dimming view of wildness, though. It was like that for a long time after I first left Edinburgh, I'd be convinced he was standing just behind and to one side of me. *Go away*, I say out loud. *Please.* Something shifts, either inside me or in the thickening atmosphere, I can't tell.

Concentrate. I'm here. Now that I've arrived, the day's decided to tuck itself to sleep. The sea's a dim band of silver beyond the sloping fields that curve away from the house. I follow a white track with my eyes and pick out another beach-inlet. *Sea on two sides.* Lift my finger as if to point and remember I'm alone. Swivel slightly on my feet, straining to make out a small loch that lies closer to the cottage. Beyond the road winding above me, mountains rise on three sides, blueish in the fading light. I hug myself.

The house is single-storey, pale in the dusk. Three windows and a blue front door. With my bag on my shoulder I push open the door and walk into a small porch. A doormat bids me *welcome*. A high, square table bears an envelope addressed to me. I smooth it over with my fingers – thick paper – and peer at the neat handwriting in blue ink before I slip it into my jeans pocket.

Inside, the first thing I see is a gaping recess in the chimney breast. *Strange.* A radiator is warm to my touch, though. There's a wooden-armed sofa and a solid chest in the centre of the room. A compact armchair sits by the window. In the failing light outside, mountains curve around the valley like a comforting arm. Approaching the door opposite the fireplace, I'm acutely aware of my sandals on the bare floor. For some reason I find myself looking over my shoulder, catch my lone reflection in an arched mirror on the chimney breast. *He isn't here.* I try and picture him unlocking the door to his own cottage. Wonder if he'll be thinking of me tonight.

And if, like me he'll be trailed by ghosts. Baby Barbara, Sheena, Granny Mary, my young self. Neil finishes up the procession. He's a combination of the old, young Neil and the new, older version. Concentrate on the house. The small dining room is painted a rather stark yellow. A clothes-pulley hangs from the ceiling. A framed map of Scotland on the wall. The fireplace is already prepared with twists of newspaper and kindling, a metal bucket of logs standing nearby. The window frames the same view as that from the sitting room.

I find the kitchen, square and simply fitted out, with two long windows, each shielded by a white blind. I lay my handbag on the worktop and pull open a door to the glassed-in porch. From here I can make out the line of the sea in the distance. The small bathroom has a deeply recessed window between the old iron bath and the toilet. A faint tracery of flowers winds from one tile to another behind the basin taps. Jiggling a metal rod, I push the window open and stand on tiptoes to peer out into the deepening dark. I can just pick out the shape of an outbuilding at the top of the sloping garden. Clamouring at the back of my head is a thudding pulse, my blood drumming a tattoo of panic and thrilled anticipation combined. *You were there, Neil. You were really there. I can't believe we've seen each other again.* I keep remembering anew. A cool breeze sweeps over my hands where they lie on the sill and I pull them in. My knee catches as I lower myself back onto the balls of my feet. I use the toilet, pull the old-fashioned chain and wash my hands lingeringly to warm my numbed fingers. I remember how cold we used to get in our flat on Cowgatehead, before the central heating was put in and how Neil used to rub his hands over mine in the chipped bathroom sink while we wasted precious hot water bringing the blood back into our whitened fingers.

There's a scullery. I haven't seen one of these since the Victorian tenement I lived in as a child – and that was converted into a bedroom for Michael. I close the door and move back through the dining room, trailing my hands on the surfaces. I think it'll soon feel like home.

I find a kettle, teabags and a packet of biscuits that have been left for me. The fridge hums in the corner. True to my expectations an unopened carton of milk sits on an otherwise empty shelf. I check the date: several days to spare. The landlord lives on the Isle of Skye – at least two and a half hour's journey from here, so I have to assume someone else has a key to the cottage.

Paper crinkles in my pocket as I shift on the kitchen chair. Reading the letter under the bare lightbulb, the neat handwriting introduces the landlord as Murdo. He tells me he will be over to discuss one or two improvements to the cottage next week and he leaves me a telephone number so I can let him know when it will be convenient. Also, my neighbour at number five (not the cottage directly above me on the track but one further up the hill) has a spare key in case of emergencies. Her name is Mrs MacLeod and she works at the museum in the community centre near Timsgarry. He writes it *Timsgearraidh*. He says she also helps out at the beach campsite.

Apparently I should visit the community centre, where *everyone is very friendly and will welcome you into their community*. Murdo hopes I'll be happy in the house as he always was. He finishes with the information that the land has been managed by his family for generations. My hands feel heavy as they hold up the letter, the weight of it bringing them down to the table with a thud. For a moment the yellow-lit air ripples and fractures around me – it feels like water. It's the shock – I was warned about that. All the shocks. I *can* breathe, I can. The angles of the room alter slightly. I squeeze my eyes shut tight and then open them again. I must have imagined the wooden cradle I thought I saw rocking on the floor in the corner of the room a moment before.

# 24

## Edinburgh, August 1987

For a couple of weeks Neil is careful. He tiptoes around Lauren. She's like a sheet of tissue-paper, transparent, easily torn. Unwritten-on. All she wants to do is sleep and think of nothing, while he brings her food and drink and calls work on her behalf. The story goes that she's had a miscarriage. *No*, he'll say to anyone who asks, *she isn't up to visitors yet*. Spreading the lie with such aplomb that before long he'll believe the baby left them of her own accord.

He brings another cup of tea and Lauren can't bear to leave her bed. His eyebrows raise as he hands over another sympathy card. "Sorry for your loss". *Poor you – poor us*, he's thinking. Hoping she'll forget it was a decision he made. He catches sight of the wet patches on her nightshirt and she sees the slight twist to his mouth. He offers again the tablets to dry the milk up (which he took upon himself to procure for her at the hospital, against her wishes). Why put up with such inconvenience? But she wants her breasts to stream the tears her blank eyes refuse to cry. She wants to lie on faintly-stinking, milk-encrusted sheets. Yet it still isn't enough. At night her body cramps as if going back into labour. Neil sleeps on the sofa.

Soon his sympathetic mouth has straightened into a firm line.

'Come on, Lauren. What's done is done.' Sounding oddly reminiscent of the midwife. 'Why not get up today, go out for a walk? We could go to Holyrood Park. Look, it's a beautiful day.'

He tuts, pulls open the curtains and sunlight floods the room. No response from Lauren. He hauls open the sash window and allows traffic noise in – excited tourist babble. It's festival season. Neil wants to go to some shows, they always go. He thought she would be better by now, having taken his annual leave to coincide with the termination of his child. Lauren blinks, transfixed by his sudden halo in the light from the window. Her former Jesus. *All my sins, I now detest them, never will I sin again.* But it's too late.

The third week post-pregnancy, Neil returns to his relentless schedule at the hospital and runs out of sympathy for Lauren. She's out of bed at least and picks a few things up off the floor but she still craves sleep, only sleep. If not in bed, then on the sofa, which smells of absent Neil.

She's still bleeding, but the milk has given up and gone. Now she's stopped hoping for a phone call from the hospital to say her baby is actually alive – it was all a mistake and Lauren can come and get her. The hope dried up, like the milk, when Neil returned to work. An unhappy coincidence – she can't help suspecting that he found out where Barbara was being looked after and killed her all over again.

---

Andrea visits, followed a day later by Ruth, who's been away at her ailing mother's in Glasgow. Ruth's shocked at the loss. She'll have to stop knitting the cardigan. She must regret, now, the cream shawl she gave Lauren when she passed the twelve-week mark. Fiona from the squat, now officially registered with the council as a co-operative commune, arrives at the flat next. Lauren almost cracks, wants badly to tell each friend the truth. But she can't. She knows they'd blame Neil and it's her who's equally to blame. She didn't have to go through with it.

She accepts their flowers and chocolates, pretends to laugh at their funny stories, especially Ruth recounting the tale of the squatter-duck that got into her boat while she was away and refused to leave when she returned. So now Ruth has a pet duck, to the delight of her little language students.

Neil comes home, strips off his pullover and skates on a sweet-wrapper. He grabs the doorframe, rights himself with comedy choreography and bangs his fist hard on the guinea-pig cage, evoking a shocked response from normally-complacent Squeaker.

'Jeez, Lauren! It's time you pulled yourself together. I thought you might at least have gone out to the shops today. Have you any idea how exhausting it is, doing a twelve-hour shift at the hospital and then coming home to misery and *no food in the house?*' A staccato ring in the air. He and the guinea-pig fall abruptly silent.

Neil moves in slow motion to where she hunches over, shaking, hands jammed between her knees.

What is grief, anyway? She doesn't understand how it dominates her so. The baby was never *here*, after all. Only briefly on the sheet between her mother's legs, half-encased in her broken sac, trailing a miniature placenta. Someone Neil never saw. *And she was there in my belly, flipping like a trapped salmon.*

'I'm sorry,' Neil crouches on the floor, tunnelling a path between her knees with praying hands. She tenses. A flash of panic in his eye, then he tilts his head sideways in a way she used to find endearing. 'I shouldn't punish you for how tired I am,' he says. 'I love you. I know you're hurting. Forgive me?' That crooked grin of his, aimed full-face now, just the right amount of rueful.

Lauren flexes one hand and forces it outwards to ruffle his hair, otherwise what was this all for?

'Of course. We're both tired and emotional. She was *your*

baby too.' He stiffens, but after a second he lowers his head to her lap. She traces the curve of his cheek. Unexpected desire in her belly but she's not sure whether for Neil or the baby. She watches the still-life of Lauren and Neil from a distance. 'It would've been so sweet to have had a little girl,' she tries.

'Don't...' Neil's fingers tighten on her thighs.

'You can't simply not acknowledge her.'

'There *was* no 'her', why can't you accept that? It was a *foetus*. It wasn't viable to survive. Look at it that way and you'll be fine!' Neil rears his head, his eyes glassy. He doesn't look like Neil anymore, with the layer of sympathy shed. He croaks, makes an effort to steady his voice. 'It'll be easier to bear that way. I'm sorry, Lauren, but someone needs to make you understand *real* life and death. I see far worse things than that at work – babies born alive, planned babies, only to die after birth – that's much worse than this. But people still manage to get over it. They carry on, why can't you?'

Shock pulses like a violent charge through her body. Her hands fly to the sides of her face.

'How can you be so cruel? I saw her, Neil, I saw my baby lying there on the bed. Miniature, but perfect. *Your* baby girl. That's the point, you say you see much worse things at work, but you didn't see *her*, you couldn't *face* it! At least allow me to grieve.' She's sobbing now. 'Don't you even care a tiny bit?'

His shaking vibrates through her own racking body, through the sofa and the walls and floor.

'I'm tired of all this.' He clambers to his feet, pushing her away. Brushes an imagined speck from his trousers. 'I see so much pain and trauma at work. You and I Lauren, we've each been through a different experience. Mine was seeing you hurt and upset. Yours was losing something you wanted very much. We've both suffered. We both need to move on.' He clenches his hands. 'I promise we can have a baby in the future. We have the house to get ready before that. Something to look forward to, let's concentrate on that.'

There's a sudden flow into the sanitary towel between her

legs. Neil doesn't know about the metal tin she's hidden at the back of the storage nook under the bath. There'll be a burial of sorts, after all. *This is my blood. And hers.* At the bedroom doorway Neil opens his mouth again, with a new face on. 'I'll order a takeaway... it's getting a bit late to start cooking now.' He steps back towards her – the old, steady Neil, reaching out a hand. She stares uncomprehendingly at it. Then her body folds in the middle, hands grasping her knees.

'Lauren?'

She drags her head up, sees that his expression's turned bleak, like the empty wastes inside her. *I can't let myself believe he really doesn't care about our baby.*

Wearily, she closes her fingers around the proffered hand and allows him to pull her to her feet, forces herself to brush his cheek with her dry lips. Gratitude floods his eyes and he grips her hand tighter. 'I'm sorry.'

'I know. Don't worry about a takeaway, I can make us a vegetable soup, it won't take long.'

Contented, he leaves her in the kitchen, opening cupboards and drawers, pulling out vegetables and equipment. Reassured that everything's all right between them again, he goes off for a shower. He'll come back with a bright smile, thinking she's all fixed. He'll offer weekend plans, excursions, or perhaps shopping. *That new dress you wanted*, he'll say. *Well, you could have it now that it'll fit you properly. You've lost weight over the past couple of weeks, I don't mean... you know. Well, anyway, you look beautiful. And it'll cheer you up, won't it? Let me buy it for you?* A dress. An honest belief that such promises can erase her sadness.

In the blade of the vegetable knife Lauren examines her reflection: white-faced, hollow-eyed. She wonders whether those empty eyes will ever shine again. There'll always be a small face in the reflection beside her own. Like mother, like daughter. She does make an effort to shape her perception around the literal truth of what Neil says, that the foetus *was* unviable outside the womb and therefore she shouldn't think of it as a baby. She really does try. And after all, she can't go back and change what's happened. Neil's right, she can only move on from here. She must remember that she did it for him. That they have a future together.

Breathing deeply, she gains calm for the duration of chopping one carrot. Then her womb twitches, a sensory memory. And she knows that the baby would have continued to grow, she would have been born, at the right time. She would have ended up alive, not dead. She would have stayed alive in Lauren's womb if they'd allowed her to. It was them, they *killed* their own child.

She breathes lightly at the top of her chest, her head buzzing. The bathroom door opens and closes. She hears the slight suction of Neil's damp, bare feet as he moves from the bathroom towards the kitchen. Tension ripples through her muscles. She touches the point of the knife into a second carrot. He's in the room.

'Hey, gorgeous,' Neil murmurs, like nothing's happened. Absolved himself with a wash. 'Thanks for doing this.'

She glances behind, sees a stilled image from a film. Neil, wearing a pristine white t-shirt which clings to his damp chest. And his favourite cut-off jeans. Jewels of water glisten on the hairs of his forearms – Neil likes to pull his clothes on after only the perfunctory use of a towel. A shard of light from the window illuminates the front of his upper body. *Sacred heart.* She whips her gaze back to the vegetables. He continues slapping ever closer across the kitchen floor on his bare feet that he hasn't bothered to dry – insensitive to Lauren's pain.

*Don't touch me.*

She brings the knife up, ready for the next chop. His hands slide roughly around her waist from behind. 'You feel lovely and soft,' he murmurs. 'I've missed your body. D'you fancy, y'know...　He buries his face in her neck. Her body goes into spasm, she doesn't even think about it. She draws the knife, forcefully, down the back of his hand on her stomach.

# 25

*Uig, Lewis, September 2016*

IN THE END bedroom my fingers discover an old photograph, face-down in the dust on the highest shelf of the alcove cupboard.

*Kenneth and Margaret MacLennan and their sons Finlay and Kenlish. 1939.* The family are sitting outside this very house. Nothing much seems to have changed since their image was captured almost eighty years ago. Even the highland cattle in the background look the same as the ones I spotted this morning.

Mathematical calculation leads me to deduce that one of the young boys in the picture is probably the father of my current landlord. In the letter he said his family has managed the land for generations. My heart beats a tiny bit faster. I frame the photograph with my hands, carry it with me into the other bedroom, the one I've chosen to sleep in. I'm tired suddenly. Achingly weary. The quilted eiderdown from my granny's Howth cottage is too inviting to resist. The shock of meeting Neil again has been flushing through me all morning, triggering a reaction in the muscles of my face which keep suffering what I'm sure must be unsightly spasms. My eyes want to close, to seal myself inside where I can replay images from yesterday's ferry journey on the screen behind my eyelids. *Neil.* How can this have happened? Why have I met him again now? I sink back onto the bed, lifting my head for a moment to shove an extra pillow behind my neck. Hold the photograph in front of my eyes and allow in the fantasy that it's Neil and myself and our own family I'm looking at, somehow in a past which is parallel to now. But it doesn't work because the two children are both boys.

Concentrate on the reality of the image in my hands. How aware of world events was this family at the time their photo was taken – did the war reach the Outer Hebrides? They would have had a radio, I suppose. I make a mental note to find out how many island men joined the British forces – perhaps this photograph was a memento of their intact family before the little boys' father went off to war. Maybe they never saw him again.

*You do let your imagination run wild.* The dark-haired father stares challengingly back at me while his wife offers a half-smile to the camera. The boys look boisterous, full of life, and yet they might no longer exist in this world. 1939. My chest contracts. I'm in their house, and they're totally unaware that I will ever exist. They don't understand that they won't be around forever. A rush of cold goes through me and I feel unsolid. The photograph flutters to the floor. I fill my lungs with air. Nip at my forearms with uneven fingernails to convince myself of my own reality. There are pinch marks all over my skin as well as a faint bruise from when I banged my wrist on the steering wheel yesterday. I close my eyes again, think of Neil's lips, red-bruised from the hot tea. *There.*

Possibly those children or their parents once slept in this bed – it looks old enough. I rake the bedroom air with my hands, pat the metal bed frame and the small wooden cabinet beside it – seeking echoes of that father and mother, of those two boys in this house. I think I hear the faint cry of a child but straining my ears, it's gone. Two more generations have been born since those children lived here, yet I feel connected to them. Time crosses over, we could exist side-by-side. What was it I read recently about parallel universes? Perhaps I've fallen into a black hole. That family and me, we walk the same floors and look out the same windows at the same mountains. There, I heard the soft sound of a woman singing, a snatch of her voice as she walked past this bedroom into the one next door.

The air snaps back to its correct tension. I'll get the photograph framed – a gesture to link me to the history of the house. In the meantime my fingers feel for it on the floor, and catching it, slip it into the bedside drawer. My eyelids start to flutter.

*Get up before you fall asleep.* So much to organise – books, clothes, my work folders. Something tickles the back of my neck when I reluctantly sit up, jolts my senses back to sharpness. *Silly, Lauren.* It's not a ghost, only a stray curl escaped from the band fastened around my hair. I get easily overheated these days and can't bear it on my neck. Perhaps I should cut my hair short. *Don't do that,* says a woman's voice – Margaret from the photograph. Much older than in the picture, sitting on the edge of the bed, tucking final strands into her long plait. She leans forward to give the non-existent embers a poke before climbing under the heavy quilts next to her husband, asleep with his mouth open. *It looks pretty around your face,* her voice says, fainter now. Pressure in my chest. She reminds me of my granny.

---

I eat a tin of soup for supper. If I don't get out of the house now I'm in danger of becoming trapped in history with my fantasy-family from 1939. I'll go for a walk.

What should I wear? *For a walk, Lauren, does it matter?* Yet the thought of Neil meeting my eyes across the table, the way I noticed him running his gaze over my upper body in my new top makes me rustle unsatisfactorily through my clothes in the suitcase. I haven't bothered much about my appearance for a long while, perhaps I'll go shopping in Stornoway at the weekend. I settle on jeans and a sweatshirt, plus a hooded woollen jacket and sturdy trainers. The light has dimmed considerably since I had the idea. But the sun still hovers above the horizon and if I hurry I reckon I'll get down to the beach in time to watch it set.

The air's crisp with a suggestion of autumn scents. The garden gate shuts with a satisfying click behind me. Feeling like an interloper, I check to see if anyone from the house up the road is watching, but nobody brandishes a fist or gives me a friendly wave, or anything else for that matter. I'm completely alone in the landscape. In the chill air stiffness creeps down my back.

My breathing grows ragged with the effort of managing the uneven downward slope on my bad knee. My heel catches in a dip and I stumble and it bloody hurts. Straightening, rubbing my knee, I wonder how wise this excursion is – too late I recall how quickly the dark fell yesterday. *I should have gone out earlier, or brought a torch.* By the time I open the second gate onto the stony track at the bottom, my knee has set up a constant throb and I'm panting for breath.

I've arrived at an empty carpark with a wooden building at one side. Facilities for the campsite that must be around here somewhere, I suppose. *Might need to use the loo on my way back.* Across the track I clamber up another slight rise, confused by the flashing white shapes streaking across the dim landscape in front of me. Are those drum beats I can hear? Am I about to stumble across a beach party, or is there some kind of ancient ritual going on deep in the dunes? A hot flush washes over me, leaves me standing in a cold sweat. Neil would tell me to stop being silly. Immediately I realise the flashing shapes are only the tails of scattering rabbits, the drumming their warning thumps as they disappear into half-hidden burrows.

Now my eyes have accustomed to the dimness I see them everywhere. The clipped grass – machair, I think it's called

– is one giant warren. I see a baby rabbit, hesitating until I'm almost on top of it before it bounds away. *Fiver*, the little rabbit from *Watership Down*. *Bright Eyes* plays in my head. I read the book one summer in Howth, when I was about twelve. Sat with my knees tucked against my chest at one end of the bench in Granny's backyard while Meg played at the other end with her *Pippa* dolls. The sound I can now hear is the sea, the same as I heard then.

My feet pick carefully between holes as threatening as landmines. What if I break my ankle out here, alone in the fast-falling dark? Most likely no-one would find me until morning, if at all. *I should have brought my phone.* I've already added Neil's number to my contacts. *I can't believe he's here, on the same small island as me.*

The light dims so fast. Boulders and clumps of grass a second ago sharply delineated against a fuzzy background have now melted out of sight. This is marram grass I feel against my legs, long and sharp, holding the blown sands of the dunes together. It scratches me through the denim of my jeans. Now the sea is just beyond a single ridge, softly lapping. I *will* reach it. My knee throbs in time to its lazy rhythm.

I push my heels into the soft sand on the gentle upwards slope. Abruptly the light switches off. I sense a pause in the atmosphere, as if all of nature is waiting to shout *Surprise*. My feet find the low clifftop just in time for me to catch the huge globe of the sun slipping below the horizon, spreading a silver line in its wake. The ocean, pale turquoise where it approaches the vast stretch of virgin sand in the foreground, transmutes to indigo beneath a band of smoky cloud further out. Violent orange bleeds upwards into the sky and the hills across the bay are inky silhouettes. The magnificence of nature swallows me. I don't exist.

My breath shudders. Why does nature evoke such grief? All the buried sadnesses erupt; not only mine. The world sobs with the relentless tide.

*Somewhere out there a mother is clutching her child in an overloaded boat, tossed mercilessly on the waves. Has she made the right decision, entering a different version of hell from the one she left? I shiver – the weight of that innocent baby is torn from my own arms by the cruel sea, as water fills that mother's mouth...*

How does chance choose its victims? In a different life it could have been me rather than her... my baby drowning. *If I had kept my baby.* Or myself as a child, making the journey my friend Phuong was forced to take from China thirty-five years ago. The wars, the creeds that fire them, all the greed and gluttony in the world, the subjecting of newborns to misery such as those refugee babies and their mothers have to endure, how can anyone bear it? I can't.

The sea whispers consolations: *it's not hurting you, count yourself lucky.* But I shake and tremble with grief, shoulders hunched up to my ears as I press my fists harder into my pockets. *Let it out. I can't hold it in.* Longing for Neil – the Neil of my past superimposed over the years-older one I met yesterday – sweeps over me like the waves smashing repeatedly over pebbles. *Hold me.*

I shudder as the ghosts file past in a solemn row. *Barbara.* Did I truly believe I could put a stop to my potential daughter with a medical termination? It didn't work – she's still here, in every breath I take. Recently I learned that cells from a woman's baby stay in her body forever: *I knew this already.*

Next, *Sheena.* You were so young, what were you thinking when you did what you did? I can only think you were trying to teach me a lesson. Well you have done and bitten off your nose to spite yourself at the same time. Consequences, Sheena – I tried to teach you about those but you were always impulsive. Remember the time you insisted you knew how to ice-skate when I took you to the rink with another girl from the Centre? You barged straight out onto the ice and fell flat on your face...

*Maw.* Just... Maw. Did I ever know you? At least you're at

rest now. My loss is more concerned with what you were never able to give, but it's still raw that you've gone. You had a hard time with your own mother locked away so young, I know. Whatever went wrong with us we'll never have a chance to put things right. I just hope you're looking after Bridie now the way she needed you to when she was a struggling teenager. *Bridie.*

While my body shudders itself to stillness I draw my sleeve across my eyes, find an old tissue in the jacket pocket and blow my nose. The tide moves inexorably forward on the breath of the sea. I listen to the tinkle and ripple of its music and it takes me a moment to realise that my hearing has sharpened only because I can hardly see anything. The thumps and scuffles from the bank behind take on an ominous overtone. *So many holes to trip me up.*

When did I become so conscious of my own fragility? Age is wearying. I turn around to face the walk home and see only pitch dark.

My knee has stiffened more, forcing me to walk with a straight leg, pressing a hand into my sore back. The new tears that threaten are no longer concerned with the rest of the world. I'm scared in the dark. *Maw, it's dark. I'm scared. 'I'll leave the door open a tiny crack so you can see the light on the landing, okay?' If Pepe doesn't shut it again out of spite.* Something must have initiated the antagonism between Perpetua and me that has never diminished. Maybe because I usurped her as the youngest girl when I was born. Or she didn't feel I belonged because of what Michael said about Da not being my da. If I'd had a family of my own I might have got over all this by now. *Don't think about that, Lauren, concentrate on staying on your feet.*

With the sea behind me I'm going in more-or-less the right direction, but my steps are so slow it could take me all night. *If it does, it does,* Granny used to say to the older grandchildren when they complained at the slowness of the little ones. It was mostly our cousins from the families with only two or three children complaining. They looked at our overblown tribe as freaks. Cousin Paddy had a fight with our Michael: 'Can yer Mammy not keep her knickers on at all?'

That summer Granny had almost twenty grandchildren and great-grandchildren staying in her three-bedroomed cottage while the parents were off at some party in Dublin – a wedding – no, a wake I think it was. I remember my great-uncle Michael sawing and nailing boards for the loft, shoving mattresses and bedding up there for the boys and cousin Jo-Jo, who insisted she was a boy.

I stumble down to the track, jolting my knee again. I'm crying out in pain. *No-one to hear me, anyway.* The dark is so thick I struggle to locate the toilet building. It's there suddenly, looming in front of me. A sensor light comes on and I push open the door and stand blinking at my red-nosed reflection, curls tangled around my face. I may be over fifty but I feel no different from when I was fifteen. *You're always alone, Lauren.*

It'll get better when I begin my new job next week, nobody knows me there or pities me like my colleagues in Edinburgh. It wasn't your fault, you couldn't have known what she would do, they said to me afterwards. I didn't deserve a second chance at motherhood. *It was all about me.* Now I'll never have one.

I wash my face at the sink, use the toilet. Silly little girl in an old woman's body, snivelling and making a fuss. *What's done is done.* Granny would give me a slap for such self-pity. And Neil, 'You haven't changed, Lauren.' Ridiculous. Of course I've changed from the girl he knew – but maybe not so much from the girl who left him with a permanent scar. Was it really only yesterday when that scar introduced itself to me again?

Back out into the dark. I fumble my way around the side of the building and launch myself on stiff legs along the fence to where I'm sure the gate must be. Up and down until my hand knocks against the concrete post. *Ouch.* Taste blood on my knuckles. *Damn, damn again.* I fumble in the dark, lift the latch with a sobbing breath of relief. Once through it, I just need to make my way up the hill and find the other gate, the one that leads into my garden. Simple, right? But half-way up the slope I trip, jam my *good* knee into a stone. Hunch over in the damp grass, crying, as if it will do any good. Both knees scream pain. I push sobs from my chest through the block of air I've swallowed. I quite enjoy the lack of control. Nobody can hear me! But I hear a sound in the pause between my healing wails and feel something nudge the back of my shoulder.

*What the...?* A huge, hulking shape – my childhood nightmares culminated in one monster. The shape looming above me bellows, rents the air. Something wet squashes against my ear – saliva, or worse, slides down my neck. When I was a kid Declan used to wake me up like this. *Boo* in my ear and a dribble of water – egged on by Pepe, no doubt. This is a real-life nightmare, yet at the same time I'm a child again.

A sharp, animal scent. A cow that's all, my inner voice tells me calmly. One of those I watched out of the window this morning, no doubt. Some were reddish in colour and others black or dun. They had long, shaggy coats and curving horns. *Fuck me, they have huge horns, it's about to gouge me.* But they must be harmless, surely they wouldn't be allowed out otherwise? The dark presses against me, along with the hoarse, hot breath of the cow and its trails of saliva. I force a final whimper from my lungs. *Stupid, wimp. Pull yourself together.*

On my bottom and with stinging hands I shuffle away from the hot breath and the trail of drool and the creature diffuses into the dark. Once I'm sure I'm clear I manage to scramble onto my hands and knees, ignoring the pain in both legs, a prickling feeling creeping down my spine. Fear that the cow will follow me – trample me. *I can't hear anything though.* On four throbbing joints I crawl to the top of the slope, grasping at tough stalks as if I'm climbing a cliff. My hands feel shredded. *Where's ma hoose?*

The cow bellows goodbye from the hill. The dark isn't as dense up here, closer to the sky. I pull myself painfully upright and tilt my face upwards to the vast bowl above me, a million stars shining down. Spin with the world.

My fingers tingle, every muscle in my body relaxes. Easy now to make out the shapes of the buildings ahead, one the cottage and the other the large shed by the back fence. There it is, the faint glint of wire. I shuffle along the fence, hand over hand until my palm fits over the gate post, holding on tight to make sure it isn't going anywhere.

# 26

FROM THE WINDOW above the kitchen sink I can only see a thin band of sea beyond the machair. It glitters in the morning sun. If I move into the glass porch my view extends around the next curve of beach. I know from the map that the white beaches of Uig Bay stretch on for miles.

A mist hung over the landscape earlier, lifting like a bride's veil from the loch. I lay in bed watching nature reveal herself in a sensual dance. It was the phone that had woken me, my landlord wanting to know if I'm at home today. He's on Lewis all day for work and wishes to come over and discuss something to do with improvements.

I was at a disadvantage, to be honest, having only just woken up. And being in the man's bed – I found a packet of condoms stuck behind the drawer in the cabinet that wouldn't close properly and I'm guessing they were once his. Now I've got butterflies in my stomach. Maybe it's the thought of the condoms which I hid in the kitchen bin under some used teabags. What if he suddenly remembers and guesses I've found them?

If my leg wasn't so sore I'd give myself a kick for having juvenile thoughts. I've spent too much time around teenagers, that's what it is.

I keep trying to picture him. He's probably old. On the other hand, so am I, or *he* might think so if he's a lot younger.

I hobble over to the sink and fill the kettle, switch it on and place another teabag in the mug I've already washed three times this morning. Apart from my bad left leg, I also have a raw graze on the right. Lurching around the kitchen using the work surface as crutches, it's hard not to feel old. I'm also foolish, *not to mention pathetic*. Thank God nobody was around to witness me making an idiot of myself. I take two slices of bread from the diminishing loaf I bought at the Co-op in Stornoway and think I ought to go shopping this afternoon at the store up on the hill.

A rap on the front door. *He's about three hours early!* My stomach tips. *I'll have to offer him a sandwich, diminish supplies further.* I hobble through the rooms, heading towards the front door. But an elderly woman is already standing in the porch, hands braced on the inner door frame, one foot in my sitting room. The neighbour with a key. *Come in, why don't you?* Tight, grey curls form a bonnet on her head and a straw tote bag dangles from one of her arms. I come to an unsteady stop in front of her.

'Hello.' She smiles, showing false teeth. *'Fàilte is fuaran ort!* That means welcome, dear. I thought I'd leave you a day to settle in before introducing myself. I'm Mrs MacLeod. Peggy, you know, from number five. I have a key to your house.' She waves it in front of my eyes before slipping it into a deep pocket in her cardigan. *She's not planning on returning it, then.* 'Young Murdo asked me to keep an eye on things before you arrived. Lauren, isn't it?' She makes me feel like a teenager, the way she speaks. 'It's lovely to meet you. I was wondering if you were all right. Mrs Macaulay who stays over by the Co-op thinks she saw you stumbling about in the dark last night. Said you seemed lost. Are you perfectly well, dear? You look a little pale.'

I'm sure I am pale, because I can't for the life of me understand how Mrs MacAulay from by the Co-op, which is a mile-and-a-half up the road, could have seen me stumbling about on the hill in the *pitch dark* last night. Unless she was the cow.

'Aye, I'm fine, thanks for asking.'

Mrs MacLeod nudges gently past me, smiling hard. I stumble after her through both rooms into the kitchen, watching her bonnet of hair shift stiffly as she moves her head from side-to-side, surreptitiously inspecting my few belongings. At the kitchen doorway she does an overstaged double-take at the boiling kettle. Her eyes gleam.

'*Iongantach*, what a lovely sight – enough for a pot in there, is there? You must have known I was coming, dear. Do sit down, you look as though you're about to fall.'

'I hurt my leg,' I offer, lame in more ways than one.

'*Gabh fois*, relax now. You'll soon be fit as a fiddle, climbing up and down all these hills. Enjoy the sunset, did you?'

*Accept it, she knows everything.* Strangely, I don't mind the way she bustles around my kitchen, chatting, opening cupboards and frowning at this and that. I've done nothing but greet like a wee bairn since I got here and now I'm oddly compelled to sink comfortably into the role. Mrs MacLeod is the person who put the milk in the fridge and left out the biscuits for my arrival. I thank her.

'No problem. We like to look after each other around here.'

She places a teapot on the table, I've no idea where she got it from. She also produces a Battenberg cake, possibly from her Mary Poppins bag. She'll bring out a lampshade next, for the bare kitchen bulb. The thought brings Maw to mind, comatose on the settee. *Nine-year-old Ardal watches the film for the hundredth time, singing along to 'Just a spoonful of Sugar'.* No wonder my youngest brother ended up in musical theatre. He's now in a long-term relationship with a well-known stage director. Ardal and Ian, the proud recent adopters of three little sisters.

'Have you a knife, dear? Oh yes, of course, silly me.' She opens the drawer below the sink and pulls one out. 'I spent many an afternoon in this kitchen with Janet.'

'Janet?'

'Murdo and Catherine's mother. I'm forgetting you don't know the family. Where did you say you were from? Bit of a mixed accent, I'd say, but I'm picking up a hint of Irish.'

'I was born in Glasgow but I spent a lot of time in Ireland as a child. I've lived in Edinburgh most of my adult life.'

'Aye, like I said, mixed.'

*Mixed-up, more like.* 'It's very kind of you to bring cake, Mrs MacLeod.'

'Ach, do call me Peggy. Mrs MacLeod sounds so old.'

She tips the pot and pushes a cup of tea over the table to me, followed by a slice of cake. My stomach grumbles and my eyes flick over to the slices of bread left out on the work top. I'll have my sandwich later.

'And will your husband be coming over to join you soon?'

I choke on the cake. We give each other a look.

'I see. Have you ever been married, at all?' An *unmarried* woman, of my age? *Maybe she's a widow*, she'll be hoping.

'I was married, for a year, once.' I married Ellis during the year I spent in Iceland. He was on the same course as me. God knows what possessed me to get married to someone I'd only known a month. I'd never got over Neil. We married in a pretty snow-covered church on a trip to the Northern town of Akureyri. We phoned ahead and the hotel organised things for us. Two locals were delighted to be our witnesses and the church choir was hastily gathered to sing us an ancient wedding hymn. They served us a wedding feast of lobster soup and the biggest slices of cake I'd ever seen. Our hotel hosted us for an extra night, free. The eight-hour journey back to Reykjavik was so romantic – I leaned my head on Ellis's shoulder as we looked out of the bus windows at the snow-covered mountains. His arm must have been uncomfortable with my weight but he never once complained. I have a sudden memory of the spigots of steam that rose from black holes in the snow.

We set up home in a two-roomed apartment on Vesturgata. He was one of those people who believed you should never go to bed on an argument. *Unlike Neil and me.* We should've been happy. We would have been if it wasn't for me. The thing was, that as the months of our marriage went by and we both studied hard for our final exams, all I could think about was Barbara. I knew Ellis wanted children, to put down roots of his own. As we prepared to return to the UK he started to broach the subject in earnest, as I'd been expecting him to do for a while.

I just couldn't see that future. The possibility was blocked by the terrible thing I'd done to Barbara. Depression swamped me again and I was frightened I'd turn out like Maw and my real grandma.

*Nobody has ever been able to replace you, Neil.*

'Oh dear.' Peggy brings me back into the kitchen. 'Of course, it isn't the same as it was in my day. We stuck at things. But you've only got to look at Janet's Murdo and Catherine.'

She stops speaking to take a bite of cake followed by a sip of tea. I lean forward, my own shameful history put to one side for the time being. I'm not the only one to disappoint Peggy, it seems.

'What happened?'

Maybe Peggy's forgotten that Murdo's my landlord, or maybe there's simply no such thing as a stranger in *these here hills*. Either way, she seems prepared to spill all.

'Such a shame for Janet,' she begins, brushing cake crumbs from her chin. 'First of all Finlay – Murdo's father, dear, died of cancer and then their Catherine hooked up with that drug dealer from Skye. Catherine ran away, you know. It sent Janet into a decline. But she was hoping Murdo and Ann would stay here in the house with her – make the place into a family home again.'

'Ann?'

'Ann MacDonald. Murdo's fiancé.'

MacDonald, the same name as Neil. *Don't think about him now, it's too complicated.* I feel like sitting with my legs crossed and stuffing a blanket in my mouth – *tell me a story.* Before she can continue, I proffer the teapot at her, remembering I'm supposed to be the host. My knee gives a particularly pulsing throb as I lean over to pour her a second cup and I work on a facial expression which doesn't give away the pain. I top up my own tea and sit back with my hands around the mug.

'Ann didn't want to go with him when he moved over to Skye.' She purses her lips and blows on the tea.

We sit in silence for a while. It seems rude to ask too many questions. I'm aware of the clock ticking and the couple of hours I'd planned to spend getting my files in order before the expected visit from Murdo this afternoon, but I see that it's equally important to become a part of the community I've moved into.

'They were a happy *teaghlach*. A family, I mean.' Peggy sits up straighter and begins to stack the plates and our empty cups. I put up a hand, indicating she must leave it for me – it's my house after all. But she ignores me. She takes the crockery over to the sink and runs the tap, squirts in some of the washing-up liquid I brought with me from Stornoway.

'I remember those two children running around this kitchen as though it was only yesterday. Murdo is the same age as my John. Murdo was happy as can be, you know. But Catherine was an odd little thing from the start. Hell-bent on self-destruction. You know the type, Lauren?'

She glances at me and I nod. *I work with them.* I wonder if Peggy knows about my job. It would make sense that she does – enquiries have probably been made by the locals about who is moving into their midst.

'It was the finish of Janet. After Finlay and everything. And it was the finish of Murdo's plans to settle down and get married as well. After Janet died, and then Catherine's troubles, he was the only one left for the girl. Her father was long gone by then. Murdo is the only person who stands any chance of helping her.'

*Murdo's sister must be a lot younger than him.* Peggy stares at her upside-down-steeple of fingers, pointing into the water.

'Ann wouldn't have her here with them. Ann, you know,

agreed to get married to somebody else not long after Murdo left, turns out she was having an affair all along.' *Did I just hear her call Ann a bitch under her breath?* 'And so Murdo decided not to bother coming back. Thought he'd stay over in Skye and rent out this house.' Peggy pulls her hands out of the water, dripping. 'There were some other tenants in here before you but it didn't work out. A young family from London, they were. But they found it too isolating. Didn't like the fact there were only fourteen children in the village school.'

Peggy rinses the bowl and overturns it. She dries her hands on the towel by the sink, leaving the pots to drain on the slatted board.

'You really shouldn't have,' I wave my hand at her finished work. 'But I appreciate it.'

I haul myself stiffly to my feet and wrap the cake deeper into its cellophane, push it back into the box for her to take away with her. But she presses her hand over mine and gives me a smile.

'It's Murdo's favourite. He used to love it when he was a little boy. You keep it for him, he's coming here later isn't he? He'll be over to my house for his dinner after but since you haven't anything in I'd best leave the cake here.'

There's nothing the woman doesn't know about me and my arrangements, not to mention the contents of my cupboards.

'Well, thank you so much for coming.' I fully expect her to get a message to Murdo about me before he turns up at my door. Still, we'll be equally informed about each other. He's not simply a landlord any more but a vibrant presence in my imagination. A saint, if Peggy's story is to be taken at face-value – who has given up his own chance of happiness to look after his young sister.

'It's no trouble,' Peggy's eyes cloud over for a moment as if she's forgotten something. Then she remembers my name. 'Lauren. I must be getting off, anyway. It's my stint at the museum this afternoon – sometimes I feel as if I ought to be an exhibit up there myself, you know. *Slán leat an-drásta.*

Goodbye for now, dear.

# 27

MY MOBILE RINGS. I knock over an empty jug on the kitchen worktop as I reach for it. Disconnecting the charger, I hold the phone to my ear.

'Hello?'

'Lauren?'

For a moment I'm swallowed by the past again, a feeling of going under water. 'Neil?'

'That's right.' His voice sounds muffled. Then I resurface, and can hear better. 'How are you,' he says. 'Have you settled in yet?'

Now I'm back on the ferry, needing to revisit the whole of our history before I can look at him again, or answer. Am I ready? Not yet. *Wake up.*

'I'm getting there. The cottage is lovely, and the views. How about you?' My hand shakes. I tuck the phone between my chin and shoulder but the awkward posture gives me a stiff neck so I place it on the table instead and press loudspeaker.

'Yes, good. Thank you. I have a nice house on the edge of town, front and back garden – garage. You know, the usual. Only a short walk across a field to the sea. I met my new partner at the surgery yesterday and she seems fine, I think we'll work well together.'

'Good, good,' I nod at the phone, softly dancing the pads of my fingers on the table beside it. *Are we just old friends, or. . . ?*

'I was wondering if you'd like to have dinner with me – say, on Saturday evening. There's a nice restaurant in Stornoway I could take you to. Or we could go somewhere more rural if you prefer?' Another painful pause while I try to think. It makes sense, I know it does. We're old friends, once deeply connected by love. We've unexpectedly landed in the same place after many years apart. We don't really know anyone else... of course we should have dinner together. But it seems to make a mockery of the pain of our split. *And yet it was still there, on the ferry, the rightness of Neil and me.*

Getting dressed up. Having to wear make-up. It's so long since I've done any of that. Do I want to start again?

'Lauren?' Neil coughs to cover the fracture I can hear in his voice. 'Would you like to?'

'Uhm. Yes – err... thanks. That would be lovely.' I let the words out with my breath. 'Stornoway is fine, you just give me a time and a postcode and I'll be there.'

'Ah, I didn't mean... I wouldn't expect you to drive all that way; I'll come and pick you up, of course I will.'

This irritates me.

'It's about an hour's drive, Neil, it doesn't make sense for you to make the journey here and back twice. I can drive myself.' How does he think I've managed without him all these years?

'Goodness Lauren, I didn't realise you were that far away. I wouldn't hear of you going all that way back, alone in your car on unlit roads, if they're anything like the ones beyond my house. I could put you up, of course, but I wouldn't like to presume... Now let me think...' Hearing the shuffling of papers, I wonder what he's doing. Is he at work, looking through his next patient's notes? I suppose they must have it all on computer now anyway, even here on Lewis. An image of Neil with his meticulous folders and colour-coded pens intrudes, the two of us sitting on the grass under the cherry trees in the Meadows. I feel sick.

'I have a pubs and restaurants guide in front of me,' Neil explains into the long pause. 'I'm looking for somewhere near

– where are you?'

'I'm in Uig, west of the island.' Hopefully Neil will find somewhere suitable between Stornoway and here. I don't feel ready to reveal my exact location just yet.

'Okay...' More shuffling of pages. 'Ah, now,' he says. 'How about this: it overlooks Uig sands, is that near you? Yes? Good. It sounds very nice.'

Neil names the restaurant and tells me he'll book a table for Saturday evening. I swallow too much air, press my hands against my stomach. But I'm relieved I won't have to drive all the way to Stornoway and back. On the other hand it means Neil will. Because I don't plan on inviting him to my house afterwards, I can't. I'm not ready. Not yet.

---

I'm home from the Co-op in time for my visitor's estimated arrival. In the store I was obliged to stop and chat with about seven individuals, all local and all curious to find out about the new tenant in *Finlay and Janet's old place*. Every one of them expressed their disappointment at the decision of the previous tenants to leave – apparently it was lovely having the young children around. However, most of the people I spoke to seemed to have already had a word with Peggy about me. A couple even enquired about my state of mind after my unfortunate incident on the hill last night.

When I was finally freed to get on with my shopping I bought firelighters, kindling, matches and a bag of sawdusty-log things for the fireplace in the dining room, which a young lad from the storeroom helped me carry out to the car. The bucket of chopped logs on the hearth is now all used up. I checked in the enormous workshop in the back garden to see if there were any there, but I only found some obscure-looking tools and an implement that I think is an actual pitchfork. I must remember to ask Murdo MacLennan where I can order larger amounts of fuel.

I've unpacked two bags of groceries from the car, including some good coffee. I fill my old yellow coffee-pot and place it on the electric hob ready for Murdo's arrival. The smell is so welcoming I wish I'd baked bread to go with it. Still, I've replenished the contents of the biscuit caddy and placed Mrs MacLeod's (Peggy, I keep forgetting) Battenberg cake into another tin I found on top of a cupboard. I remembered to bring in the photograph I found in the bedroom cupboard, too. I'm oddly fond of that couple and their children, as if they're my own distant family, not his. Crazy I know, but I conversed with Margaret yesterday evening while she attended to her knitting on a rocking chair in the dining room. She's much older than the Margaret in the photograph. Reminds me of my granny. Perhaps Murdo will be able to tell me about the woman I'm hoping is *his* granny.

I bite my nails, stand up and hobble through to the sitting room to inspect myself in the mirror. Lick my fingers in an attempt to smooth the wildness of curls around my face. Rub at the dark shadows under my eyes. Holding onto the windowsill I attempt some physiotherapy, creaking my leg slowly backwards and forwards a few times. It doesn't work, just makes it hurt more.

Next I watch cattle gathering by the fence at the other end of the garden. One rubs its rump aggressively against a post. That post could have been me last night. Another swings its huge head from side to side, trying to shake the fringe from its eyes. I stand there wondering which one I had my encounter with. Perhaps I can make friends with them and they will guide me home in future. Across the road and over the gentle slope of a field, the loch is black as oil under a fresh bank of clouds. The mountains hunker above the winding road, shadowed by the change in weather. I tap my fingers on the windowsill. It's not my place to feel concerned about Murdo MacLennan's long journey here from Skye, or back again.

I straighten and point myself in the direction of the kitchen again. Check the coffee and remove the pot from the stove. If I go to the toilet, surely that will precipitate an inconvenient knock at the door? But though I take my time washing my hands with the moisturising handwash I've just bought, there's still no sign of my visitor when I emerge back into the kitchen. He'll be lucky to get here before nightfall at this rate.

I shuffle into the glass porch and stand looking out at the now monotone landscape behind the house and down to the empty beach. I give myself a sharp pinch on my wrist to remind myself that I'm really here. Trace a circle around it with my fingertip, rough despite the moisturiser. Squeeze my eyes shut until I see the freckled skin over Neil's wrist bone on the ferry and now I'm rubbing that instead of mine. *Stop it, Lauren, the landlord will be here soon.* I open my eyes again. I can just make out flashes of rabbit tails on the machair above the sea. The image is grainy, as if from a film.

To the left, there's a cemetery on a hill. I need to go there. As a child I had a morbid fascination with graveyards. I searched them for names for my future children. After Barbara, I spent a lot of time in Greyfriars Kirkyard imagining that the baby's monument I'd found was hers. I picked wildflowers and laid them beside the other baby's memorial and once I buried a poem, an apology to Barbara, in the soil at the edge of that other child's grave. I also buried a metal box, one I'd been hiding in the nook under our bath at the flat. I buried my pregnancy remains one evening after the final tourists had left the graveyard. I took the trowel I'd used that spring to plant daffodil bulbs in the window box outside our bedroom. There were traces of graveyard soil in my fingernails for days after I planted the metal box. This time I'll have to search out the grave of a teenager as well as that of a baby. It stings again, the way her mother finally crawled out of the woodwork for Sheena's funeral. I bet she never felt her daughter's presence deep inside in her heart like I do.

*Ach.* I know how to absorb grief, break it down and

distribute the weight until it's comfortable to carry. I can do that again. But I miss my colleagues. They understood. Young Angel, the wee lassie in training who amused everyone with her Yorkshire accent. She was the one who'd promised to look after Sheena for me and the one who frantically searched the streets with me that night after I received Sheena's text. Big Dave, our gentle giant, loved by the kids but they don't mess with him because of his size. Caroline, older even than me – she was like a grandmother to our young clients. I guess I was the mother. *The mother who never was.* On Monday I'll have to walk into a different office, get to know new colleagues. They might resent that I've been selected for a job they probably applied for themselves. What if they hate me?

My face is wet. I've done nothing but greet since I got here. I can't make sense of anything.

I grab the roll of kitchen paper. Collapse onto a chair. *Let it go,* as the song from the children's film I took Sheena and a couple of other girls to see advised. No-one will hear me, however loud I howl. But the knock on the door comes just as I lift the sodden tissue up to my nose for about the eighth time. I've been hiccupping, which must be why I didn't hear the approach of a car.

Jumping to my feet with another howl – of physical pain this time – I gather the tissues and drop them in the bin, face burning. Wash my beetroot-coloured fizzgog at the sink and pat it dry with a tea towel. *Shit, shit.* What a sight I must be. How could I have forgotten about my visitor? *This is no way to greet your landlord.*

I quickly run my hands through the mess of my hair a final time and hobble through the two rooms to the front porch.

# 28

THE DARKNESS SURPRISES me when I open the door. Will I ever get used to such sudden nightfall in the mountains?

Then, in an instant, I'm thrown back into the past. I once stood beside Neil in the National Museum of Scotland. We'd gone to see an exhibition of Pre-Raphaelite paintings and I was transfixed by this one particular painting: *The Light of The World* by William Holman Hunt. A luminescent painted Jesus, wearing an elaborate gown of jewelled colours, holding a lantern in the night. But this is a real person holding a lantern at my front door. I take a shuddering breath, hastily closing my mouth which has fallen open like a child's, spellbound by magic after an exhausting greetin' fit.

'It's an oil lamp,' the figure explains, proffering the flickering object at me. 'I brought it for you as a house warming present. *Tha mi toilicht do choinneachadh.* I'm happy to meet you.' I still can't speak. 'Thought I'd light it to surprise you. It comes from this house anyway – it belonged to my grandmother.'

'Margaret?' I ask, half in a dream. I only now think to switch the porch light on. 'Thank you.' My hand reaches out and grasps the wire handle of the lamp and I hold it aloft in the style of *Little Bo Peep*, blinking. Short of air.

'Aye,' he's saying. 'Margaret was my gran. Have you been talking to Peggy MacLeod, by any chance?'

The flame in the lamp gusts to one side, straightens again. I try to answer but my voice is reluctant to come out so I cough, to clear my throat. 'I have. She told me about your ma and da, but I also found a photograph of Margaret on a shelf in the cupboard. I just sort of guessed.' My voice is still hoarse. 'Hello, by the way.' I transfer the lamp into my left hand and extend my right for him to shake. 'I'm Lauren.'

In the harsh porch light, his face breaks into a grin. 'Pleased to meet you, Lauren. I'm Murdo. How are you settling in?' He takes my hand firmly. His grip makes me feel safe but also confused by the long moments I spent staring at Neil's hand on the ferry. Our hands detach and I can't resist the impulse to scan the back of Murdo's for a scar but there is none. My chest loosens. Stepping back I stand aside so he can enter. He dips his head through the two doorways and stands in the sitting room looking me over. He's younger than me, I guess – forty, maybe. Strong and tall, wearing a black jumper and jeans. A frown appears between his eyes.

'Are you all right?'

I'd forgotten how red my eyes must be. Puffed up like two balloons. I place the lamp on the low wooden chest and fold my hands in front of my body.

'It's not as bad as I probably look. I've always been an ugly crier.' I let out a bark of a laugh and he shifts his feet. 'I, err, had some sad news lately and it just got on top of me temporarily. I feel a right doowally now. I'm *fine*, honestly, very happy to be here. I love this place of yours.' I force another laugh. 'Go on through into the kitchen, I've got some coffee on.' *Although it's probably ruined by now.*

'Are you sure you're all right?'

He stands, miles ahead of me in the kitchen doorway, practically looking at his watch, I've taken so long to get there.

'Stiff knee,' I collapse onto a chair. Then I remember the coffee. 'Oh, damn.' Huffing and puffing, I start to get up again.

'No, no, sit down. I'll get it.' He looks embarrassed. I must seem such a *queerie* to him.

'Thanks, you'll need to pop it back on the stove.' My mouth breaks into a smile. 'There's some Battenberg cake in the tin.' Murdo raises an eyebrow. With the black hair hanging down the side of his face and the way his mouth turns up at the corners, he reminds me of that guy in the TV series, the one set in Cornwall, with the copper mines.

'You've definitely been talking to Peggy.'

'She actually left this here for you. She must know you very well.'

He hooks a strand of black hair behind his ear. 'Aye, she does. She watched my sister and me grow up. She grew up with our mammy as well.' He blinks a few times. It's too awkward to ask after the welfare of his sister and her 'troubles'. He places the coffee pot and some mugs on the table along with the cake tin. When he turns to fetch a knife from the drawer, I wave an imperious hand at the worktop.

'There are some chocolate biscuits over there as well. You must be hungry after your journey from Skye.' If I'd known he was going to arrive this late I'd have offered him a proper supper before his journey home. That's if there are even any ferries scheduled for the evening. I hope he's not... just because it's him who owns this house.

'Ocht, it's not that far. I had a delivery to make on the way here anyway. Which reminds me, I've got something in the truck for you. Well, for the house, I mean.'

'You've already brought in the lamp.' I pass him his coffee, push the cake and biscuits across the table.

*Tapadh leat!* Thank you.' He dives into the tin. With his mouth half full he explains that he's brought me a wood burning stove for the empty fireplace in the front room.

I catch my reflection in the black window. The muted image smooths away my wrinkles and grey hairs, makes me look like the young Lauren again – or perhaps that's what I want to see. *You haven't changed, Lauren*, Neil said on the ferry. But there's so much he doesn't know about me.

Murdo pours himself another strong coffee. The upward

twist on one side of his mouth draws a dimple to his left cheek. *'Sláinte mhath!'* He raises the mug and I clink mine against it. My stomach was hurting and so I've offered to cook him a meal. He swallows coffee and I watch the motion of his Adam's apple as it goes down. 'What have you got in then, food-wise? Always happy to eat, if a meal's on offer.'

'Hmm.' I picture the afternoon's shopping. 'Plenty of veg, eggs and cheese. I could knock up an omelette?'

'Sounds good. I'm definitely hungry. Peggy'll have a full-on dinner for me later but I'm not in a hurry, unless you've got something you wanted to get on with?' He must have noticed my files and laptop on the dining room table.

'Nothing that can't wait.' My chair scrapes on the tiled floor.

'Great, okay. Hey, wait.'

'What for?'

'I feel bad, putting you out like this, with your sore leg and all. I can make the omelette, why don't you just put your foot up, take the opportunity to have a rest?'

*He probably thinks I'm about ten years older than I actually am. Another Peggy.*

'Not at all. It's much better now, anyway.' I wince, my face hidden in the cupboard. 'This'll be the first meal I've cooked for a guest in my new home. Appropriate that it's for you.' I offer a beaming smile, arranging pans and the box of eggs on the counter. 'So,' I continue on with our conversation about life on the island. 'You lived here your whole life? I mean before...'

Sure. I was born in this house and so was my sister. My father's parents had the land returned to them after the First World War and this house was built on the site of our ancestral blackhouse. If you go up to the top of the garden, behind the workshop there, you'll find a rectangle of stones. That's all that's left of the blackhouse. In the eighteen-forties my family were cleared off the land...' He stops and raises his black eyebrow at me. 'Are you actually interested in all this?'

146

'Definitely.' I finish chopping an onion and begin on a tomato. 'One of my aims is to embark on an essay, or a study or something – possibly even a book if I can make it interesting enough – on the enduring links between Hebridean people and their land.' I slide the onions and tomatoes into the pan and throw him a glance. Begin grating cheese. *Don't want to sound like I'm boasting.* 'I did a similar study in Iceland for my post-graduate degree. There must be some similarities between all northern islands and islanders, is the way I figure it.' I don't tell him I had a book published on the back of my PhD. *He might think I'm snooty.* I whip the eggs vigorously. 'I brought a few books with me to look at but I'm much more interested in *living* history, if I can call it that.'

'Eh now,' he laughs, rubs at a mark on the table. 'I'm not that old.'

Heat spreads up my neck and into my cheeks but at least I can put it down to the hot oil in the pan. 'You know what I mean.' I pour egg mixture on top of the onions. 'So what happened when your ancestral family was cleared off the land?'

'My great-great-grandfather's wife had died, and their younger daughter died shortly afterwards, only a wee baby, she was. A lot of people got sick at that time due to being forced out of their homes and onto barren land. The conditions were terribly overcrowded. Great-great-grandpa Murdo married the orphaned daughter of his best friend fairly soon after his first wife died, as much for the girl's protection as anything else, so the *sgeulachd* goes. Both her parents had died. His new wife was the same age as his own daughter, Isabella, and apparently the two girls didn't get along. There was some sort of god-awful *pleigh* one night between them and after the fight Isabella ran away.'

'Anyway, I'm the eventual result of Murdo's remarriage, through a line of male descendants.' I watch Murdo's Adam's apple bobbing again as he tips the mug right back and swallows the last of his coffee. He wipes his mouth with the back of his hand and the movement reminds me of an otter. He shifts the base of his mug on the table. Steam from the pan heats my cheeks. Reaching down for the bin, I hold it open while I sweep onion skins into it. Murdo settles the mug squarely on top of a gnarl in the wood.

'Old Murdo worked for the *maor*, the factor on this island – that's the guy who looked after the landlord's business – a bit like what the estate-agent in Stornoway does for me.' Murdo gives me a wicked grin which I can't help returning. 'So anyway, Murdo at least had a means of earning a living here. Even with most of the tenants gone, there was maintenance work and arranging for the sheep to be transported and accounted for. He wouldn't have been too popular with the tenants who stayed, mind.'

Something's nagging at the back of my mind. Perhaps it's that their voices are similar. Even as I stare at Murdo I'm back in my past on Granny's Green Steps in Edinburgh, the first time Neil and I kissed. His voice drifts up to me through the layers of the years as a blue scarf flutters to the ground and I look deep into the blue eyes that match it. 'I'm Scottish too, you know.'

# 29

THE RESTAURANT SITS in the dunes, suspended on an overhang above the beach. The wide, white stretches of Uig sands spread out on three sides. Wind blows through the marram grass and rustles sand into clouds that coagulate and resettle like fairy dust in the golden light. I spot a seal – then another and another, morphing from the boulders on the inlet beach, each one slipping smoothly into the water, heading for an outcrop of rocks in the sea.

If I were to stand at the narrow end of the massive bay window and crane my neck to the left I'd be able to glimpse my house on the slope of a hill the other side of the bay – I experimented when Neil went to the loo. *Ma hoose.* It tickles my stomach, like when I was a bairn and my uncle's dormobile, stuffed full of us children, went flying over bumps on the roads in Ireland.

Neil was already here when I pulled up in the car park. As we greeted each other I had an odd feeling of wanting to pick a fight, he was so familiar to me. He started scanning the mountains and asked whereabouts I live. I made a vague gesture towards the foothills. But as his head turned in the direction of my sweeping hand the back of my neck prickled at the sight of the soft fuzz of hairs on the back of his.

*I don't want to lose the sense of self I've been building.* I've enjoyed my time alone. Every day I took an early-morning walk around the loch and returned home to the cottage for breakfast. Sat at my laptop for a couple of hours and then went out again to perch on a rock by the sea, from where I watched white birds divebombing the choppy waves, sand blowing into my hair. At home again I ate a hefty ploughman's lunch, followed by another hour at my laptop, catching up with emails. Most afternoons I would usually walk down to the machair and sit quietly amongst the rabbit burrows with a book until sunset traced shadows on the mountains. Time to go inside then, for a warm by the fire. My skin has been whipped rosy gold by the wind and the September sun. *I don't believe autumn will ever truly arrive.*

The rabbits now hop unconcernedly close to me like the ones on the grass below Edinburgh castle did when I first met Neil. On my way back to the cottage I make friends with the highland cattle on the pasture next to my house. Rip up handfuls of grass and feed it to them from the palm of my hand, thinking to stay on their good side.

Yesterday I visited the museum at the community centre, just up the road from the Co-op. Peggy proudly introduced me to everybody and showed me around. She left me with a pile of historical documents to sift through in a side room – touchingly excited by my interest in the island's history. With this much evidence at my fingertips I may write that second book after all. Afterwards we ate soup and shared a pot of tea together in the community café.

I sit reading by the wood stove after dark. Murdo made it, that's what he does for a living. He told me the family who rented the house before me specifically asked him to remove the old one so they could put an electric fire in its place. We shook our heads in disbelief and I fell into a laughing fit, maybe due to the wine I opened – the bottle from the estate agents. It was late by the time Murdo finished installing the stove but he said it would be worth the scolding he'd receive from Peggy to see it burning cheerily away before he left.

And now I'm here with Neil. I have to keep swallowing a lump in my throat. We both watch the seals from our table in the restaurant, perhaps focussing too hard on the outside because of the tumult of feelings under our skin. Under mine, at least. Neil keeps rubbing at the scar on his hand with the tip of his finger, I'm not sure if he's aware of it. The glass ceiling is angled beneath the dome of the sky. The first stars are out and the moon waits patiently in the wings while the sun makes an exotic disappearance under a violet and orange shroud. Twinkling lights, strung up below the glass ceiling, flicker on. A chorus of *ooh* and *ah* ripples round the room. The wave of human breath wafts through me, a chill. Nothing is solid, it's as if water rocks me. My fingers clutch the corner of the tablecloth, bunched on my lap.

'Are you cold?' Neil leans forward.

'No,' I rub my arms. 'Something walked over my grave.' An old saying of Granny's. 'I'm fine, now.' But it's still hollow in my chest. I breathe out slowly. They've only just taken our food orders. Neil keeps apologising as though it's his fault but I don't mind. We sit with the candle in a red glass bowl between us, my tall glass of spritzer, olives in a blue dish. My hands spread themselves in front of me on the table. I press my palms down to ground myself. There's the silver-blue sea, the sky turning cobalt. And then I look back at Neil's hands opposite mine. Once or twice I risk his eyes but they make me shiver.

We skim our pasts: how it felt for him to go back to Canada and rebuild his relationship with his brother. His feelings for his father. What it was like for me to be the only Wilson to make it to Granny Mary's funeral. I lived with her in Howth in the months before her death, helping pack her belongings away in preparation for her move to a hospice. Even Maw couldn't make it over to Ireland – the hospital she was in refused to allow her to travel. She ended up locked away like her own mother who I barely knew. The bitter memory rises into my throat. I swallow it, consciously uncurl my fists into relaxed lines again on the white tablecloth. Neil waits, tidying a pile of olive pips to one side of the dish. I tell him about my mother dying and how things have never really improved between me and Perpetua.

We haven't yet discussed our marital status – I'm reassured that whether or not he's been married since he last saw me, he isn't any longer. He hasn't mentioned children. I haven't told him about Ellis. Neil doesn't ask me about my childlessness or otherwise, either. Maybe it's too painful a subject for both of us. We discuss a few mutual friends from University and our jobs, but when I try to tell him about Sheena, the words dry up. I could never explain her importance.

I gulp down a mouthful of Spritzer. We both turn our heads to stare at the sea.

'Imagine being in a boat out there,' Neil murmurs, and jolts a little in his seat. I get the feeling he's surprised that he's spoken out loud. He keeps his eyes on the sea. 'A fragile, wooden boat, like a rowing boat. Or a dinghy. Crammed into it with far too many others. I mean, look at those waves. I sometimes try to picture it, I feel I should. Sort of... to kind of bear witness, you know? To all those desperate people who'd be prepared to do that. Put their family through that.'

My heart warms. He clears his throat and our eyes meet. Mine brim with tears because I think about the same things so often.

'I know.' Neil says as if he can read my thoughts. 'You can't help thinking about it either, can you? You were always a caring person. I think it took me a lot longer to develop genuine empathy – a medical degree doesn't train you for that.' He spears the remaining fat purple olive from the blue dish, a crease on his forehead, meets my eyes again. I glance away, at the olive disappearing between his lips. It takes me a while to speak and then it all comes pouring out.

'I went over to Calais, you see. To the so-called Jungle. I was granted a secondment from my job, about a year ago. The conditions there were disgusting. But what may happen if the authorities go ahead with their plan to dismantle it will be even worse. All those children on their own.' I pick up the napkin from beside my plate and dab it carefully under my eyes. 'I went there to work with a group of young girls.'

I can't seem to stop talking now – the spritzer's gone to my head. 'I made particular friends with a twelve-year-old named Israa. A lovely girl. We just seemed to click.' I bite my lip. 'She was so brave. Looking after her mother. Her baby sister was born in a caravan there. She and her mother had somehow got separated from her father and two little brothers – somewhere on the road between Greece and France. This was after they'd all nearly drowned in the sea. There was so much violence at the borders that Israa fell down in the crush and she couldn't get up. People were walking right over her – can you believe that?' I twist a corner of my napkin into a point. 'She thinks her father and brothers were swept along with the crowd and she and her mother got left behind. When I met them her mammy was suffering from terrible depression and Israa was trying to hold them both together and ensure her mother cared for the baby. What d'you think happened to those little boys?'

I stare at him as if he can answer me. My vision is focussed beyond his candlelit face in the restaurant. Instead I see a vignette of Israa and the other teenage girls. Sitting in a circle on the floor of a makeshift library, the wind rushing through the tarpaulin walls. The girls were delighted to be holding books and practising their English. Neil shakes his head helplessly.

'Israa still had an infectious smile,' I tell him. 'After everything she'd been through. But when she stopped smiling her eyes went dark. But do you know what she said to me?' I wet my lips. He shakes his head again, his mouth pressed into a line. 'She said, after having to stay indoors in her house in Syria because it was too dangerous to go outside, and she would hear bombs going off nearby and never know if they were going to hit her home – she was happy to be walking in the pouring rain on their trek across Europe.' I pick up my glass, long stem pinched between my fingers, swirl it absently. 'Against all the odds they made it safely from Turkey to Greece in that crappy little boat and they were delirious with gratitude. Yet they still had another long journey before them on foot.' I search his eyes. 'She had a few short hours of being a child again during our games workshops.' Now the tears slide out faster than I can wipe them. My eyes will be smudged. Sometimes I can't bear the world.

'I feel guilty that I don't even know what happened to her. I tried to write, I meant to go back, Neil, but things got in the way, they always do. I should have tried harder.'

'I know. It's okay. I know difficult it is.' Neil gives me a tight smile. 'You won't believe this, but I've recently been there myself.' His chin juts forward, catching the candlelight and looking strangely extended. 'To the Jungle in Calais. I too spent a month working there. I was with Médecins sans Frontières. Almost a year after you. Imagine that.'

'Oh my God,' I breathe out. If we'd been there at the same time. If I'd gone this year instead of last, not had my leaving do at the Centre. Everything would have been so different. 'Bloody hell, Neil.'

We clink glasses in a mutual salute. We must appear a long-married couple, celebrating an anniversary perhaps. We'd have spent the first half of our lives bringing up children and dedicating ourselves to work and now we'd be free to embark on an arbitrary lifestyle. To live in this isolated corner of Heaven.

A young couple sit at a table in the window, hardly more than teenagers. They're on their honeymoon. We know this because a balloon floats above their heads, emblazoned with the words *Newly Married*. The balloon and the bouquet and the bottle of champagne in a bucket of ice was all set up before they arrived. When they walked in, at a nod and a wink from the head waiter the other diners including Neil and myself were encouraged to give the couple a round of applause. The youngsters lean across the table towards each other now, hands entwined, and my heart aches for them. It aches for the young Lauren and Neil too, and for all the young people with an uncertain future ahead of them. I catch Neil's eye.

'You look happy,' he says. I resist the urge to bristle. To qualify my current contentment with the events that have built my resilience. Instead I form my lips into a contained smile and say nothing.

'*I'm* happy, especially to see you again,' he says. 'I can't tell you how often I've thought of you over the years.'

'Have you?'

'You sound surprised. Of course I have. You were,' he swallows rather off-puttingly. 'The love of my life.' He takes a deep sip from his large glass of red wine, it must be that which has diminished his reserve – or our shared experiences. Perhaps he's booked himself a room in the hotel. Neil's not the sort to drink and drive. He replaces the glass on the table, twirls the stem between his fingers and thumb as I recently did with mine. The wine rocks wildly in the glass, but never quite over-spills.

'Have you thought of me much, in all these years?' He raises one eyebrow. I hold my own glass with the stem slotted between my fingers, the bowl cupped in my palm.

'Lauren?' He's used to getting difficult information out of patients. I'm spared for the time being because the waiter finally arrives with our main courses. Mine's half a lobster and I need my wits to fight my way into it. Neil pierces the glossy pastry casing of a salmon wellington with his fork. *A crime not to sample the local seafood*, we'd both agreed. I squeeze lemon juice on my lobster, pick at the white flesh with an instrument of torture. A messy operation, too late to back out now. Eventually I withdraw a morsel from the lobster's claw. Pop it into my mouth. I keep my eyes on the table, wiping my greasy fingers on the napkin.

'Of course I think about you. If you want to put it that way you were, well... the most important relationship I've ever had, too.' My marriage to Ellis cowers in a corner and I pull a mental cloth over it, avoiding the memory of the hurt in his eyes when we met up to discuss our divorce.

As Neil gazes at me a crystal-drop appears at the tip of his nose. I turn away and study the blacked-out view from the window while he trumpets into a hankie. What I'm actually looking at is a reflection of the young couple, still with their hands clasped, superimposed onto a reflection of Neil and me. Both in real life and our reflections, lights twinkle above our heads.

I turn back to Neil as he folds the large cotton handkerchief into his palm, not the disintegrating length of overused tissue from days gone by. He secretes the handkerchief away out of sight.

'Sorry. Still not cured, I'm afraid.' The back of his hand faces me. *We ought to acknowledge the scar.* My stupid lower lip trembles, my sinuses prickle again. Neil waits, like a doctor. He probably wishes there was a box of tissues on the table to push towards me. I dab under my eyes again with the napkin, supposing there must be no makeup left on my face by now. I don't know why I bothered. I give Neil a fleeting smile and, to put off the inevitable, occupy myself with extracting a further morsel of lobster from the shell. Neil takes a few more bites too and we both chew. I wince at the sound of Neil's knife on china. Finally he looks up from his food.

'Go on. You want to say something else, don't you?' He wears a prepared expression of understanding. I lay down my implements of extraction.

'All right. I never got over it. Over... the abortion. Over Barbara. That's still who she is to me, although I doubt I would have named her that if – no offence, of course. Maybe I would have given it to her as a second name, after her grandmother.' I see him wince. I take a breath. *Angel.* The name appears out of the blue. *I might have called her Angel if she'd been alive.* Though perhaps I'm thinking of the young social worker back in Edinburgh. Sniff. Barbara's more of an angel dead, of course – could be another reason the name came to me in retrospect.

'But Barbara is who she's become. I never got over the loss of our baby, Neil, and the guilt. It was *my* fault, ultimately. It was me who went ahead with the crime. It's not that I blame you, exactly. I can't, really – because it wasn't you who did the deed.'

My reflection distorts in the curve of my glass. The updrawn hair at the sides of my stretched-out face, the exaggerated slash of plum lipstick – a clown's mouth. The remains of my eye makeup, applied as an attempt to redefine the lost clarity of my formerly full upper lids in the smudged and smoky way Neil would remember. I had to dig deep in my rarely-used makeup bag to find the eye cream and the mascara – God knows how out-of-date it is. *All this effort, and for what?* It only reminds me of a girl who disappeared a long time ago. Tiredness assails me.

The jury's back in.

'Lauren. I... I'm sorry. I think about that time too, about what I persuaded you to... have done. I *am* sorry, honestly. I wish I'd never asked you to do it.' He scrapes the last dregs of Hollandaise sauce from his plate with the edge of his knife and transfers it onto his fork before popping it into his mouth. He brings his lips together satisfyingly.

My mouth must have fallen open. A drop of lemon juice trickles down my chin. I wipe it off with the smudged napkin.

'Really?'

'Yes. I'm so sorry it happened.'

I play his apology back in my head. 'You're actually saying you wish we'd never aborted our baby?'

'I am now – now that I'm sitting here looking at you again.' He has tears in his eyes, too. He slides his hand over the table and takes my wrist, very gently. The way we're looking at each other we must appear to be the grown-up version of the couple sitting in the window, still gazing into each other's eyes. Now that we've spoken about Barbara – that Neil has acknowledged her – I can actually perceive of us taking up where we left off.

'You look beautiful tonight,' Neil says. 'I remember you so well and how much I loved you. I wish I'd never done anything to make you leave.'

I can't believe he's saying all this. My head buzzes. I can't help being suspicious. Is he only saying he's sorry about the abortion because it was the cause of my leaving, or does he mean he wishes we'd had our baby after all? It's important. The tingle travels from the back of my neck into my shoulders and down my arms. My fingers reverberate in the cup of his hand.

'What exactly is it that you're saying, Neil? I just need you to clarify. Are you sorry now that I had the abortion – do you mean you wish I'd kept the baby?'

If he does, then we can go forward, we can regret our past mistake together, it will be all right. The shared experience will join us again, rather than it being something lived from two different perspectives, a thing that'll always come between us. After all, we have so much in common. The old feelings are still there. A twitch in my belly confirms it.

His fingers close more firmly around my hand. I swallow as I allow my own fingers to curl up inside his. *He's still my Neil, and I'm still his Lauren.* I can feel my eyes shining.

'Yes, I am saying that.'

A flush spreads up from my chest, floods my neck and swamps my cheeks. There's the slightest pause.

'I wish I'd let you carry on with the pregnancy. I wish I'd supported you the way I should have done.' His eyes brim over with moisture. 'If I'd truly known what it would do to you, I would never have asked you to get rid of it. Of... her.' He squeezes my hand. *He's admitted that it wasn't just a foetus. She, her. Our daughter.* There's a faint tremble in his jaw.

'Thank you.' Warmth hovers over my solar plexus. He smiles sadly, takes another long sip of his red wine, gulping slightly. Then he fusses at the corner of his napkin with the fingers of his spare hand, as I fussed with mine earlier. He leans in even closer. Again he swallows nervously. The warmth begins to drain from my face and chest, leaving me feeling isolated, despite him still holding my hand. I hold my breath. A single bead of sweat materialises above Neil's eyebrow.

'It was only when Naomi was pregnant with our first,' comes out of his mouth. 'That I really understood what it meant to a woman to grow a baby inside her and give birth to it. And the way I felt when I first held baby Helen in my arms... I realised I could have had that, with you. *Your* baby was my first daughter.'

He looks stricken. But not as stricken as me.

# 30

MY HAND SHAKES. *Why am I bothering, anyway?* I look like a woman trying to recapture her youth. My reflection's tinged green. Lipstick bleeds into the hair-thin lines around my mouth. I blot with a tissue but it still looks awful. Tutting, I wipe off as much as I can. *Cannae turn myself into a twenty-year-old.* My eyeliner's already smudged. Stepping back, sunlight highlights a downy coating of hairs on my lower face. One particular hair, thicker than the rest, stands proud in the centre of my chin. *Neil must have noticed it on Saturday night.* I pull ineffectually at the hair with my thumb and forefinger, the way I wanted to pinch and pull at his skin when he told me about his daughter.

Granny Mary used to say *there are worse things happening at sea.* She would have been thinking of the fishing boats that never came back to her village but I think of a tiny boy on a Turkish beach. The enduring image, symbolising all the individuals washed in on the foam of the sea. In this day and age. *So stop being pathetic about facial hirsuteness. You're lucky to be alive, lucky to have your imperfections.* What do the kids at the Centre say? First world problems. With a hashtag.

I wonder if the island teenagers will be any different from their mainland counterparts – cheeky, arrogant and over-sensitive for the most part. Pains in the ass but rather that than so broken they don't speak at all. I open my handbag and take out a pair of tweezers. *Chris*, I think, grasping the rogue hair between the flat silver ends. I pull. The hair becomes longer before it pops out. Fuck.

Chris was red-haired, a freckle-faced boy of fifteen, kicked out of the family home when his mum got a new boyfriend. I'd worked with Chris's family on and off since he was six years old, knocked unconscious by a fall – or a push – down the stairs. He spent a week in a coma that time. I was one of the social workers who convinced his mother she should begin calling him by his name instead of 'it'. We worked intensively on the relationship between her and her child and when Chris's father moved out, things improved.

I inspect the root at the end of the hair, the hole left in my face, God, I can't go out like this! *Arrghh, I'm gonnae be late.* Hurrying back through the dining room and kitchen I open the bathroom cabinet and take out a bottle of tea tree oil, knocking a box of Paracetamol off the shelf at the same time. Unscrew the top with butter-fingers, tip a couple of drops of oil onto a ball of cotton wool, dab at the hole in my chin, press down to stop the bleeding. *Better.* I close the bathroom cabinet. Despite the wasted time I move deliberately back through the rooms, treading the footsteps laid down by generations of one family, but what I'm really thinking is why did you have to ruin our evening, Neil?

*I can't think about that now.* I button my jacket in the porch like a child on her first day at school, except that I'm the one in charge of the key to the house – apart from Peggy MacLeod – and Murdo, perhaps. On the doorstep I stand and admire the mountains, girding myself for the fifty-minute drive into Stornoway and all the new faces to become acquainted with when I get there.

The woman up the road stands by the open door of her front porch as usual, arms folded across her aproned chest, staring at me as I drive past. I offer a wave, keeping the other hand firmly on the steering wheel, but she doesn't respond. In the rear view mirror I notice her head turning, sense those black bullets of eyes burning through the windows into the back of my head. I try not to let it bother me. The woman's name is Mrs McLean, Peggy told me, and she was *dropped on her head as a baby.*

Pushing the always-intruding Neil aside, my thoughts return to Chris, the boy who wouldn't speak by the time he came back into local authority care. His mother had remarried and the stepfather abused him. The stepfather was convicted, Chris was given due counselling and things improved for a second time. Then his mother took up with another new boyfriend, and this one attempted to strangle Chris. This time when it came to a choice between his mother's boyfriend and her son she voted for the boyfriend. Chris was ejected from home. As his key worker, I found it hard to deal with his passive-aggression, enough to turn any social worker to stone. *Give me a gobby cow like Sheena any day – you know where you are with them.* I tighten my hands on the wheel for the wide bend that begins the climb into the mountains, taking care to avoid the potholes at the edge of the road. I already feel homesick for my new house and for Neil, despite his betrayal.

---

Edging my car around the small parking area at the back of Children's Services, sweat prickles on the back of my neck. Where is it? I've been informed there's a spot signposted with my job title. On my second circuit I find it tucked away in a corner. Several attempts at parking under the mocking eye of the security camera later and I'm convinced there must be a row of workers standing by the windows watching the new girl make a total fuck-up of things. Because surely they have nothing better to do? I'm required to squeeze out of the car, having left a much wider gap on the passenger side. *Ach well, I'll be able to offer someone a lift home.*

Grasping the handle of my briefcase more tightly I head towards the only door I can see, at the top of a short flight of steps. *You're a grown woman, Lauren. You've been in this business more years than you care to mention, you've worked in Dublin and Reykjavik and Edinburgh, handled cases other social workers refused to take on. You've even spent time in a refugee camp, for Heaven's sake. So stop acting like a baby on her first day at nursery school.* Why am I so nervous? Maybe it's because it's the first time I've been back to work since. . . Someone pulls the scruffy blue door open at point-blank range.

'Hello there, Lauren, is it? *Fàilte!*' My body catapults backwards in shock and my foot slips on the top step. I make a sort of *ouff* noise. A young, blonde woman dressed in a navy suit stands in the entrance, clutching her stomach.

'Sorry,' she giggles. 'You just looked so funny. I wanted to offer you a welcome but I can see it was more dangerous than I expected.' She has the soft, lilting accent of the Western Isles. 'You *are* Lauren, I take it?'

'I am. Lauren Wilson.' I try to soften my vowels to be more like hers. 'And how nice of you to greet me at the door. Pleased to meet you.' I put out my shaking hand and leave a question mark at the end of my sentence.

'Jessica,' she takes my hand in a firm grasp. 'Jessica MacDonald. Family Placement. Substance Misuse is looking forward to having you. We've all been covering the position since Stella left.'

'Substance Misuse – that's a more compact job title than the one I was given.' I glance down at the glaringly-new ID card hanging from my lanyard. 'I've never worked in such a specialised bracket before. I ran a youth centre in Edinburgh, mainly.' Jessica's about twenty years younger than me. Her lipstick perfectly demarcates her cupid's bow of a mouth and her eyeliner is impeccable. But I like her immediately. *MacDonald.* She could be a distant relative of Neil's.

'We've all been looking forward to your arrival,' Jessica stands back to usher me into a dark hallway at the bottom of a tall flight of stairs (*oh no, my poor knee*). 'I'm sorry about the reason for your delay, though. That poor wee girl, it all sounds so awful. She was quite special to you, I gather?'

I swallow the lump in my throat. 'She was. But it's time to look to the future now and keep on doing the best I can. Right?' I need this child-woman's endorsement.

'Absolutely right!' She offers me an intense gaze from her grey eyes, then her face breaks into another smile. 'Your office is on the first floor, if you want to follow me up?'

---

I drink my third cup of coffee of the morning, hoping I don't regret it later. A young filla with scarlet hair and silver studs dotting the outline of one ear goes through my caseload with me, they call him Rab. Wearing a burgundy jumper his gran must have knitted, a loose thread trails from one sleeve. *Ach, the lad canna be more than twelve!*

'You'll need to watch out for this one,' he tells me, pulling a file out. An angelic-looking boy with pale hair and jade eyes. *Jonnie*, I read. 'Totally messed-up, unfortunately,' Rab says. 'One of his habits – just one of them, mind – is that he likes to lick middle-aged women's faces. Takes you by surprise. Sorry.' Rab colours, glancing sideways at me. 'I didn't mean to imply you were –'

'Don't be daft.' I dig him gently in the ribs. 'I can hardly be called young, now, can I?'

'If you're not young, then what am I?' A silver-haired man, must be in his sixties and he's heavily overweight, stands by the coffee machine. He's been drinking the black stuff all morning. Holds one of those e-cigarettes between the first two fingers of his left hand. 'Want another?' he asks, raising a mug.

'No thanks. In fact from tomorrow I'll be drinking herbal tea instead. I'm not supposed to have caffeine.'

'You should have said.' An elegant black woman about my age walks past, balancing a china cup on a saucer. Peppermint-smelling steam wreaths around her, weaves into the dust-motes floating in the light above my desk. 'Did Jessica show you the kitchen? It's that way, just past the toilets. We have a variety of non-caffeinated drinks in there. John.' She glares at coffee-man.

'What, me?'

'Yes, you.' She points a finger. 'Your doctor warned you to cut down on the coffee and we all know it. We lost a colleague to a heart attack last year.' Nodding at me. 'I'm Louisa, by the way. Teenage Advocacy.'

'Lauren,' I repeat for the umpteenth time. 'Substance Misuse.'

Louisa loosely grazes the tips of my fingers with hers. Winks at Rab, who turns a darker shade of red. He watches her move across the black and white linoleum tiles, leaving a gust of peppermint in her wake.

We continue through my cases. 'This one,' he pulls another folder from the pile. 'She's from Lewis originally but her Mammy took her to live in Skye. Seemed to be going okay, she was even taken off our books at one point. Then her mammy overdosed and this young lady's now in a care home. Her uncle lives nearby but she's not cooperating with him. You'll have to see how you get on with her.'

A tingle of my old 'feeling' for the job makes itself known, anticipation of making a difference. The boy with jade eyes who hit his father so hard with an iron that he suffered brain damage (the father was beating up the mother) didn't set off that flicker in me, nor, strangely, did the Asian girl who's kept a teddy-bear stuffed up her jumper since she gave birth to a stillborn baby. It doesn't mean I won't give them the best I've got. But for some reason this girl's the one who flicks my internal switch.

I lean in front of Rab, catch the scent of nicotine on his breath and the slight muskiness of his skin. Now it's my turn to flush. But never mind that. I want to look more closely at the girl. Her startlingly blue eyes in a pale face. The long, black hair hanging in front of her shoulders. She has the blanked-out expression of so many of my clients, struggling to close the windows on their souls.

'She's not officially a user,' Rab says. 'But the staff at the home are worried she's experimenting. Concerned she could be going the same way as her mother. Intervention's considered pretty necessary at this point and they want you to see her as soon as possible.'

Something about those blue eyes, staring out of the photograph. Does the girl remind me of Sheena in some way, different though she is in skin colour and the lack of attitude in her gaze? She doesn't look *gobby* like Sheena, that's for sure. But she does look somehow *mine*, as I always felt Sheena was. I take off my reading glasses and give them a wipe on the hem of my blouse, then replace them on my nose and peer closer at the sheet so I can read the name under the photograph.

*Catriona MacLennan.* 'She has the same surname as my landlord.' I turn the page and glance over the girl's history – pretty similar to many of the children I've helped look after in the past. They don't know where her father is. Neglected due to her mother's addiction.

'It's a common name around the islands,' Rab says, pulling another folder from the pile. 'You'll find MacLennan's everywhere.

# 31

I HAVEN'T FELT this exhausted since the night – since the night... I've got to try and help other young people now, the boy with jade eyes who only wanted to rescue his mother from his abusive father, for example. The girl named Catriona.

But right now I need to get safely home. Once I've negotiated my way out of rush hour in the town centre the roads are quiet and so dark. I have a long drive ahead. Was it a mistake to choose a home so far from Stornoway? I tighten my hands on the wheel and try not to look for the turnoff where I think Neil's house is. I feel so hurt when I think of him being a father. I progress along the calm roads south of Stornoway. At the sign for Calanais I remind myself to take a trip to the standing stones some time. *I'll go one night when the moon's full.* It's supposed to be magic. My turnoff is at Garrynahine. From there I drive on towards Miavaig, the lyrical sound of the place names rolling through my brain as I read the signs. And yes, I plan to learn how to pronounce them in Gaelic.

Through the tunnel-like valley – *Gleann Bhaltois*. In my headlights the landscape is reminiscent of a film set, another planet. The baaaaing of sheep rings out into the dark. I bring the car to a stop. Headlights off. Savour the teeming silence of nature. *I'm alone in the world.* The last person left. I get out of the car. The sky is purple velvet, the stars like those miniature silver balls Kathy always put on our birthday cakes. The mountains echo with the soft shriek of the wind and the baaing of a mother sheep close by – echoed by the amplified bleat of her well-grown lamb.

Feeling my way around the car I notice a ripple in the grass at the side of the road. I jump back as a bulky shape bursts from it, blunders in front of the car. The shape skids to a halt by the warm metal of the bonnet. It stares right at me, close up, a deer as big as a horse! Antlers spread like the branches of a tree. I can smell it, musky and earthy, feel the moist of its breath dissipating around me. The animal inspects the bonnet with its snuffling nose before gathering itself into a leap. I press myself against the side of the car, heart going ten-to-the-dozen. The stag bounds gracefully into the grass on the other side of the road. I let out my breath with a *whoosh*. Dreamily, I feel my way back around the car and lower myself into the driving seat. Pull the door shut. Restart the engine, switch the headlights back on. The prehistoric environment transitions back into a manmade road. I'm acutely alert. I drive out of the confines of the steep-sided valley and into the open again, mind full of the magnificent deer with a pelt the same colour as Neil's hair. Freewheeling down the hill from Timsgarry, tiredness sweeps through my muscles. I picture the hot water bottle I'll take into bed, the novel I'm reading about the Second World War, told from the perspective of a blind French girl. I'll think about Neil even if I tell myself I don't want to. At the bottom of the hill, the wide bend in the road leads onwards to the sea but I turn right onto the narrower road, indicators flashing to no-one. Purr down the track that leads to my house (and the house of the woman who was dropped on her head).

She's not standing on her doorstep. Her curtains are tightly closed. Peggy's car is on the road in front of my house though. I brake just in time, narrowly avoiding a crash. *She could have fecking parked further along.* I stall the engine twice, attempting the narrow gateway with no manoeuvring space. It would serve Peggy right if I left a scratch on her paintwork.

I don't know why I even bothered locking the door. Peggy

awaits me in the porch, showing herself at the moment I finally position my car on the concrete by the house. *'Ciamar a tha thu?'* she calls out. Whatever the fuck that means.

I try a haughty voice. 'Can I help you, Peggy?' But it washes over her.

'Ach, no, hen. It's me who can help you. There's a little something in your kitchen for you, I knew you wouldn't mind.' *Ach weel...* There are advantages to a member of your community having a key to your house – and feeling free to use it whenever the mood suits them. My stomach grumbles. A still-warm casserole, perhaps? Or a pie. Peggy must have brought me something for supper. How kind of her to realise I wouldn't feel like cooking by the time I arrived home from my first exhausting day at work in the big city.

Peggy smirks, backing indoors ahead of me as I dump my bag on the floor and shrug off my coat in the porch. 'You'll like it,' she promises. 'It'll be just the thing to keep you company as the nights start drawing in. You've no idea how windy it gets down here in the bay.' My tired brain attempts to make a connection between the supper she's brought me and the company it will provide – plus the references to wind and night drawing in. She's still staring at me with a fixed grin on her face. The grin falters as we both hear a sharp bark from the direction of the kitchen. Peggy must have noticed my face darken. What the...?

'She'll be great company, aye. That she will.' Her ingratiating expression grates on me. My hand twitches. She closes the door to the porch behind me (I've pushed past her rather roughly) and her footsteps hurry after me through to the kitchen.

A small dog sits on the table. Despite the distraction I can't help hastily scanning the surrounding surfaces for the supper my stomach's promised me. My nose points itself hopefully at the oven but there's no delicious smell coming from it, and the small red light of cooker-consciousness is not lit. Burning starts up behind my eyes. *It's not fair.*

The dog lets out another sharp bark, a pair of black, beady eyes fixed on my face similarly to how Peggy's were when we stood in the porch. My communication skills return. 'Fuck me, Peggy, what's this? It's on the bloody table.'

Peggy winces. I *hate* dogs, hence not having one. If I'd wanted a dog, I would have chosen a dog of my own and not an almost sausage-shaped one like this, its bottom replacing what I'd hoped would be food at my eating-place. My stomach growls. The dog's ears prick up.

'Get down!' I jab my finger at the floor. I must admit to some surprise when the dog obliges. It jumps onto a chair and from there to the floor, a worried expression on its face. *I must remember to keep the chairs tucked in to the table in future*, I find myself thinking. Followed by a mental slap in the fizzer – as if I'm going to keep it!

The dog tiptoes towards a basket Peggy must have placed in the corner. It circles the cushion a few times before collapsing, staring accusingly at me. I refuse to be affected by its wrinkled velvet forehead. Peggy wears a similar expression. She stands in the opposite corner of the room, hands clasped over her stomach. The moment stretches and I feel weightless, like I did when I was a teenager. Untethered to reality. I gasp for more air, pinch at the ample flesh around my waist. Once I'm certain I won't float away I make my feet walk over to the sink and persuade my hands to turn on the tap and run hot water into the bowl. The smell of bleach brings me round. I scrub the table. *Dog's bottom*, I keep thinking. I don't want a dog. And anyway I don't deserve to have anything of my own to look after.

A whisper reaches my ears from the human in the corner of the room. I unstick my mouth.

'What was that you said?' Empty the water down the plughole, spray disinfectant on the cloth and leave it in the bowl to soak.

'Her name's Titania,' Peggy repeats, stronger this time. 'She belonged to a cousin of mine from Bearnaraigh. Maura died and they were looking for a new home for the dog. I told them at the funeral that I knew just the person.'

I sink into a chair at the table. From the corner of my eye I see Peggy fluttering her hands before she draws herself up. How does she make herself taller like that? She marches over to the kettle and switches it on. I refuse to look at the dog but there's a sort of trembling in the air. It's trying to telepath how much it wants to stay. My stomach growls even louder.

'You should have asked me,' trips out of my mouth.

Peggy releases an audible breath. 'Aye, I see that now, hen, but I thought it would be a nice surprise. Look, will you be all right for a wee minute? You see, I've got your dinner in the car.' Now *my* ears prick up. 'Why don't you have a bite to eat,' she says, 'while you mull it over, have a wee think about it, eh?' *Blackmail, pure and simple.* It might just work.

'She's a good dog, mind, used to being on her own, she is.' Peggy's managed to leave the kitchen and return without me noticing. Now she bustles about fetching plates and cutlery and I'm still sitting zombie-like at the table. My knee throbs. 'Sometimes my cousin could hardly get out of bed, you see. And the dog had to sit on the windowsill all day, looking out at the world. She wished she could be a part of it, poor thing.' *Jabber, jabber, jabber.* 'She'll love it here, the wee madam. I just thought about you, you see, Lauren. All those walks you like going on, why would you want to do that by yourself now?' She makes her best puzzled face. 'One thing I do know, dogs love a walk, that's for certain. This dog will have a new lease of life with you. You two are a match made in heaven, that's all I'm saying.'

---

*'Ith gu leór!'* says Peggy, a smug look on her face. She doesn't know I've loosely learnt some phrases from my Gaelic dictionary. 'Enjoy your food, too, Peggy,' I reply. The casserole's still hot within its insulated container, so no oven needed. All the time I'm eating, I'm aware of the suspenseful

anticipation of my potential housemate and its bringer. When I've finished wiping my plate with the bread Peggy also brought along from the community café – *sell by date was today, we wouldn't have been able to use it at the café tomorrow* – Peggy whips the plate out from under me and carries it to the sink. The smile-crinkles are back at the corners of her eyes and she's confident I'll have changed my mind by the time she sits herself down again, cradling her mug of tea and placing mine in front of me.

'Mr MacLeod will be wondering where I've got to,' she simpers. When I don't answer she adds, 'Never mind, he can be sorting himself out, for a change. Now, about the dog.'

Finally, I turn my head to look at the creature properly. It considers this to be an invitation, slithering out of its basket, slinking along the floor towards me. Warmth pools over my foot, the dog's pointed nose sniffs at me. Peggy pushes her seat back, tilts her head to peer under the table with an indulgent smile, her bonnet of hair never moving. She's sensible enough not to make a smart remark. After a few beats of time I make a 'harrumph' noise, find myself asking, 'What did you say her name is?'

'Titania,' Peggy pronounces it in an oddly English way, *Titarniya*. I leave another expectant pause during which Peggy breathes deeply. Finally I break it.

'Tatty will do.'

Peggy lets out her breath as quietly as she can.

'Hello, Tatty,' I give the animal a stern gaze. 'I'm your worst nightmare of an owner. I'm not going to take any crap from you, mark my words.' I mean it quite literally. 'If he,' I say to Peggy, 'I mean she, thinks I'm planning on picking up anything that comes out of her bottom, she's got another think coming.'

Peggy purses her lips but says nothing. The dog sits up and stares unflinchingly back at me. A terrier of some sort, I guess from my limited knowledge. Perhaps a Dachshund? But the ears look wrong. Perpetua had a Shi-Tzu when she first got married, but this is not one of those. Tatty's short, smooth coat is a mixture of brown and black. Her ears are silken-looking and folded over. Her body's elongated but stout and she has a thin, upcurled tail. I like her eyes though, bright like shiny berries, and the wrinkle on her forehead. She has a small, sharp nose.

'You will never, ever, *ever* climb up on this table again, do you hear me?' I rap the table sharply with my knuckles. Tatty hangs her head, trembling. My guess is she's only pretending to be ashamed. 'Never,' I repeat menacingly. 'Will she need anything to eat?' I ask Peggy.

The dog perks up again, tilting her head on one side. Peggy jumps to attention. 'Ach, most of her things are in the scullery already. A bag of those nugget things, two bowls, one for water and one for food. I've hung her lead on the peg in the back porch for you.' A hint of her usual self-satisfied smile at the corners of her mouth. 'She even has a little coat with a fur hood, it was a present from my cousin's daughter.'

'No dog of mine will be wearing a coat.' With this statement I claim ownership. 'You can give it to the charity shop at the community centre.' Peggy looks disappointed but the dog gives my ankle a lick. 'Don't think you can get round me like that.' I put my stern face back on. The terrier – or dachshund, whatever she is – smiles.

## 32

MY EYES SNAP open with the alarm. The first thing I see is a pair of urgent eyes. It takes me back to the flat on Cowgatehead when the builders knocked down an internal wall to install the new boiler. I felt something running over my feet in the night and nearly battered Neil unconscious with my flailing arms. After that I would open cupboard doors and come face-to-face with similar glittering beads of eyes as the ones regarding me now. We had to put down a special box baited with poison. *We were good at killing things, weren't we, Neil?*

When I recognise my dog a sensation suspiciously like affection warms my stomach. *Bah, humbug.* The dog angles her head in such a way as to show the whites of her eyes, triggering responses from me like shots going off. Well, any dog looking at any person like that would have the same effect. It'll disappear the minute she chews the carpet or climbs on the kitchen table again, I'm sure it will. Tatty evidently feels it's now appropriate to deafen me with a high-pitched, musical whine. 'You can go out in the back garden. We're not taking a walk until I've had my shower.'

I swing my legs out from under Granny Mary's eiderdown, feet on the cold floor, feeling around for my slippers. I'll have to teach the dog to fetch them. I open the back door for her on my way to the bathroom. Tatty throws an offended look over her shoulder, laps her water with a delicate tongue and plonks her bottom down in the porch. She's still sitting in the same place when I pass her on my way back to the bedroom. She stares pointedly at her lead and then at me. We walked in the dark last night, just as far as Mrs McLean's house. Tatty dutifully performed her business directly opposite. I pushed it into the long grass with a stick. I'm not sure whether I imagined it or whether the woman-who-was-dropped-on-her-head was peering out from between her curtains, but it made me nervous. I locked and bolted the front door before I went to bed.

At least I've got a dog to warn me of intruders now. This isn't as paranoid as it sounds. The father of a kid under my care – the truth is, it was Sheena – once broke into my house at night. I woke to find him standing at the foot of my bed. He'd climbed the drainpipe and entered by the open window of my first-floor apartment. Sheena's da stood with his fists bunched, threatening me with grievous bodily harm if I disclosed any information that could put him in jail. I tried to keep him talking because, as it happened, I had a panic button behind my headboard for just this reason. One push of it and he ended up in jail anyway. The police told me to keep my window shut in the future. I hate sleeping in a room with a closed window. *Sheena.* Her da disappeared shortly after he was released from jail. They tried to get in touch with him after – but he never turned up. I stare at myself in the mirror. I'll never be any good to anyone if I crumble every time I remember the night she texted me to tell me what she was about to do.

'Come on then.' Back in the kitchen, dressed in a jumper and jeans, I shrug on my waterproof jacket and peer through the porch windows at the weather. Silver-and-gold sky with a heavy bank of grey clouds in the distance, heading our way if the blanketed tops of the mountains are anything to go by. The kind of weather I'll need to get used to, as both Peggy and the woman at the Co-op remind me every time I mention how lovely the blue of the sky is, or that it's not as cold as I'd imagined it would be in the Outer Hebrides.

I pull on my boots, balancing with a hand on the shelf. 'You're going to make me late for work.' I unhook Tatty's lead. I want to go out as much as she does, especially as it'll be getting dark by the time I arrive home. She wags her funny, curled-whip tail and I snap the lead onto the collar, my fingers stiff and complaining. I straighten my back and flex my hands. I'll take Tatty over the fields and keep her on the lead because I don't know how she is with cows, or if she would run away and never come back. She may have not got many walks with her previous owner but surprisingly she doesn't seem overweight. 'Maybe she just didn't feed you, eh?' Tatty looks hopeful at the mention of food.

I must let out a grunt as my knee jolts because Tatty flicks me a concerned look. I reassure her that she'll be hearing these kinds of sounds from me regularly, so not to worry. *You look just the same*, Neil said at the restaurant. Nice sentiment, Neil, but totally untrue. I do *not* look the same as when I was at University. That would've made me an excessively wrinkled twenty-year-old. Perhaps so many middle-aged people get together with past partners or childhood friends because they still see the young person within the older one. Neil might be seeing me as the embodiment of our youth and former happiness but do I still see him as Jesus from the film? No. *He's more like Judas.* He *betrayed* me. He had children after making me get rid of mine. *It's not fair.*

My legs are jelly by the time we get to the bottom of the hill. The dog wags her whole body. Spins in a full circle, prances backwards, hopping on her hind legs. If she was a person I'd be afraid I was falling in love. How did Peggy know?

---

We slip through the gate into the field opposite. Out of breath, I realise how slowly I must have walked before I became the owner of a dog. Tatty strains on the lead but I daren't let her go. Shaggy-coated cattle huddle at the top of the next hill, gazing down at us with gloomy expressions. One or two of them are lying down. Perhaps I'll soon find out whether the old adage about forthcoming rain is true. We circle the base of the hill. Tatty rasps for breath on the end of the lead, ears twitching backwards and forwards. Every now and then she lets out an excited bark – or rather, a high-pitched yip – and rabbits thump at the entrances to their burrows. *They train terriers to hunt rabbits, don't they?* 'You'd better leave them alone, when I do decide to let you off the lead.'

The dark water of the loch mirrors the unsettled sky. A fine mist of rain needles the oil-like surface. Tatty lifts her feet daintily on the soft moss at the loch's edge. I squidge happily through puddles in my wellies. *I'm eight years old again, dragging Bridie by the haund through the puddles in our local play park. Bridie greetin coz o' the hole in her welly. Both her feet wet anyway coz the water went over her boots. That was Declan's fault for splashing us. But Maw'll nip my heid when we get back to the hoose, fer oor Declan can do nae wrong. Pepe'll stick her tongue out at me from behind the curtain of the boys' kitchen bed like she always does when I get in trouble.*

'What is it, hen?' The dog's stock-still. A ripple runs through her short fur. One of her feet – with long, feminine toenails – curves delicately above the ground. Her tail has straightened and sticks up into the air. She looks at me, then back at the water. I follow her gaze and in an instant, one of my childhood dreams comes true. An otter – *no, two otters*. Two round, sleek heads dipping in and out of the metallic ridges on the water, wet black orbs followed by the semi-circles of their backs, the level rulers of two thick tails. I bring my finger slowly to my lips and press it there, willing Tatty with all my heart to keep still. As if reading my thoughts, Tatty sinks slowly onto her belly. She remains there, trembling, eyes never leaving the water.

One of the otters senses us: quick as a flash it somersaults in the water and swims away in the opposite direction. *Don't go*, I think to the other otter. *Please.* I've waited my whole life to see an otter in the wild. Treading water, the bold wee man peers at us from about fifteen feet away – at me, certainly. I'm not sure it can see Tatty though it must be able to smell her. Cool as you like the otter rests there, bobbing up and down with the current. I hardly breathe, taken back to childhood again. *Ah curl on ma top bunk that Da made me in the bed-closet. Ah'm reading* Ring of Bright Water. *Later I stand fer 'oors at the railings along the Clyde, wan'in every shadow and piece a driftwood tae be an otter. Da's sent oot to search fer me and fetch me in for ma tea.* My skin tingles beneath the waterproof jacket at the sensory memory of Da gripping my arm as he dragged me back to the tenement house. *I get another slap on the leg from oor Michael fer making Da have a proper* Annie Rooney.

The otter twitches his whiskers at me and makes a decision. In a snakelike movement he streams out of the water and lands on a long, low rock a couple of metres away. He preens himself, running miniature paws down his long whiskers, using those tiny hands to groom the back of his neck, his ears and face. Presentable now, he swivels in a graceful movement and faces me again, his nose twitching. His eyes are round and as wet as the loch. He can't be more than six feet away. I can see the definition of every claw-groomed hair on his face. His whiskers vibrate. The tip of his tongue pokes from his mouth. I've been holding my breath and I let it out incredibly slowly, forming the word *stay* on a hiss of air for Tatty, who trembles at my feet. Still holding my gaze, the otter rolls onto his back. I breathe in again, out again. He rolls from one side to the other, keeping his eyes on me, regains his feet. He stands briefly up on his hind legs as if to inspect me more closely, balancing on his long tail. Then, as swiftly as he arrived, he slips into the water and swims in a straight line back to the other side of the loch to join his mate, never once looking back.

'Oh my God, I can't believe it!' Tatty jumps to her feet, too, dancing to the tune I sing out. She yaps, tangles my legs in her lead. 'You were a good, good dog. Thank you!' I make a mental note to get some treats for her from the Co-op in Stornoway.

# 33

TATTY JUMPS ONTO the back of the armchair. 'I've left all the doors open so you can get to your basket and your food. And Tatty, please, if you *must* do any business make sure it's on the newspaper by the back door?' The dog sighs, rolling her eyes like a teenager. I open my handbag to check my keys and my mobile rings. Something slips inside me when I see the screen. My fingers tremble as they hover over the two options, then one of them twitches without me having to make the decision. I cough to make sure I sound confident.

'Hello, Neil, I can't talk for long. I'm just heading out to work.' The keys dig into my palm.

'I understand,' he says in a careful voice. 'I'm just about to begin morning surgery myself. Hi, anyway, Lauren. Just a quick call. I was wondering if you're free on Saturday and if so whether you'd like to have lunch with me? We could have a chat, you know. About everything.'

Seconds tick away on the clock on the sitting room wall, the one I bought from a jumble sale in the community centre. I also bought a new dress that I'll probably never wear – I mean, I don't go to tea-dances often. But it was for a good cause. I can't remember what. My outward silence transmutes into the squabbling of a crowd of crows outside the house. Or are they rooks? Anyway, crows are supposed to be extremely intelligent – and good luck. Perhaps I'll leave some food out for them. Am I ready to meet up with Neil again? Not yet.

Yet I haven't been able to stop thinking about him since I

turned my back on him in the hotel car park, tears sneaking out of my eyes faster than I could wipe them away. I looked as if I should be chewing bamboo shoots when I caught a glimpse of myself in the porch mirror on my arrival back at the cottage.

But Neil... His crown of thorns has slipped. He's a *father*.

'Lauren?' I can hear him breathing.

'Yes, sorry.' My palm stings, engraved by the keys. I open my fingers slowly. 'Yes, okay, if we make it after one or so – I don't want an early start on Saturday.' I could make no effort at all, allow Neil to see me without makeup, shatter his illusions of my preserved youth once and for all. Maybe that'll be the end of it. 'I have to walk the dog and everything first...'

'You have a dog?'

'What? Oh yes, she came to live with me yesterday. Her name's Titania. Anyway, I really must get on. Text me and tell me where you want to meet, and – well, thanks. Bye.' After I disconnect the call my throat feels as though I've swallowed something bulky – it's not going to choke me but it'll take a long time to digest. Like the chips I ate on the ferry.

---

'We had another call from Pine Tree House.' Rab rolls his chair over to my desk as soon as I sit down with my peppermint tea. I'm satisfied with myself this morning after only a forty-five minute drive to work and a perfect parking manoeuvre when I got here.

'Pine Tree House, err, remind me?' My mind's full of dogs and otters and my upcoming lunch with Neil. *How will I avoid ever mentioning his children?* Let alone meeting them, if we ended up getting back together.

'Catriona MacLennan.'

Ah, yes. The girl with the same surname as my landlord and half the Western Isles apparently.

'What did they say?'

'Here, I wrote down the gist of it but essentially she disappeared yesterday evening and they had to search her room. They discovered evidence of drugs. By the time they found her she'd broken into the kayak club, taken a boat out into the bay and couldn't get back to shore by herself. She was rescued by the lifeboat crew and taken to hospital for a quick check-over. She's fine. Grounded in her room today. They want you over there tomorrow to talk to her.'

'What, to Skye?'

Rab nods, sucking the end of his pen, a habit I noticed yesterday. 'There's a ferry at nine from Tarbert to Uig – that's Uig on Skye, not your Uig,' He laughs. 'It will get you there at ten-forty, and you can catch the ferry back at two-thirty. Or if you miss it there's another at five, they should allow you to change your ticket. I can book it for you.'

The palms of my hands are clammy. 'So, uhm, the ferry's from Tarbert, you say. How long will it take me to drive there from, err, from *my* Uig, here on Lewis?'

'An hour and a half? Better set off about seven in the morning, just to be safe. I'll email the tickets to you, okay? Then you can print them out or just show them on your phone – save paper, you know? Don't worry, the ferry staff are all very laid-back. Show them your badge, they'll look after you. It'll be a relaxing journey, honestly.' His freckled forehead creases as he adds, 'I promise.' He pulls a sympathetic face and lays a hand on my arm. I must look like the scared novice I feel like right now. And it's not just the unfamiliarity of the job, either.

*Don't worry, your families will be fine...* Israa and her father were assured by the sellers of useless lifejackets and later by the smugglers. Visions of rubber dinghies and fragile wooden boats, laden with people, tossing about on the waves, the same old pictures crowd my head. *A drowned child washed up on a beach, symbol of them all.* I hear roaring in my ears. A choking cough bubbles up in my chest.

'Are you all right?' Rab's earrings flash in a spear of light from the tea on my desk. Jessica turns from her computer screen, narrows her eyes at me. John laughs, over by the coffee machine as usual. 'Seasick, are you, dear? Don't worry, the forecast is fine for tomorrow.'

*Something about water.* What's going on with me? I never used to be afraid. It must be the aftershock of what happened after my leaving do.

'I'm fine.' I glare at John and shrug Rab's hand off my shoulder to concentrate on my own screen, the distraction of a new email coming in – *ping*. Rab rolls his chair back to his own corner.

My inbox is busy all morning with notifications of various cases that need my attention. It seems the adolescents of the Western Isles are not so very different from the kids I worked with in Edinburgh after all.

---

I leave work in the early afternoon to get home before dark. Pale sunlight caresses the slopes of the distant mountains, glinting off seaweed on the beach only a few hundred metres from the road. The sky is dun-coloured. I drive out of Stornoway, ignore the turnoff to Neil's at the same time as wondering if he's also finished work for the day. Indulge in a short fantasy of us sitting on the deck he told me about at the back of his house. Looking over the flat field to the sea. *The feel of his hand around mine, just before he betrayed me in the restaurant. His eyes when he told me about his daughter.* My heart's heavier than when I drove into the office this morning. I put it down to the case I was reading before I left, a fourteen-year-old addict who recently dropped out of school, though the staff seem to have done their best to support her. She's now in hospital, recovering from a heroin overdose administered by her older brother.

And I admit it, I'm nervous about my meeting with Catriona tomorrow. Fearful of a potential struggle with professionalism. Another girl of Sheena's age. *I should have resigned from this job before I even began it.* Sheena begged me not to leave, even at the end of my leaving party. I told her I'd think about her every time I read a book on the Kindle. I said I'd always keep the cover she embroidered for me, even if it fell apart. We could Skype and she could let me know how young Angel was getting on as her key-worker-in-training. The truth is I could never have become a proper mother to Sheena. There was too much family stuff to get in the way at the beginning, when Maw was ill and Da was drinking himself to death. Once I'd turned down the opportunity to foster her it was my responsibility to keep our relationship professional. *And you failed, Lauren.* I didn't realise Sheena had slipped ahead of me out of the Centre that final evening, and was planning a grand gesture.

Turn the radio on. The station is Gaelic and I can only understand the odd word of it but the sound of the language lulls me. So much that I'm soon sleepy. I stop the car in a lay-by above Miavaig Pier on Loch Rog. The water is faintly orange from the lowering sun. Arrows of gold pierce the stillness between currents. I close my eyes for sixty seconds but it turns out to have been five minutes. Neil's face had loomed through my sleep and I'd forgotten how hurt I felt at the restaurant.

Now I remember. I start the car again and continue towards home. Flip the sunshade down against the afternoon light glinting off the road. As I drive, my troubles slowly loosen like released balloons but I still feel attached to them by long threads.

---

At home Tatty leaps into my arms, trying unsuccessfully to lick my face. 'Okay, get down,' I say after a guilty minute of indulgence. 'You need to behave like a dog, not a spoilt brat.' I have a cup of tea then grab her lead and we head off down the hill and along the stony track to the inlet beach.

With the tide out, the beach is a white cloth spread right over to the other side of the bay. Reminds me of a story Granny Mary used to tell us, *The Sea Baby*. She said her own grandmother had told it to her. Granny Mary used to go off into a sort of trance, almost, when she told us the story of the sea baby – as if she was channelling her grandmother.

*A dreadful storm blew up one afternoon, the biggest storm the village had ever seen. The sky was as black as night and when the real night came nobody could tell the difference. The wind blew so hard it took the roof off the hall at the back of the church and a huge chunk of cliff fell onto the beach, we all heard it breaking away with a terrible rumble and a roar. But by the following morning the storm had blown over and the sun had turned the beach to gold as far as the eye could see – further than ever before. The tide had receded so far out that an old, submerged village was revealed.*

Granny Mary had us spellbound, crowded three-to-a-bed under the rafters in her cottage above Howth Bay.

*We ran across the miles of sand,* she said in her own grandmother's voice. *To explore the uncovered houses with their neat front gardens, the cobbled streets and the alleyways, the deserted shops. The people of the lost village were fast asleep inside their houses. All except for one.*

Granny Mary's own granny had told her that she was a little girl at the time, and she was the one who discovered a single baby awake in her cot, chortling and waving her arms, while all around her, the baby's sisters and brothers slept in their beds.

*Outside on the street one of my friends shouted a warning that the tide was coming in and we must hurry to get home before the waves overtook us. But I wanted to carry on playing with the baby, Mary. None of my friends noticed I wasn't with them when they all ran back across the sands towards the safety of our own village. A while later I glanced out the window of the cottage and I saw that the sea was dangerously close, and I was frightened. What was I supposed to do about the baby? So I grabbed her and carried her out of the cottage because I couldn't leave her there, could I? We were chased across the beach by the waves until the froth was soaking the backs of my heels. I was so afraid and out of breath. I made it to the bottom of the cliff just as the water lapped up to my knees, and when I had struggled to the top with the baby in my arms, I found that everybody had been searching for me. My mother did scold me!*

*I kept that baby for a whole week, Mary, since my parents could think of no way to return it to the underwater village. It was obvious from the start that there was something peculiar about her. She never slept, only laughed and wanted to play all the time. I looked after her as best I could, but she wouldn't eat and she wouldn't drink the milk I tried to give her from the bottle we had used to feed Uncle Patrick's orphaned lambs. And as I said, she never closed her eyes at all. At night the little baby lay quietly beside me in my bed, with her eyes wide open. But one night, about a week later, there was another storm. Not as bad as the first but with a wild wind and a lot of rain nonetheless. Eventually I fell asleep with the wide-awake baby beside me. I was woken by a tapping at the bedroom window. I saw a woman, swimming through the dark night of the storm. She had her eyes closed and her hair blew about in the wind. The window blew open and the woman swam straight into the room. Mary my love, I swear to you that she set her feet as gently on the floor as if she was standing at the bottom of the sea. Then, still with her eyes closed, she reached across me in the bed. I was so afraid. But all she did was lift the wide-awake baby into her arms. 'Shh-shh, shh-shh,' she whispered, and it was like the sound of the sea washing over pebbles on the shore. My head began to feel heavy and I noticed that my sea-baby's eyelids were beginning to droop, too. I fell asleep then, because that mother's voice was so soothing. I didn't see her swim back out of the window with the baby, but that must have been what happened, because the baby was gone in the morning.*

I take a shuddering breath, the story of my female ancestry rippling through me. *Greetin again, Lauren.* When my vision clears I scan the hill opposite for the community centre and beyond that the restaurant where I ate with Neil. *Oh, Neil.* The orange sun sits in the sky just above the tops of the mountains. Turquoise lies above the band of orange, higher still scribbles of charcoal clouds. Soon dark will fall. My chest aches with the echo of Granny Mary's story – my story. The dog stands poised at my feet, like a small statue. Water laps gently at the stones on the beach. Tatty fixes me with one of her intent stares and jerks the lead out of my hand, *little sod*. She sets off, legs flailing, across the machair in pursuit of a rabbit. Her high yips ring through the near-dark.

'Tatty, get back here,' I brandish my fists with no thought for my dignity. To my surprise her dark form spins on the spot. Before I know it she charges back towards me, dragging the lead through the damp grass. Sits at my feet, panting. My stomach turns over. I know it's impossible – Tatty is six years old, Peggy told me – but the way the dog looks at me reminds me of Sheena when she was the scared ten-year-old I first took under my wing. I bend to unhook the lead from her collar. 'Go on then,' I say. 'Now I know you'll come back, I can let you have a run.'

# 34

THE SUN RISES above the mountains, pearlescent clouds edged with gold in the smoke-grey sky. I pull the front door closed behind me. The path is wet with a slick of rain and I concentrate on not slipping, trying not to hear Tatty's whines. But I can't help glancing up at the window before I leave. Her nose is pressed miserably against the glass, a patch of mist blossoming around her face. Did I need the extra stress of a dog? Whether I did or not, Tatty's mine now.

I reverse carefully onto the track and change into first gear once I have the car pointing forwards. *She-who-was-dropped-on-her-head* is – unbelievably at this hour, on her front porch as I drive past. Her arms crossed over her chest as usual. I lift my hand in a cheery wave but it's not returned. I make a two-fingered sign at the rear view mirror and then go hot all over at the thought that the woman might have noticed. *O.M.G.* as Sheena would've said. No wait, what was her most recent expression? *Da Fuk?*

Oh empty road, oh wide, wide sky and bouldered mountains high. Stroke the wheel lightly and the car seems to drive itself. A John Denver song much loved by Maw fades into my head as I drive up the road past Timsgarry and then Miavaig, then on a downward trajectory around the bottom of Loch Rog. Heading back towards Garrynahine, I turn right on the A859 southwards to Harris. I'm not trusting the journey entirely to my holey old brain – my Satnav, programmed to an Irish male voice I named Greg Mulligan (after a character in a novel), gives me lyrically-pronounced instructions throughout the journey.

The landscape widens and becomes rawer as I approach Harris. The mountains here are stonier and more prehistoric. I feel the strength of the wind tugging the car and I take the mountain bends slowly. When a car approaches from the opposite direction – sometimes two or three cars or trucks or motorhomes in a row – I'm the first to pull into a passing-place and let them by. Sometimes when I come around a bend I find a car or van already tucked snugly against the mountainside, waiting for me to crawl past. A long stretch of road follows the curve of a loch, the sky perfectly reflected. Nestled on the banks and spread out along the sweeps of ridged land are the remains of croft houses, broken monuments to the past. *Blackhouses*, like the one Murdo's ancestors were forced to give up to sheep. Since I learned about that pile of stones at the back of the outhouse I've been fascinated by the historical way of life here. Not dissimilar to the people who lived in the turf-roofed houses I studied in Iceland for my PhD.

I wish I had time to pull in to the viewing spot, watch an imagined reel of the lives of people past. Women and men carrying creels of kelp on their backs, nutrients for their ridged potato beds. Peat stacks towering in front of the houses, fuel for the fires. A family huddled together in the smoky darkness of the blackhouse interior. A life almost of slavery, of early death from overwork – from blackened lungs or from starvation when the potato crop failed. So why do I experience a painful nostalgia? Glancing at the ruined settlements on the banks of the loch I choose to hear the high, fine voices of women singing at their spinning-wheels rather than the pitiful cries of hungry children. *You're a dangerous romantic, Lauren,* as Neil used to say. *Concentrate on the job you're here to do.*

On a straight stretch of road I sweep the romantic scenes aside and hit the mental refresh button on my knowledge of

Catriona. Her mother died from an overdose. Catriona refused to move in with a family member for reasons which are unclear. She'd been working hard at school, even when her mother suffered a heavy relapse after being clean for a year. Catriona is musical and enjoys art, but since her mother's death she's involved herself with 'bad company'. The staff at Pine Tree House were already concerned she was experimenting with drugs and now they have evidence that their fears were well-founded. I need to try and find a way to reach her.

*You won't be able to. You let Barbara down and then you did the same thing to Sheena.* I glance accusingly at the Satnav but the display only shows an unimpressive ribbon of grey road and Greg Mulligan's voice is absent. The voice was me – the failure inside me. *Failed mother, failed social worker.* I remind myself that I've helped some people. A tinier voice (with a lisp) reminds me I've won awards for my work... Still, I'm taunted by the memory of Sheena's dancing eyes, the amused curl of her messily pierced lip – the look on her face the day she came into the Centre and noted my shocked reaction to her visible self-abuse. *She knew I loved her.* Then why did I let her down?

Anyway. I need to stay positive if I'm to begin again. I focus my attention back on the steering wheel. I need all my concentration for an everlasting bend around a fat mountain. The vista of another loch greets me on the other side and more traffic has appeared on the road. The world's waking up and setting off for work. I see a sign for Tarbert, only eight miles away. I should have a good forty minutes' spare time to visit the toilet and consume a forbidden coffee before boarding the ferry.

---

I'm waved to the front of a virgin traffic lane.

'Weather's been treating us kindly, hasn't it, now?' The steward inspects my ticket as if it's the most interesting thing he's read in a while. I agree that the weather has been fair – we could almost call it an Indian summer. 'Business or pleasure, Madam?' – After a steady stream of chit-chat. I tell him business and think about the pale, defiant girl with straggly black hair.

'Are you heading for Portree, by any chance?'

It must be written on my face, or he's telepathic. 'Yes, I am – quite near there.' The man's speckled grey eyes crease at the corners. 'I was wondering if you could deliver a package for me.' He taps his fingers on my open window, pulls a brown paper packet from his back pocket. I feel prickling under my skin. Sweat breaks out on the back of my neck. I swivel my head from side to side – is this some kind of test? Here I am, going to talk to a young girl about drugs whilst the ferry staff try and persuade me to carry an illicit parcel across the water.

'Oh, dear me, Madam.' The man's in stitches. 'Don't look so worried, it's nothing bad. My daughter has had a baby, you see.'

The heat washes away from my cheeks but I'm still suspicious. Light rain starts to fall and I allow my eyes to be distracted by the soft mist covering my windscreen. So what if the man's daughter has had a baby? He pokes his head further into the car and hands me back my ticket. 'My wife has knitted the baby a little jacket – pink for a girl, you know. We're not going to be getting over there to visit until the weekend and I promised the wife I'd find a nice young woman such as yourself to take a present over to our daughter. Ahead of our state visit, you know. You look like just the person, and it's on your way after all. It'll be no trouble, now.'

'Well. Okay then, I suppose I could do that, I don't see why not.' I fumble with the ticket and put my hand out awkwardly for the parcel. 'As for both nice and young I'm not sure about that.' At last I'm able to get into the jocular spirit of things.

'You're as young as you feel, hen. And you're younger than me at any rate. It's kind of you to help us out. I said to my Mary, I'm bound to find the right person travelling on the morning ferry – and along you came. Here's the address, I've written it down on the back of a postcard, see? It's directly on the road to Portree. If you'd just pop it through the letterbox for us that will do nicely. Or if you fancy a look at the new baby and a chat, I'm sure our Katie will be happy to let you in.'

The brown paper crinkles under my fingers, rippling over the knitted garment inside. A pink baby cardigan. *Like the one Ruth was knitting for me.* 'That sounds wonderful, but I don't think I'll have time to stay. I've got an appointment, you see.'

'Aye, well, you're doing us a favour by dropping it off, at least. Thank you kindly Mrs...' He studies my face. 'Miss...?'

'Miss Wilson, Lauren. Just call me Lauren.' I never took Ellis's name. The steward and I shake hands and I can see him wondering why I'm not married. He presses his other hand to his earpiece and straightens at the same time as the hooter blasts on the ferry. 'Oops, that'll be us, now. Right, since you're at the front of the queue, you can be the first on. Just follow the directions of the young lad over there.' I start the engine and give him a wave.

'Goodbye, then, and don't worry about the parcel, I'll make sure it gets there safely.'

'Goodbye, Lauren. See you at the other end.'

---

It takes me about twenty-five minutes to drive from the ferry port at Uig on Skye to the outskirts of Portree. Greg Mulligan issues me with straightforward directions in his soft Irish burr. I keep my hands on the wheel and enjoy the view of gentle slopes and trees – so many more trees here in the 'Inners' than in the Outer Hebrides. I sing along to the music on the radio and try not to be nervous about my extra mission. A mission of goodwill, probably much more pleasant than my first meeting with the recalcitrant Catriona.

On a quiet residential estate I pull in to the curb and get out of the car. The curtains of the house are drawn. I picture the new mother inside those walls, cuddling in bed with her tiny baby. The way I used to lie on the sofa in our flat, stroking my tummy. Hoping Neil would change his mind. You'd think after all these years I'd have forgotten those feelings. It can't be normal – perhaps if I'd joined a support group or had some counselling in the early days I'd be rid of them now. *Yet I don't want to be rid of them. Barbara was my baby.*

I open the gate as quietly as I can and tiptoe up the path. There's a porch with a letterbox in an outer glass door but I don't want to crumple the package further so I try the handle. The door opens obligingly. I lay the brown paper parcel on the mat and pull the door gently shut again, tiptoe back up the path to my car. Whatever her father said, the woman doesn't want to be disturbed by a stranger desperate to take a peek at her new baby. This much I do know.

# 35

THE THREE-STOREY BUILDING was evidently once white but is now a stained, mossy grey. Lined with rowan and pine trees, the drive's covered in fallen leaves, splashes of red and orange. Leaves squish under the car wheels. I roll forward and pull up by a low wall next to the house. Pine needles crunch under my feet as I get out and stretch my back. Collect my bag and lock the car, careful as I move around it not to slip on the wet leaves. The skirt I pulled out of my suitcase and wriggled into this morning feels tight and uncomfortable but it gives me what I hope is a professional authenticity. Kids expect social workers to be dressed like hippies and I prefer to surprise them with a smart appearance.

I straighten my suit jacket, fasten the top button but leave the other one open to allow my stomach breathing space. Stand with my back to the car and assimilate my surroundings. My legs feel naked in the thin sheen of unfamiliar tights. I miss the loose jeans and jogging bottoms I've been wearing lately, clothes pulled on for comfort.

A car horn blasts from the main road, making me jump. I push myself away from the car and move to the front door, lift the solid knocker. It falls heavily onto peeling green wood and lands with a resounding thwack. I repeat the process twice. Eventually footsteps sound beyond the door and it's pulled open by a white-haired woman with tired, greenish eyes. From the tint of her eyebrows and freckles on her cheeks I'd say she was once a redhead. A single shout of

*'Bastard!'* rings out into the tiled hallway as she ushers me inside.

The woman smiles and I can see how she might have a motherly influence. 'Not to worry about that.' She offers me her hand. 'It's only our Bradley. Coming to the end of his allotted two hours on the latest apocalyptic computer game. He likes to be the first of the day. I'm Christine. You must be Lauren? Very pleased to meet you.'

'You too. This place has a lovely feel.'

The hall, large and open-plan, is warm and the smell of cooked breakfast makes my stomach grumble.

'It does sometimes. Sometimes it's not such a good place to be. None of the residents chooses a life here, of course.' Christine waves me forward with a sweep of her arm. 'Actually, I take that back. Catriona, whom you're here to see, did of course choose to come here – but only because of a fallout with her uncle. She had the offer of an alternative home with him though I'm not sure he'd be able to manage her. Wind him around her little finger, she would. But we're working towards a reconciliation, as we must. Maybe you can help with that.'

The smell of breakfast grows stronger as she steers me down a corridor to the left of the entrance hall. My stomach growls. Christine looks at me over her shoulder. 'Are you hungry? Breakfast is finished but there are plenty of leftovers. Only be thrown away, otherwise. *Unfortunately.*' She makes a tutting sound. 'Health and safety. If I had my way we'd be teaching them to make do and mend. Not waste food. After all, most of them will end up living in poverty, sad to say.' She stops and peers at me in the gloom of the corridor. 'I bet you haven't had breakfast, have you?'

'No.' Warmth rushes to my cheeks. 'I meant to have breakfast on the ferry but the queue was so long and, well, you know. I thought I'd better go through Catriona's notes again instead.'

'Now aren't you the conscientious one?' As if I'm about

twelve. I can't decide whether I like Christine or not. Of course I'm conscientious, it's my *job* to be. And hers. She leads me into the bright warmth of a large, square kitchen with a long table in the centre. Trays contain the remains of scrambled eggs, sausages and toast. On a countertop are boxes of cereal and a couple of clean bowls. Christine gestures. 'Help yourself. I'll put the kettle on – tea or coffee?'

'Tea please.' I fill a plate with eggs and toast. While I'm eating I watch leaves spiralling onto a lawn through the high, narrow window. Near the end of the long garden is a tall climbing frame, a high metal slide and a robust set of swings. Also a trampoline. Outdoor table-tennis and a basketball hoop are closer to the house. Two youths and a well-built teenage girl lean against the trunk of a pine tree, smoking.

'They're not supposed to.' Christine places two mugs of tea on the table between us. 'Smoke, I mean. But they will anyway. As you must know, we're wise to choose our battles carefully. Marijuana, now that *is* banned from the premises. Doesn't always stop them though, as we found out with your girl Catriona the other night.'

An altercation's going on somewhere along the corridor. Christine puts her mug down and covers her ears. It doesn't sit right, a gesture more suited to a teenage resident than their caregiver. The tendons in her neck stand out. Then, as if changing a mask, she takes her hands off her ears and brushes them over her face, replacing the smile that dropped off a second ago. Not for the first time I'm glad my job enables me to go home at the end of the day. I can sit alone in glorious solitude. Well, I could before Tatty arrived. *I could always lock her in the barn if she got too much for me...* Joking, I hastily add to my indignant counter-self. No. I'd insist Peggy take Tatty away again, that's what I'd do if she got too much. I'm not trapped by anything. *Or anyone*, my mind adds, thinking of Saturday's date with Neil. I could still change my mind. The skin of the back of my right hand burns, for some reason, but when I check the skin is unmarked.

'Bradley's time on the computer's obviously finished,' Christine looks so weary. Raised voices and bumps from down the corridor. 'I'll let Dereck deal with it.' She sits at the table with her hands folded in front of her, like a praying nun. Perhaps she *is* praying. She glances at me from time to time while I eat. Closes her eyes as the raised voices dim. When I place my knife and fork side by side on the empty plate and dab my lips with a sliver of tissue from my pocket, the movement makes Christine open her eyes and look up.

'Now – about Catriona.'

---

I follow Christine up two flights of stairs. Brightly-coloured wallpaper peels off in places. The red carpet's threadbare at the edges, the banister chipped. From behind closed doors I hear snippets of conversations, laughter and arguments. A boy with spiky hair comes out of a room with his arms full of bedding. He sees me and scowls before heading down the curved flight of stairs I've just come up. Christine catches my eye and makes a slight movement with her head, flattens her mouth. She says nothing. I follow her up a few more steps. A damp patch flowers in the join between the decorative coving and the ceiling. We follow the angle of the first landing and begin climbing the second, straight flight of stairs, my knee shouting at me.

'Impossible to keep up with the maintenance of such an old building.' Christine's slightly out of breath. Surprisingly, I'm not. Must be all the walking I've been doing lately. 'Too expensive. Plans are afoot to rehouse us in a more modern facility but it's a shame really. Still,' she huffs as we continue climbing the steep stairs. 'It'll be one less thing for the kids to get teased about at school. It's not cool to live in a dilapidated mansion, apparently, even worse than living in a care home.'

At the top – in what must once have been the servants' quarters – I follow Christine along a narrow landing with a high ceiling and a window at one end. We pass one closed bedroom door and walk a few steps towards the next. All seems quiet up here. She raps sharply on the door with her knuckles.

'Catriona? I've got your new social worker here – Lauren. Can you let us in, please?'

I hold my breath. Let it out again at the sound of something sliding to the floor, maybe a book, or perhaps an iPad. A creak of a mattress and then the sound of a handle turning. The girl from the photograph stands impassively in the gap between the barely-opened door and its frame, lank black hair hanging either side of her peaky, narrow face. The outlines of her cobalt eyes are smudged with mascara, further dark shadows creating half-moons below them. She doesn't look as though she's washed this morning. Possibly not last night either. A musty smell blows out of the room. Catriona glances at us with disinterest before dropping her gaze to the floor, muttering, 'Don't know why you're bothering to knock, you weren't concerned about my privacy when you broke in here the other night.'

'That was different, Catriona, and you know it.' Christine lodges her hand on the doorframe and edges her foot in as if she thinks Catriona's going to close the door on us. 'Now, may we come in?'

Catriona looks from one to the other of us. She studies me a bit longer than she looks at Christine, breathing noisily through her mouth, which hangs open. *She's been crying.*

'*She* can. She's my social worker. You see me every day as it is. I'll talk to her if you insist.'

'Well, fine. Make sure you're co-operative, then. We don't want any more nonsense. Be nice, Catriona.' Christine waggles her finger. I can see how it would get on a teenager's nerves. Actually, it gets on mine. Still, I give Christine a smile which she returns as she steps back from the door and moves behind me to retrace her steps along the corridor.

'If you're lucky, Lauren,' she calls back, 'Catriona might

make you another cup of tea. There's a kitchenette just down the landing.' She nods at me, then Catriona. 'She makes a good cup of tea, don't you, hen?'

'Oh, I might, *Lauren.*' But Catriona doesn't look my way, spitting a glance at Christine instead. I taste a million exchanges of sarcasm in the air between them. I straighten my shoulders. Catriona transfers her gaze to me. 'If you're good.'

The way she says it gives me the creeps but I smile anyway, my lips quivering at the corners. *She mustn't be allowed to see how weak I am.* Catriona drops her hand from the door handle and takes several backward steps into her room. I follow. She grabs a hard-backed chair from the desk and swings it around. I hold myself still. But she's not planning to attack me and places the chair at the opposite side of the room from her bed. 'You can sit there.'

I've been told.

# 36

I SIT, RELEASING the briefcase to the floor where it rests against my legs. I need to appear open and accessible, not self-conscious. My straight back and calm gaze aim to project a sense of control – I've taken classes in this sort of thing. Now that I'm practising my profession again, the rhythm and flow returns to my body like remembered bars of music.

Catriona bends to pick up a fallen iPad, hair draping her face. She flips the cover closed and places it on a shelf. She's thin, maybe too thin. She moves to sit on her narrow bed – slouched, back curved against the purple-painted wall. She shoots glances at me. Neither of us speaks for a while, each assessing the other.

I have to remind myself that I'm probably an old woman to her. It's funny though, because inside I'm taken back to the Edinburgh squat on the first night Andrea and I stood there, ready to fight or fly. The other residents gave us the same look, a kind of *what the fuck?* Still, inhabiting my younger self endows me with the confidence to meet Catriona's expression with a similar one of my own.

'So?' she says.

'So?' I return. My older soul soon takes over.

'You know the score. I'm here to talk to you about the drugs you were taking the other night and ask you why you felt the need to run away.'

'Drugs!' She sniggers. 'Hardly that. I didn't run away

anyway, I simply felt the need to escape from this shithole for a while.'

'Why?'

'Oh, why d'you think?' She answers as if she's been asked a million times. 'This isn't where I belong. I'm only here until I'm *old enough* – as if I'm not already,' she sniggers again, a laugh devoid of emotion, '– to look after myself. Who do they think looked after me all those times my mum was using? Anyway, I...' She clamps her lips tight shut, as if she's said too much already, picks at the skin around her nails.

'Where do you feel you belong?'

'Stupid question. You do know my mum died, right?'

'Right. Sorry.'

I turn my hands over and study the backs of them, remember the need for a relaxed pose and turn them over again so my palms face outwards. She presses her back against the wall and I hear her spine click. I ask a few more pointless questions about school and hobbies and what music she likes. She mutters under her breath in response. Her chin dips further. While she's examining her nails I scan the room, keeping my hands open on my lap. A guitar in a corner. A shelf full of books. *Try another line of questioning.*

'What's your favourite book?'

'Huh?'

'Your favourite book. What do you like reading?'

She scowls, like it's a trick question. She's right of course – if anyone asks me to reveal why, even though I'm exhausted, I'll still stay up late into the night reading I can't tell them what kept me so gripped without having to give away my inner self. Catriona lifts her head slightly and flickers her eyes over me.

'None of your business.'

I almost smile, but hold it back. She'd think I was laughing at her. 'Touché.' Watching for a flicker of response. She shifts position, wrapping her arms around long legs in black skinny jeans.

'It's stuffy in here, don't you ever open the window?'

'You saying it stinks?'

'Only of stuffy air.'

'Open it then, if you want.'

She digs her chin more firmly into her knees. Picking my way through the clothes and books on the floor I spot an open sketchbook, allow my eyes to graze over it briefly before leaning across the cluttered desk to heave the sash window up a few inches. Fresh September air floods my lungs.

'That's better.'

'If you say so.'

I plonk myself back on the chair, knees neatly together, palms up again. The black brogues I bought in Edinburgh's New Town have rubbed my heels, and the soreness is an almost pleasant distraction.

'Why do you sit like that?'

'Like what?'

'You look like you're bloody meditating.'

'What if I am?'

'Looks bloody stupid.'

She resumes picking her fingers. I keep my back straight and my head still, read as much information as I can from the room, from the hunched girl on the bed, the items strewn around the floor. Her breathing has quietened – air enters and leaves through her nostrils now instead of her mouth. A long stretch of time ensues. *Hold your patience*, I tell myself. This is my tried and tested breakthrough method.

'What are you even here for, anyway?'

I jolt on the chair. 'I told you. Just, you know... To have a chat.'

'Why aren't you having this *chat* then?'

'A chat takes two people, otherwise it's just a lecture.'

Her chin makes an unconscious nod.

'I'm waiting until you're ready.'

Actually, I could do with a pee, but I don't want to get up and leave the room in case she won't let me back in.

'What if I'm never going to be ready?'

'It doesn't matter. I'll stay here for a reasonable amount of time, to show I made an effort and give you a chance to make that decision. If you don't want a chat today I'll come back another day.'

'Fine. You'll be waiting a long time.'

'I don't mind.'

I make a physical effort not to cross my legs. Now the thought's in, my bladder responds with a clamour for further attention. *Sorry bladder, you too will have to wait.* Not to be left out of the bodily chorus my knee aches harder than ever. It's all the driving, I expect. I try to shift it without attracting Catriona's attention. *Stay patient.*

*When Ah was a wean Ah used to watch out for a catfish that someone had released into a pond on the grassland behind oor tenement. It would only reveal itself at night. Ah had tae sit utterly still at the edge of the pond, shining Da's torch intae the water, waiting tae glimpse the catfish's silver belly if Ah wiz lucky. A sighting could nae be guaranteed. There was a fine sense of satisfaction when the wee wild creature consented tae be seen. Ma granny's exhortation that 'patience is a virtue' wiz proved right every time.*

I must have gone off into some kind of genuine meditative state. Brought back to myself by an indignant voice.

'So, d'you want a cup of tea then, or what?'

I blink. 'Ah, yes please. That'd be lovely. Thanks. I'm fussy how I take my tea, mind.'

*'That'd be lovely. Well, I make it a certain way and if you don't like it, tough titties.'*

I suppress a giggle. Maw used to say that. Catriona glowers and unwinds herself, springs up from the bed – passes me in two short strides. I notice scabs on her pipe-cleaner arms, black sleeves rammed up to her elbows. Push myself up stiffly from the chair and gather my briefcase, sling the strap over my shoulder. I can't prevent my limp as I take the first steps towards the door. Looking over her shoulder she notices and gives a derisive sniff. Fair enough, the old woman is clearly overriding the eternal teenager inside me.

'There's a bathroom next to the kitchen,' she points out. 'You're obviously dying for a piss.'

*Incontinent* old lady, then. Hey ho. 'Thanks. I thought you'd never offer.' Did she just smother a smile? Maybe.

I hear the clanking of kettle and cups as I pee with immense relief. Then footsteps. The clatter is interrupted by the mutter of conversation. I wash my hands and enter the kitchen. The girl from the garden and a boy wearing a skull-and-crossbones bandana crowd into the small area with Catriona. They all stare at me, standing in the doorway.

'Who's this then?' asks the girl.

'My social worker.'

'Fuckin' social workers.' The lad curls his lip. 'Rather you than me, Cat. I'm off. See ya later, there's a bad smell around here.'

'A *very* bad smell,' chips in the large girl, finger under her nose. She bumps deliberately against me as she leaves. I try not to take it personally – she'll have her own problems, many of them no doubt enhanced by social workers. None of them would be here if they didn't. Catriona glances at me as if she ought to apologise, but she doesn't. I break the awkwardness with an inane comment. 'Steep it for long, do you?'

'What?'

'The tea. What's your secret?'

She hooks a strand of hair away from her forehead, shaking her head at the same time. 'You want to think yourself lucky you're getting a whole teabag to yourself. 'S not always the case. Plenty of teabags here, though.' Gifting me the mental image of empty cupboards and one dried-out teabag to be reused later. Still I say nothing. The more she gives of her own accord, the less I'll have to take.

'Thanks.' I pick up the steaming mug, blow over the top. There's a slight film on the tea.

'We can go back to my room if you like.'

'Okay, whatever you want.'

'I didn't say it's what I want. I don't get much choice. Just better not to have nosy spectators around.'

'You're probably right.'

She rolls her eyes. Back in her room, she waves me to the same chair while she hovers on her feet, looking out the window onto the garden. The same view as from the kitchen window only much higher up. A flock of starlings swoops above a thicket of trees at the end of the narrow lawn, marking a figure-of-eight in the sky. A grey bank of clouds hangs over the surrounding rooftops, punctuated by watery sun. As I sit here I can't help thinking about my long journey home.

Catriona tilts upwards on her toes and lowers herself back down again. She's wearing thick socks. Up, down, repeat. Like the exercises Bridie used to do at her dance class. *She was so dedicated. She could have been a ballerina – retired by now.* A respected dance coach, perhaps. With her back to me, Catriona rolls her head gently on her neck, black hair hanging limply down her back. Maybe someone taught her relaxation. I think back to the notes in my file, one year since her mother died. She must've had some counselling. I cough gently. 'It's not a bad room you've got up here.'

She turns her body ninety degrees while her feet stay put. 'I suppose.'

'Get on with the other kids, do you?'

'None of your business.'

'No, I suppose you're right.'

'I generally keep to myself, anyway. Prefer it that way.'

'Yeah. I know what you mean. I do too, I suppose.'

She looks into her mug and blows on the tea, takes a sip, looks at me sideways.

'Not married, then?'

'No.'

'Why not?'

'I'm just not, that's all.'

'At your age? Lezza, are you?'

'No, Catriona.' When I use her name she jerks her chin slightly. *Now I've got her attention.*

'I'm not a lesbian. Even if I was, I could still be married – to a woman. It's legal these days, you know. Or I could still choose to stay single. It would be up to me.'

She thinks about this, freeing one of the hands wrapped around her mug to pull at the skin near her nail with her teeth. It'll bleed if she's not careful. I notice her teeth are yellowed and stop myself from asking when she last cleaned them. Her finger ends are torn and scabbed. She spits out a tiny tag of skin that catches on the sleeve of her black jumper. I wish she'd notice and brush it off. After further consideration, she narrows her eyes.

'Devoted to your job, are you?'

'I *like* my job. Not sure I'm devoted to it, though.'

Devoted surely means you think about nothing else. I'd save that for individuals, not a career.

'Shouldn't be doing it, then.' She sniffs. 'Live all on your own?'

Shades of Sheena in the interrogation, but without her spark. Without her flashing eyes and lightning-quick wit. It took a long time to build relationships with my kids in Edinburgh and now I have to start all over again.

Catriona's watching me closely. I let out my breath. 'Yes. Well, no. I live with my dog.' I must have smiled at the thought of Tatty. I catch the reflection of it on the girl's face. She looks at me fully. 'Nice. I wish I could live only with a dog. What's your dog's name?'

'Tatty. It was Titania before she came to me but I thought that was a bit pretentious.'

'Why? It's from Midsummer Night's Dream, isn't it?' Catriona blushes and backtracks. 'I only know that from school. 'S not like I read Shakespeare or anything.'

'I'll let you into a secret. I've only had Tatty for two days but it feels like forever already. She's a great little dog.' I sip my tea. Catriona opens her mouth and closes it again.

She narrows her eyes in my direction, then places her tea on a bookshelf and runs her fingers over paperback spines. From behind a curtain of lank hair she says, 'What kind of dog is she?' She pulls out a torn book, holding it against her chest, facing the bookshelf still – her body tense. I watch surreptitiously. Wait until she's ready to share. Meanwhile I keep talking.

'Some kind of terrier, I'm not sure what. She's brown, with a black stripe down her back. And a funny, whippy tail.'

Catriona moves her head, cocks one ear. 'Hmm. Probably a... a, maybe a Border terrier or something like that. Not a Yorkshire terrier? A Cairn terrier maybe – what kind of ears has she got?'

'Little silky... folded-over ones,' I say.

She pushes hair away from her face, thinking. 'A bit like a Jack Russell, do you mean?'

'Yes. She has quite a long body, if that helps?'

'Hmm. Like a sausage-dog. Sounds like a mixture to me. Mongrels are healthier than pedigrees, you know.'

'Oh? I didn't know that.'

She takes a step towards me and places the book in my hands.

'This is how I know about Titania. This was my mum's book, see. She had it from when she was at school in Stornoway.'

I place my mug on the desk and open the book at the first page. An inscription is written by hand in black ink. *Stornoway High School. Prize for English presented to Catherine MacLennan, November 1984.*

Catherine MacLennan. Same name as the sister Murdo's looking after, according to Peggy. He and I didn't discuss his reasons for moving to Skye. But I learned from the museum, not to mention my files at the office, how names are repeated over and over again through the generations and across the islands. Even the school in my tiny township is full of children who share a handful of traditional names – with an Arya and

210

a Rocky sticking out like sore thumbs – incomers' children, Peggy told me.

Catriona retrieves the book from me, turns the pages. She angles the book towards me. 'She was clever, my mum. This is what I got the book out for – Titania, see?' She runs her finger under a pencilled underline on the page. 'She was the Queen of the fairies.'

'Ah yes, I remember this from when I was at school.'

'A bloody long time ago,' Catriona closes the book. She moves other books aside and slides the Shakespeare carefully back into its gap on the shelf. Then she picks up her tea again and takes a loud slurp. Plonks herself back on the bed.

'Too right it was. A *very* bloody long time ago.' I smile at her. 'Thanks for this, by the way, it's a good brew.'

She makes a sort of harrumphing noise – a bit like the one I often make myself.

'Aren't you going to get a folder about me out of your briefcase, then? About bloody time we got on with this chat of yours – the sooner we start it, the sooner we can finish and I can get my room back to myself again.'

---

Driving back through *Gleann Bhaltois*, a red deer steps onto the road ahead of me. Trembling, I slow down and change into second gear, thinking he'll move out of the way. But I get closer and closer and still he stands there, staring at me through the windscreen. I change down into first and roll to a stop, only metres away from the animal. Could it be the same stag I saw last week? My senses sharpen. I notice individual hairs on his thick hide. I'm so close I can see the moisture gathered at his nostrils. It makes me think of Neil. The stag doesn't move, only regards me steadily through the windscreen with his deep, brown eyes. I stare back at him, mesmerised, feeling as though every hair on my body is standing upright. I've stepped into a scene from A Midsummer Night's Dream. Or a Disney film.

It's probably only seconds, but seems more like minutes. Long minutes. The deer dips his antlers before taking a step towards the opposite side of the road. The air around me is sucked into a vacuum. Tall grass at the edge of the road ripples like water and the hair on the deer's hide trembles too but I can't hear the wind that must have surged through the valley. The deer takes another step, still with his face towards me. Then his movements speed up. He points his antlers to the hills and takes a running leap, scattering a knot of sheep in all directions. Their bleats ring out into the released air. I breathe again. Soon the stag disappears into the ferns and I wonder if I merely imagined his magnificent spell of attention.

# 37

SATURDAY COMES AROUND, brought to me by what sounds like a battle of crows outside my bedroom window. *Neil!* I can't face him. But I can't live with the constant jitteriness of anticipating our meeting, either and at least by this evening it will be over. Despite Tatty's intense gaze from her blanket near the fireplace I stay under the covers until I can focus my train of thought on a reflection of the past week. As well as Catriona on Skye I went to see a boy struggling to maintain a manageable lifestyle with his recovering-addict father on North Uist. Both the father and son acted defensively and hostile – it'll take perseverance to make any headway with either of them. Then there was a young mother, Anna McIver. Aged only seventeen, she's recently moved from the mainland to live with an aunt on Harris in an effort to escape the threatening behaviour of her drug-pusher boyfriend, the baby's father. There've been concerns about the health of the baby, but Anna's auntie is jumping through every possible hoop to keep the girl and her baby together. I left their home beneath the bouldered mountains at sunset, just as the whole landscape turned red.

Tatty continues to stare at me, a faint noise like a damaged squeaky toy coming from her throat. I'm going back to sleep. Later, I shove her out the back door with my foot and take myself back to bed with my morning pot of tea on a tray and read for a while. *I'll let her in soon.* My eyes close and I reopen them to find my book face-down on my chest. The highland cattle have gathered at the bottom of the hill opposite, nudging shoulders along the fence. They seem to be staring in at me.

'Peeping Toms.' I allow myself to drift in and out of sleep. I'm woken by a sharp rapping on the front door. *What?* It takes me a while to get my head together. With fog in my brain and a nasty taste in my mouth I stumble out of bed, shove my feet clumsily into slippers and drag a dressing gown onto my shoulders. Fighting to get my arms into the armholes, I weave with the unfocussed gait of the shockingly-awoken through the dining and sitting rooms to the front porch and struggle with the key and the bolt.

*Yap*, Tatty announces. Regards me smugly from the arms of She-who-was-dropped-on-her-head, apron and all.

I'd swear Tatty's laughing at me. She-who-was-dropped-on-her-head isn't. She's not even smiling. "Er gotten out.' She sounds like a character from *The Vicar of Dibley*. She shoves the dog at my stomach, turns on her heel and marches down the path, slamming the gate a little too roughly, in my opinion.

Tatty gives me a sheepish look. I give Tatty a hard, silent glare. She whimpers. I dump her on the floor and walk away. On second thoughts I call back to her over my shoulder. 'Don't ever show me up like that again, otherwise it's the rescue kennels for you.' I don't even know if they have such a thing in the Outer Hebrides.

---

I find myself applying moisturiser with particular vigour after taking a long shower in the chilly bathroom. I bring out the dreaded eyeliner pencil again and hope the wrinkles around my eyes have smoothed out overnight. They haven't. Instead I transfer my wishfulness to the desire that Neil's eyesight will have deteriorated at the same rate as mine and he'll therefore view me in soft focus. My stomach liquefies and I strengthen my grip on the hairbrush. My hand hovers over the side of my head with a hairclip I found in the bottom of one of my cardboard boxes – *so eighties* – Indeed, he might even have recognised it had I actually worn the thing. The clip goes in the bin. My heavily conditioned curls fall loose around my face as I pull on a navy smocked dress (falls clear of my stomach) and black leggings.

I shut Tatty in the kitchen. She's had enough adventure for one day and has probably already done a poo on Mrs Dropped-on-her-head's lawn. At the front door I push my feet into chunky black boots and shrug on my Arran wool coat, check my lipstick in the mirror.

---

*There he is!* Outside the restaurant in Stornoway town centre, a short step away from the main shopping area. I wish my heartbeat would calm down. *Focus, Lauren.* The sky is bright but sunless, an opaque white – turning the shop windows reflective and outlining the rooftops' sharp edges. I can smell the sea.

I wobble on my feet. Neil's hands are jammed into the pockets of a grey duffle jacket, his tawny hair – speckled with grey – lifting from the top of his head in a ruffle of breeze. He stands in profile and in the stark light of early afternoon, from this short distance away I notice the lines etched into the skin of his face. *He's vulnerable.* My stomach drops and my hands curl into themselves. Shoppers pass between the two of us, pulling children by the hand or pushing them roughly over the curb in buggies. One child drops a toy and its father, occupied with his mobile phone, ignores the son's cries and continues to pull him along. The toy looks sad, lying in the gutter.

Two youths call to each other from the harbour wall across the main road – their conversation echoed, amplified down an alleyway to where I'm standing. A woman with her arm linked into a man's stumbles. She nudges me as she rights herself. She apologises to me over her shoulder. Time is suspended.

Neil turns and looks directly at me. He smiles but at the same time I see concern in his furrowed brow. I'm over-conscious of my pulse – still not quite regular. I feel it in my throat. My own weight seems to pull me down. Or perhaps the metaphorical weight of what was lost – Neil as my *homeland*. I could have sailed unerringly back into the comfort of his harbour, were it not for his children. They block my way home, pirates in immovable boats. He reaches me.

'Neil.'

'Lauren.' We place our hands on each other's shoulders and he brushes his lips on both my cheeks and I brush mine on his. I try not to grip too tightly.

'How was your first week at work?'

'Good, thanks. How are you finding the practice?'

'Fine. *Good.* It's great to see you again, I thought... I wondered...'

'Wondered what?'

'Whether I'd upset you. It felt a trifle awkward when...'

'When you were eating your trifle,' I laugh.

'My Eton Mess, yes.' Neil has always been so literal, not to mention unintentionally poetical. I smile but my insides are jittery. 'It was a shock, hearing about – you know.' I can't say the word *daughter*, nor mention the son he then had the effrontery to wax lyrical about.

'I suppose it must have been. I was crass Lauren, I'm sorry. I've thought about it since. I *assumed*, and I know that's the wrong thing to do – that you would've been married and had your own children by now. I didn't mean to hurt you.'

'I know.' I also know that he'll never truly understand about Barbara. How can he feel the way I do? She's been real to me all these years. I'm a mother but my child – my *children*, if you count Sheena, and you may as well, are lost and I'm bereaved. It's a loss no-one else can share. In almost thirty years I haven't breached the top of the arc and I don't think I ever will. Would we be able to build a bridge over the rift?

'I *was* married, for a short time,' I blurt out. But we're walking now. He places one hand gently on my back and gestures towards the door of the restaurant with his other. 'You were?' He pushes open the door. We enter a dim passageway, slate walls and faintly blue lighting. Metal fish glimmer all around us. It's like being in a cave under the sea. Aproned staff await us at the other end of the passage, one of them steps forward to take our coats. Another leads us up a short flight of steps and around a corner into a bright room. Floor-to-ceiling windows look out onto the street. More fish shimmer from the walls and dangle from the lamps, hanging low over the tables. The waitress takes our drinks order and places menus in front of us while I toy with a corner of a linen napkin. His eyes are so blue.

'So, you said you were married?'

'Yes, for about a year. I met him when I was studying in Reykjavik – Ellis, his name was. We married somewhat in haste, I suppose.' At the look on Neil's face I quickly add, 'And no, I wasn't pregnant.'

On the flight home from Reykjavik with Ellis, deep in my depression I prayed my husband would forgive me for what I was about to do. We disembarked from the plane and collected our bags. I was watching them outside the men's toilets, thinking up ways to tell him I couldn't go on with the marriage, when something made me panic. I couldn't speak to him, I just couldn't. Instead I deserted his bags and ran. As I reached the glass doors to the outside I heard a tannoy announcement about abandoned luggage.

I've been divorced for twenty-three years. *But Sheena*. She reminded me of the children Ellis and I might've had together. They would have had coffee-coloured skin and wiry, dark hair like hers.

*I've never been pregnant again, not since Barbara*, I tell Neil with my eyes. 'I married Ellis because I liked him – that's all.'

'Didn't you love him?'

'Of course. He was a good, kind person.'

I want to say *but not in the way I loved you.* I want to tell him that Ellis reminded me of him, in his manners and his introversion. My body aches. Neil hands the menus to the waitress when she returns with the drinks, and he gives her our orders. After she moves away again he asks, 'What happened then, why do you think you didn't stay married?'

'I can't really say. We never argued, as such. In all honesty, Ellis bent over backwards to make me happy.'

'Hmm,' Neil says, his mouth creasing down at the corners. He'd better not be deducing that I was a demanding madam – the best insult he could once come up with for me. I try to explain.

'We were both studying, we were both busy. We lived happily alongside each other. And there was nothing wrong with... you know...' A hot wash to my cheeks. Neil looks down at the table. 'But when the time came to return to the UK, things started to go wrong.'

'Mm-hmm?' He looks up at me again, sounding annoyingly like the doctor he is. I don't have to say anything more, I tell myself. This is not Neil's business. But I can't help it, I tell him anyway (he must be a good doctor). 'He wanted children and I couldn't do it. I hadn't got over my baby.'

If I'd had children with Ellis – and I wish I had, now, even if Ellis and I wouldn't have ultimately stayed together – they might have looked like Sheena. Ellis was North African, very dark-skinned, whereas I've always been as white as a pickled egg. If I'd had those babies of my own, Sheena might never have... Perhaps I would never even have gone back to Edinburgh. Perhaps Ellis and I would've been happy, and would still be married now. Or perhaps, even if we'd split up after having children, I would still have moved back to Edinburgh, and I might have ended up adopting Sheena after all, adding her to my family. *But there still wouldn't have been Barbara. Stop trying to rewrite your life, Lauren.*

Neil appears stunned.

'I'm sorry again, I mean it.' *Words that will go round and round forever.* I'm certain the scar on his hand lights up as he lifts the glass of sparkling water to his lips. At least you can *tell* he's been hurt.

I sip from my own glass. The absent presences of his children hover between us. I should ask... but I can't.

'So tell me about this dog of yours.' It's him who keeps the conversation going. We're finishing the main course – sea bass for me and a prawn and rice concoction of some sort for Neil. 'Where did you get it?'

I lay my fork down at the side of my plate. 'A neighbour brought her to my house the first evening I came home from work. The owner had died. I couldn't really say no.' I dab my mouth with the napkin.

'And how are you enjoying dog-ownership, does it suit you?'

*A family dog in Canada, a Labrador.* I can almost see it. *He most likely has regular Skype-sessions with it (and his children).* I lift my fork again, glance quickly at my plate and choose a boiled potato. I don't want to know about his other life. I swallow the food and take a sip of water. 'It does suit me, actually. I was reluctant to take her at first but already I can't imagine being in the cottage without her. She was naughty this morning, though...' I recount the tale of Tatty and the woman who was dropped on her head. Neil laughs out loud and it brings tears to my eyes. *In our young days I expected this: us to be sitting here together, or somewhere like this, at the age we are now. This was always to be the future of Lauren and Neil.* I picture our daughter at the table with us, sitting opposite me I decide, next to her father. *Then I could look at her.* She would have a baby on her knee, or a toddler in a highchair. There might be a son-in-law too, and older children. Our daughter might have had sisters and brothers – this could have been a family get-together. *See, this is how I live my life, as a fantasy, the abortion's cause*

219

*and effect.*

'Is everything okay?' The furrow reappears between Neil's brows. 'You know, with us. Have you forgiven me?' He does the kind of cheeky-boy grin middle-aged males are adept at. *Oh Neil. If only it were that easy.*

'It's not about forgiving you.' It's all I can think of to say as I reel back to reality. 'It was never about that.' I know he'll never understand.

The waitress comes to take away our plates.

## 38

THE SUN'S OUT. We wait for the green man at the pedestrian crossing.

'Shall we take a stroll around the harbour wall?'

I nod, swallowing. We trail our hands on warm, yellow stone and admire the boats in the harbour. Cross a bridge and walk into a park. The ground feels solid under the chunky soles of my boots. Trees line the edges of wide lawns and a woodland path embarks on a steep climb up a hill. I learn from Neil that these are the grounds of Lews Castle.

'The castle used to be a college, until quite recently in fact. Originally, of course, it was privately owned – built for Sir James Matheson. I don't know whether you've noticed, but the name Matheson is common on Lewis.'

'Yeah, I've heard it. There's a Matheson who lives near me, in fact.' The name MacDonald is common as well. I glance at him sideways.

'Lord Leverhulme bought the castle after the Matheson's sold it. He did the whole place up and eventually gifted it to the parish for civic purposes. Cool guy, huh? It's owned by *Comhairle Nan Eilean* now. That's the Islands Council.'

'Okay, how long did you spend practising that?' He's about to answer but instead nudges me, pointing to a squirrel chasing another into the trees. *Tatty would love it here.* Now I need to concentrate on breathing as the path climbs upwards even more steeply. Clutching my bad knee at the top, I'm panting. Neil doesn't sound out of breath at all. I picture his healthy Canadian lifestyle – jogging along the edge of some clear-aired lake with his Labrador. *Or his super-healthy children.* Straightening, I focus on the magnificent vista of treetops below us.

'Want to sit down?'

'Okay.'

He brushes leaves from the bench with one end of his scarf. Closes the gap I leave between us.

'Are you warm enough?'

'Yes.' It doesn't stop me shivering, though. Neil unwinds his fine wool scarf and drapes it around my neck, touching my lips. The scent of his skin tickles my nostrils. 'I like that you've got yourself a dog,' he says.

'Why?'

'I worried about you, living in that house, deep in the mountains. Now you've got someone to bark for you, I feel better.'

'You feel better? I've been living on my own for years, Neil. I don't actually need anyone to look out for me, dog or otherwise. Besides...'

'Besides what?'

'Well. You weren't there. All that time. I could have been in all sorts of danger – sometimes I was, and you didn't know.' I press the scarf closer to my nose with my knuckles. 'I'm uncomfortable with you saying things like that. I'm not used to someone else worrying about me, I suppose.'

'That's sad, Lauren.'

'Oh really! Just because I haven't been ensconced in a cosy family situation like yours it doesn't mean – maybe I wanted to be alone.' I glance at him. 'Sorry, that sharpness was uncalled for. But it's not your business, to be honest. I mean, we can start from *now*, and you can be concerned about me now, if you must, if you want to. But I don't want you making judgements on the life I chose to live all the years that have passed.'

'You're right,' he says quietly, and settles his hands in his lap. The scar winks palely on the back of his browned skin and my stomach flips. *That was me.* A hot bolt of desire leaves me winded. I turn it into a cough and busy my mind with an examination of the leaves, individually rustling, distinct and separate in the carpet of treetops on the hill below. Every leaf with its own stem, each dependent on the tree it belongs to. The roots of all the trees tangled together under the soil.

A family walks by, the young mother wearing a hijab. She pushes a baby in a buggy. A tiny girl holds onto the handle. She's wearing a red velvet dress and white lacy tights with shiny patent-leather shoes. The father carries a boy on his shoulders, a child with the glossiest black curls I've ever seen. The little girl drops her toy rabbit as she passes and I lean forward to pick it up and hand it back to her. She giggles and the mother flashes me a smile. Prickling starts up behind my eyes, they look so happy. The sound of the children's laughter dies away. Neil and I glance at each other. I'm shocked by Neil's eyes, they look like burning embers.

'What is it? Are you okay?'

'He reminds me of Hassan,' he says. 'That father.'

'Hassan?'

'A young guy I met in the Calais Jungle. Looked just like him. He was a father too, but he had to leave his wife and baby daughter behind in Syria. It's so fucking unfair, the way young men are criticised for leaving.' Neil's not the type to swear. He mutters something I can't hear, then turns back to me. 'This guy who was delivering food to the camp cut his hand on a palette. Hassan helped patch him up and they got chatting. Afterwards the driver called Hassan a coward – not to his face, of course. He said nothing would have made him leave his wife behind. Some people's ignorance is so depressing.'

I allow my fingers to creep towards Neil's knee, make contact with the denim. His leg feels warm beneath. An image of this same leg unravels, my younger hand on his bare knee, moving towards his thigh, creeping upwards. Maybe we could...

Neil gathers himself, seemingly unaware of my hand.

'Hassan was training as a doctor in Syria.' He speaks in a deliberately calm voice. 'He helped me out in the medical centre. We used to chat during our brief breaks. Every night Hassan walked out of the camp and tried to jump on a lorry. One night he even swam out towards a boat in the harbour with the intention of stowing away, but there were too many searchlights, so he came back. He became progressively more depressed as each of his friends made it to the other side, one by one, and he was left behind. Told himself he was a failure and if it wasn't for his family he would have killed himself by now.' His fists are bunched on his thighs. My touch is ineffectual and I allow my hand to slip off. Neil continues in a tight voice. 'I had to treat Hassan's wounds more than once after he was beaten up by the Police on his way back into the camp. Did you know about that – about the police brutality?' His eyes are angry. I swallow and nod. *Shh*, I want to say. *Try not to get worried. Jesus Christ, Superstar* is back.

'Once Hassan was blind for a whole evening after he'd been tear-gassed by those bastards.' Neil turns towards me and my body involuntarily leans closer to his. He trembles faintly. 'People ask why the 'migrants' are mostly young men. Vilify them for leaving their families behind. Hassan would have been dead if he'd stayed in Syria. He showed me his torture-wounds.' He presses his hands briefly against his eyes, as if trying to blot out the memory. 'Bloody hell, Lauren. Bloody, *fucking* hell. If they don't leave they're rounded up and conscripted by the terrorists. Is that what people here want? More terrorists? I've read the bloody *Daily Fail*, the pure and spiteful ignorance. It was Hassan's wife who begged him to leave, for fucks sake. Begged him to try and reach somewhere safe for them all. Sorry,' he looks at me properly. 'I don't know why I'm spouting all this at you. It's not your fault. Sorry – some date this is, eh?'

He looks me up and down as if he's just realised who I am. I remember the long conversations we had in the past – how he introduced me to so many causes. What I am is partly due to him.

'No, it's all right,' I say. 'Carry on, it's important. Important for me to listen. Carry on, honestly.' I try and manage a smile. Push aside awareness of his children, my resentment. This is the Neil I fell in love with. His passion, the fury of *Jesus in the temple.* Neil licks his lips.

'If his wife and small child had been washed up on a Greek holiday beach because he'd brought them along with him, he would have been equally vilified. To leave them behind was an act of great bravery, I think. Like an old-fashioned quest. It can take years but it's worthy. Not cowardice – why can't people see that, Lauren?'

I kiss him, suddenly and hard. Taste salt from the tears running down his cheeks and into our mouths. I pull away. His moisture on my upper lip. Neil occupies his hands with a handkerchief. My body tingles but now I feel oddly emotionless. Neil blows his nose loudly and puts the hankie away in his jacket pocket. Looks at me and smiles. 'Sorry.'

'Don't be. I'm sorry too, about the hell those people are living through.'

I should ask him about his family, but Neil's children are the elephants in the room, in the landscape. In our *universe*. What was I thinking, kissing him? I don't know how it could work, me and him. I ought to have said no to this date. I definitely shouldn't have kissed him. Am I ready? Not yet.

We wouldn't even have known we were destined to end up on the same island if we hadn't both been in the ferry cafeteria at the same time.

My chin sinks into the wool of his blue scarf though. It smells of him and I like it. Suddenly I have to peel it away. Heat blazes behind my skin while at the same time cold explodes in my chest. My outer layer prickles, like a million insects crawling up to my skull. It's Neil's turn to ask if I'm okay.

'Hot flush.' Flap myself with the scarf's tassels. Three months without a period, the longest I've been. *I'll never have another baby...* If we'd met again even ten years ago. But it still would've been a betrayal of Barbara.

'Are you, err, taking anything?'

I wrap the scarf around my shoulders, for the comfort more than the need of warmth.

'No. Nothing much has happened yet.'

'Forever young.' He nudges his shoulder against mine. 'You always will be to me.'

I look at him properly, study his face – which has smoothed out again. Something slips and slides inside me. I start to gabble. 'How did the years hurtle by so fast, though? As if a whole bunch of pages was turned all at once, and somehow... I don't know how... I missed what happened in between.' I notice a patch of dry skin at the side of his nose. 'The worse thing is that nothing much seems to have changed except our bodies and faces – whatever you say, Neil.' My mouth twitches. We hold each other's gaze a moment. He presses his shoulder against mine, his face too close now for me to make out any detail. I lean away and smile. We both gaze out across the treetops, over the harbour and down at the town in the draining light of the afternoon. I wrap my hands around each other, compelled to keep talking.

'Take the UK, for example. Same type of Government now as we had in the eighties, the same *Victorian* differences between the rich and poor. It's the same uncaring, *me, me, me* attitude. And anyone who argues for compassion is ridiculed and lambasted for being weak.' Neil nods. My mouth won't stop running away with me. 'I even think the tide of refugees is similar. Fleeing wars that *we've* played a part in. And then you've got the same bloody arguments over nuclear weapons – we now have the same fucking fear of a final, apocalyptic war happening as we did then. Especially with... Oh God. What kind of world are we living in?'

---

A cloud of seagulls screeches overhead, aiming for the harbour. *White birds on the foam of the sea.* Phuong materialises in my mind. 'I remember all these worries from my twenties, Neil. Don't you? I mean, why did I even go to Greenham Common?' I pause to take several breaths. 'Can things turn around again, do you think? Back then, things did seem to improve, didn't they? The Berlin wall came down, Nelson Mandela was released. We were so hopeful, weren't we?'

But Neil and I weren't together anymore by that time. Our separate histories lie within those stuck-together pages of our pasts. What was he doing while I was a post-graduate student who attended a memorial for Tiananmen Square? When I went on *Free Nelson Mandela* marches, and established myself in my career? I should ask him, but I can't bear to hear about Helen and the son whose name I can't remember.

'I feel the same way as you. You know I do.' He hums softly, and I strain to catch the tune – *where have all the flowers gone?* A lump jams my throat. I cough and swallow.

'Does the world have to suffer utter devastation before things can get better?' Did we?

'Remember Phuong?' Neil has apparently caught my thoughts.

'Phuong, aye. *I am haunted by numberless islands, and many a Danaan shore.* That was from a Yeats poem. She learned to speak it in perfect English. Wi' a Scottish accent, o' course. She came to the United Kingdom on the foam of the sea, like in the poem. Weel... More-or-less.'

Phuong was probably the reason I became a social worker. The face of the numberless Vietnamese refugees on TV and the ones Da told me about when he worked on the reception centre in Port Glasgow. 'She married a head teacher, you know. Last I heard she lived in a fancy cottage in the grounds of a boys' boarding school. I think she taught there – did something related to teaching anyway. Also, I heard she'd become a grandmother – quite young. We lost touch a few years ago.'

'You are funny,' says Neil. 'Did you know your accent grows much stronger when you talk about the past? Anyway, not anymore – Phuong, I mean. Well, I expect Phuong's still a grandmother but she isn't at the boys' school in Hertfordshire anymore. She split up with her husband. I met her recently at a conference in Nova Scotia. Amazing coincidence. She's working in women's global health now, what a change in circumstances, eh? She was about to set off for Afghanistan. Small world, though, isn't it?'

'Oh my God, yeah, small world indeed. Did you know Phuong's parents cashed in all their savings to find their safe life? They were once very well-off. They just happened to be born in the wrong place at the wrong time and I guess during the wrong war – not that I think any war is *right*.' My fingers flex involuntarily and I see Neil's hand heading for mine across the denim of his leg and my woollen coat.

*We're on the ferry, the scar on the back of his hand burning a warning – or an invitation – I haven't looked into his eyes. Not yet.*

After the slightest resistance, my fingers tapping on my leg, I allow his hand to take mine. But it hasn't stopped me ranting. 'More than thirty years later, millions of refugees from other parts of the world are having to do the same as Phuong's family. Fucking risk their lives to set out on flimsy boats in hopes of reaching a safe harbour.' I want to bring him into it. 'Like your Hassan.' I trace the veins on the back of his hand with my thumb, avoiding the dangerousness of the scar, though I seem to feel its heat. I can hear a slight whistle in his breathing. 'Welcomed by tear gas and water cannons.' I squeeze his hand, shake my head. 'Phuong. She'd been through so much. And now Afghanistan.'

'I know.' He squeezes my hand in return. On the outskirts of all our worthy words, I'm aware of this... the silent but far more eloquent dialogue of our fingers and palms. 'It's the people who have suffered that do the most to help others, I think. One of the doctors in my practice in Canada was also a Vietnamese refugee. It turns out his family knew Phuong's, they came from the same area of Vietnam.'

'Small world,' I echo.

---

We emerge from the bottom of the track and follow the pathway back along the edge of the harbour. The sky is red where it touches the buildings and masts. Sails absorb varying degrees of sunset hues, the water is coloured red. We're holding hands, Neil and I, as though we'd never stopped. I feel displaced in time. When I look out across the coloured water it's as if veils of images from different chapters of my life shift and stir in front of each other like voile curtains. A breeze rustles the trees behind us and chops at the incoming tide. Our bodies stop moving at the same time. We lean against the harbour wall, watch seaweed and gulls rocking on the swell of the water.

'Wow,' Neil waves his hand at the evidence of elemental forces, so much more powerful than us. But my eye is drawn once again to the scar on the back of that waving hand, as if its force is more powerful even than nature.

*Let the past go – or bring it back.*

My body turns towards him, I swear it has nothing to do with my consciousness. He unhooks his other hand from mine and pulls me against him but I'm caught in an attitude of fight or flight, hovering between the two. He kisses the top of my head. And then it's no different from when we were nineteen and twenty, standing on Granny's Green steps. Or when we were twenty-four and twenty-five and I gave him the scar. Someone must have erased the script of all the missing years – resealed us in our proper places. We've reappeared at last on the stage of our entwined lives.

# 39

I ARRIVED LATE this morning. I kept getting static shocks as I was driving and I don't feel completely settled in my body – haven't all weekend. Maybe part of me stayed behind with Neil as we reluctantly separated in Stornoway on Saturday evening. I rest my face in my hands, elbows pressed into the desk. *Neil.* It's hard knowing he's only a mile or so away but we've agreed not to see each other again until the weekend.

I haven't been in the office long when Rab hands me the phone. It's Christine from Pine Tree House. I make polite enquiries as to her health, but she's not one for standing on ceremony. She cuts me off with the purpose of her call – Catriona has absconded from the premises again and got herself into a state after smoking marijuana. 'Skunk, to be more precise. I'm at my wits' end with her,' Christine snaps. 'Most of them I can build up some sort of a relationship with, but Catriona refuses to give an inch. Maybe it's just a clash of personalities but I can't seem to get through to her.'

Funny, I'd felt the girl would be easy to get to know, *on her own terms.* Again I remind myself that it's easier for me because I can walk away. There's been trouble between her and her uncle after all – maybe Catriona's not as straightforward as I'd smugly allowed myself to believe.

'Would you be able to come over and have another talk with her?' Christine asks. 'I mean, she gets on particularly well with one of our younger care workers but she's on maternity leave at the moment. I don't know who else to turn to.' Christine's voice wobbles. I wonder what Catriona said. Of course, I say, I'll have a look at my diary.

'I meant today if possible?'

'Err, that's a bit sudden. What's the emergency?' A now-familiar prickling begins under the skin of my face and heat floods my whole body, settling in the small of my back. I'm a radiator. I swivel my chair slightly in a bid to escape Rab's probing gaze. The tiniest stress sets these flushes off. I try to breathe regularly, let it wash over me. Sweat cools on my face.

'We're short-staffed,' Christine goes on. 'They've sent a cover but the lad's ineffectual, he's not much older than the kids. You seemed to have a calming influence on Catriona. The thing is, she had a visit from her uncle yesterday and they had an argument, she ran off after he'd left and she came back stoned again. This morning she won't talk to anyone.'

I glance at Rab, picking his teeth with an unravelled paperclip. 'I'll call you back in a minute,' I say to Christine. 'Can that meeting with the teacher at St Margaret's be put off until tomorrow?' I ask Rab. I turn the diary page back to today and run my eyes over it. 'I have a couple of hours available this afternoon, I see. Christine wants me over in Skye today but I won't be able to do anything else if I go to Pine Tree House. In fact, will I even be able to get to the island and back at all?'

I could just say no to Christine – fit tomorrow's appointments in today and set off early to Skye in the morning. But I want to go. I want to continue discussing Shakespeare and Catriona's mother and find out what the quarrel with the girl's uncle was about. *Don't let yourself get too involved.* I don't heed the warning in my head. Christine believes Catriona will open up to me – *I'm needed.* It's a satisfying feeling.

Rab checks the ferry times. He concludes that I'll have to stay overnight on Skye but there's a budget to cover the cost of a recommended B&B. *What shall I do about Tatty?* There's always Peggy, she has a key to my house after all.

It's an adventure. Rab taps away at the keyboard. 'You'll have to hurry if you're going to catch the afternoon ferry.' He hands me a print-out. 'You can buy your overnight essentials on the boat. These are the details of the B&B you'll be staying at, it's in Uig (on Skye) so handy for the return trip in the morning.'

---

'Christine tells me you have the opportunity to live with your uncle if you want.' I continue to talk into Catriona's thick silence. 'Do you not feel that's an option that would suit you at all?'

*'Do you not feel that's an option that would suit you at all?'* Catriona keeps parroting me, the only method of conversation we've yet engaged in. She keeps her eyes fixed on her knees. A different girl from the one I met a week ago. She's shaved the sides of her head, a move which, rather than making her look tough as I suspect she intended, gives her a heartbreaking vulnerability. In the dim light of her bedside lamp I see a crust of dried blood under her nose. This is due to the metal bar she's had forced through the cartilage.

Christine says she hasn't eaten, at least not at the home, not that they know of. Hollows under Catriona's eyes give her a Halloween appearance.

'What was the argument with your uncle about? Have you only fallen out recently, or have you always had a difficult relationship?' Ineffective. *What can I say to her?* 'Christine tells me he visits you every week. Your mother's brother, isn't he?' I drop words like stones into her apathy. She barely flickers an eyelid. I haven't been offered a cup of tea this time. My mouth is dry. I heave myself off the hard chair and move over to the window, jerk the closed curtain aside. The metal rail vibrates with the rattle of curtain rings. *Try a different tack.*

'It's actually a lovely day. Would you like to go out for a walk? We could go for a drive, even, if you fancy it.'

She touches her nose gingerly with a fingertip, examines the fingerprint for blood. Sniffs, squints at the light, shrugs. 'If you like.'

I do. It smells horrible in the room and Catriona's presence is dark in more ways than one.

'Come on then. You'll need a jacket.'

*I'll take her to a café I spotted along the road.* The thought of a cup of tea and cake cheers me up no end. She won't tell me what the quarrel was about, still hardly speaks at all – merely mutters an odd yes or no in answer to my questions. Yet it's an achievement to have got her to come out in the car with me. I allow her to settle into a less guarded silence. The look of relief on Christine's face when I came down the stairs with Catriona tagging behind, pulling on a grubby hooded jacket, was palpable. I can understand it, the girl's depression is weighty and it settles on me as I drive. Added to by my failed years of trying to help Sheena. Sheena needed my total commitment and I refused to give it to her when all's said and done. I mustn't make the same mistake again.

Glancing sideways I note the fresh scabs on the side of Catriona's head – I'm guessing she dragged a disposable razor over her scalp. I haven't mentioned it but I mourn the loss of those dark wings of hair she had. Catriona gazes fixedly ahead as the road unravels before us.

I cross the centre of the island and drive along the west coast, heading northward, having decided to bypass the café I saw on my way to Pine Tree House. It feels too soon to break the drive and have to settle ourselves all over again. Past the *Skye Museum of Island Life* at Kilmuir. Perhaps I should offer to take Catriona there next time – maybe she could teach me a thing or two about being an Islander. Right now she's not talking and I leave her to contemplate her own thoughts. Before we round the top of the island we pass the ruins of Duntulm Castle, stark on the skyline over slate-grey water, beyond which lie the mountains of Harris. After that we drive through the scattered township of Kilmaluag. The monument to Flora MacDonald reminds me of Neil. My insides twist.

The view on our right reveals the full glory of steepled mountains with bare, jagged peaks that score the leaden sky. The *Cuillin*, my recalcitrant companion tells me after some probing. Catriona settles back into her seat, lulled by the drive. I don't want to disturb her by stopping the car at the next café, the one I see signposted down a narrow track, so I carry on despite my dry mouth.

*Might it have felt like this if I hadn't killed Barbara? Lulling her in the pram I'd picked out from Mothercare, the one I was going to pay for in monthly instalments. I had it all planned out before Neil persuaded me to do what I did. Pushing her up and down the streets of Edinburgh to keep her asleep, maybe late at night so as not to disturb Neil and put his patients in danger by depriving him of his much-needed rest.*

The steering wheel becomes a pram-handle in my hands, the one I never got to push. I will take care of *this* daughter. I can almost see Barbara's sleeping face in that pram. Oh, how I wish she'd had the chance to become the twenty-eight-year-old woman she would have been by now. *Why* did I allow Neil to persuade me to get rid of her? *Why did I, why?* Weariness overtakes me – that eternal theme tune in my head along with the rumble of car tyres on gritty road surface.

'Watch out, you stupid cow!'

Catriona's right, I *am* a stupid cow. A car towing a caravan heads towards us on the narrow road, no doubt the driver had expected me to pull in to the passing place just now disappearing from view in my left wing mirror. I snap back into the present, jam my foot on the brake, followed by the clutch, seconds before a collision would have taken place. The driver of the caravan-pulling car shakes his fist at me. Somewhere in my brain I'm fascinated to discover that people actually *do* that. With my own shaking hands I steer the car backwards into the passing place I missed. The car growls past with its caravan rattling behind it, uncomfortably close, the driver still apparently shouting at me through our two closed windows.

Sweating, I engage the handbrake and slip the gear into neutral. I turn the engine off and we remain stationary in the passing place, my hands clammy on the wheel. My face prickles with sharp pin-jabs, heat floods under my skin like water from a boiled kettle. My scalp crawls.

'Bloody 'ell,' says Catriona.

'I feel like I am. In Hell,' I respond, panting. She regards me with interest. 'You look like a beetroot. Purple.' She giggles, twitching as though having some kind of fit. I watch her laughing until a strangled yelp bursts from my own throat. After giving in to a hysterical peal I bring myself under control and wipe my eyes. 'Yes, well. You wait, one day it'll happen to you too. The joys of being a woman.'

She goes quiet, I wonder what she's thinking. A few drops of rain patter against the windscreen but the sun still bleeds from beneath a ridge of clouds. It'll brighten up again soon. I start the engine.

'Let's find a tea shop, shall we? I could definitely do with a cup of tea after that.' She doesn't respond. I take it as a yes. 'Somewhere with a nice sea view.' I groan inwardly as the car springs into life and I check my mirrors a hundred times before pulling back out onto the road. *A nice sea view.* I sound like someone's grandma. Not Granny Mary, she had a sea view the whole of her life.

'*Harrumph.* If you insist.' Catriona pulls her hood up, the top half of her face disappearing under black cloth. I suppose she'll be embarrassed to walk into a tea shop looking the way she does. She balls her fists and shoves them into her pockets, stretches the jersey fabric until it covers her knees and the hole in her black tights. I'm aware of the thump-thump of her fists, within the pockets, on her knees. We drive in a new silence. I miss the banter I once enjoyed with Sheena. I miss Sheena... Stop it. *Whenever I feel afraid, I hold my head erect, and whistle a happy tune...* I only realise I'm actually whistling when I finally become aware of Sheen – I mean *Catriona's* incredulous frown from under her hood, feel the scorch of her eyes on my left cheek.

'What the actual fuck?'

'Oops, sorry. Not the most tuneful, I know. Would you prefer the radio on?'

'No, I was enjoying the quiet, actually.'

I keep my eyes fixed on the road. High above the sea we glide past a signpost that tells us we are passing through *Flodigarry*. Catriona sits up straighter in her seat. I flash her an enquiring glance, but she keeps her gaze angled through the windscreen, pulls her hood further over the front of her face and doesn't articulate her sudden burst of animation. *Flodigarry*, it rings a bell but I can't think for what it tolls.

Then I see a signpost for a hotel, advertising afternoon tea. I indicate left and drive down the road towards the sea.

---

In the hotel's garden, indeed with a sea view, we drink tea from china mugs and watch each other pick scone crumbs off our plates with the tips of our fingers. She wolfed hers down in a few mouthfuls but I still have half a scone left. I slide it onto her plate. She grunts what may be a thank you.

'More jam?' I say. She looks me full in the eyes. I take my chance.

'What was the argument with your uncle about, then?'

'Nosey cow, aren't you?' Her gaze slides away. She takes a bite of scone and stares out to sea.

'Haha. My... another young lady I worked with used to call me that.'

*Damn. Why did I have to bring Sheena into it?* Catriona must have noticed something. Her eyes slide back towards me. She licks jam off her fingertip. 'What was her name?'

'Who?'

'The *young lady* who called you a nosy cow.'

'Oh.' I breathe carefully. 'Sheena. Anyway, we're here to talk about you, not her.'

'It takes two to have a conversation, you told me that last time you came. A bit of give and take is only fair, isn't it?' She picks up the last bite-sized portion of scone and shoves it in her mouth. I brush crumbs off my lap, trying to look unconcerned but I can feel my shoulders rising around my ears. *Relax.* Catriona swallows her food. 'I'll tell you what the argument was about,' she says. 'If you tell me why you're uncomfortable talking about this Sheena girl?'

'What d'you mean, uncomfortable? I'm not.'

A long pause.

'Fair enough. Just tell me one thing about her, then. Bit of give and take.'

'Fair enough,' I echo. 'If it's so important to you. Okay. Let me think. She was –' I stop myself. 'I mean she is the same age as you.'

'Was? You said was. What happened to her?'

'Nothing.' Someone's turned the furnace on inside my cheeks again. I claw at my scarf and allow some air onto my neck. She spreads out her hands, her eyebrows raised. The heat continues to boil under my skin. 'Now that's enough,' I say, flapping with the ends of the scarf. 'I told you one thing and that's not what we're here to talk about, anyway. Come on, it's time we were getting back.'

I stand up too quickly, knocking my knee against the metal leg of the table. 'Ouch!' The backs of my eyes burn. *Pull yourself together, Lauren.*

'Chill out, Lauren,' says Catriona. 'You're turning purple again. Sit down, for fuck's sake, you haven't even finished your tea. Sorry for asking about *Sheena*. She's clearly off-topic.' She gives me a challenging look.

'That's enough,' I say again. But I sit back down and top up my tea, proffering the pot at Catriona while I get myself back under control. She shakes her head. I imagine a rod being threaded through the bones of my spine. *Sit up straight.* There. I'm calm again.

'It was about going to live with him,' Catriona says unexpectedly. 'Same old argument. But I don't want to, so he needs to stop going on about it. *Idiot.* Him, I mean, not you.' Though she looks me up and down as if she's not sure.

I let my hand rest, palm up on the table. 'Why don't you want to live with him? Surely it would be better than the home?' I consider saying something about Christine but think better of it. *Stay professional.* Instead, I wait.

'I *would* have agreed to, eventually. If he hadn't bloody moved to a different island. It's all his fault.'

'What do you mean? He lives on Skye, doesn't he?'

'That's what I mean. He's an *idiot.* He should never have moved over here, to that poky new house. He got rid of the only place I ever really thought of as home.'

There must be a breeze coming off the sea because I can feel the hair at the back of my neck stirring, leaving a chill on my skin. I pull my scarf tighter again.

'Where was that, then?'

'It was my grannie's cottage on the Isle of Lewis,' Catriona says. 'I want him to get it back!'

---

*She's familiar to me, as though I've known her a long time. Not what I would have imagined a daughter of mine might become, but I suppose many people's daughters aren't. They grow to be their own people, don't they? This is what I've learned from talking to parents: some disgruntled about their child's individuality, others heartbroken, or indifferent, or keen to absolve themselves of responsibility. I don't often meet the happy ones.*

*Sheena grew on me slowly. She started off as another routine client, though our eventual mutual affection was stronger than I'd developed for any other child. But Sheena had a mother of her own, however neglectful. Catriona doesn't, not any more. The first moment I saw her photograph I had an insight into the complicated emotions she'd evoke in me. Maybe I'm still too raw to have come back to work. Social workers are supposed to remain detached. But how can you do the job properly if you don't care enough?*

We sit in the dark car outside Pine Tree House. Catriona fell asleep on the journey back from the hotel but she's awake now, refusing to go into the house. I saw Christine tugging the curtain aside ten minutes ago, peering out into the gloom. She must wonder what we're doing, though she's probably grateful for a few extra minutes of relief from this quietly difficult child.

When Catriona told me about the Isle of Lewis, I suppose that was the moment the ridiculous, un-thought-out, completely unfeasible idea came into my head.

It's only because of Sheena. I know this, and yet the new, stupid idea has planted itself in my inner ear, chattering constantly as I sit motionless in the car's quiet. I speak out loudly, to silence it.

'Come on, Catriona, you need to get out of the car now. We can't sit here all night.' I open the door with a determined flourish.

She turns her head to glare at me. In the glow of the interior light I see that she's broken the scab in her nose – a small trickle of blood pools in the dip above her upper lip. It must have happened when she rubbed her nose with the back of her hand earlier – and explains the exclamation she let out, followed by an expletive when I enquired as to its cause. I touch my own upper lip and waft my hand gently towards her.

'Here, have a tissue.' I find them in the well under the steering wheel. 'You can keep the whole packet if you like.'

'You're too bloody kind.' She presses a tissue to her sore nose and with her other hand stuffs the packet into her jacket pocket. 'Go *on* then,' she says, after she's examined the dotted pattern of blood on the used hanky. She scrunches the tissue and stuffs it down the side of the seat. *Thanks for that!* 'Go and give Christine your report. I've got things to do in the house of fun, can't sit out here in the car all night.'

*So, all it took was a packet of tissues.* My eyes sting as I get out heavily, stabilising myself with a hand on the back of my seat. I follow her to the front door, limping slightly. The raw sides of her scalp glimmer, pale in the half-dark.

Can she be fixed? Can I do it right this time?

---

Catriona slithers past Christine with her chin tucked into her neck. She clomps up the stairs with her hands shoved into her jacket pockets and her shoulders hunched. There's a ladder in the back of her tights and her short, stretchy skirt has ridden up at the back. Christine gives me a flat smile, shaking her head from side to side.

'I don't know how you put up with her.'

When I don't answer she adds, widening her eyes for a response, 'Surly madam, isn't she?' I still don't say anything and her eyes harden. She blocks the doorway with her elbows, apparently doesn't intend to invite me in. She fishes in the pocket of her long cardigan, withdraws a packet of cigarettes, tips one out and ignites it with a lighter fashioned from green plastic, the rudimentary shape of a lizard – or perhaps it's a crocodile. Not that I smoke, but she doesn't offer me one anyway.

I allow my bag to slide to the ground and bend to open it. Balancing the folder against the wall I sign the report sheet, tear it off and hand it to Christine. She takes it from me with her free hand, folds the thin paper with two fingers and a thumb and slots it into her baggy cardigan pocket. 'There'll be a case meeting in about a week,' she says, releasing a puff of smoke from her lips. 'I'll let you know the date and time.'

My mind ticks over rapidly. Straightening, I give her my best attempt at a smile.

'Well, I'll be off to my B&B, then. Early start in the morning. Have a pleasant evening, won't you?'

Christine nods, lips making an 'o' shape as ash falls to the damp ground. Light from the hallway behind her illuminates stray wisps of her hair.

---

The B&B room's double bed is placed alongside an old-fashioned window with a deep sill and a metal frame. Sliding my shoes off I lean over and push one side open, breathing deeply of the cool, damp air. It's not enough to stop the tide of heat that washes over me. In the tiny bathroom mirror my skin from the neckline of my blouse to the roots of my hair has turned cerise. A heater must be blowing hot air against my lower back. I pull off my outer clothes and swill my face and neck with cool water, run wet fingers through my hair. I unfold the smallest towel from the pile of three folded on the tiled surface next to the sink, cursorily dab my skin dry. *That's better.* Unhook my bra from inside my vest top and slip first one arm out and then the other. How will Neil react to the softness of my well-fed belly? I try to hold it in in front of the mirror. Heat floods me again. I practise my pelvic floor exercises.

*Think about work, Lauren.* In vest and pants I climb onto the bed, Catriona's file tucked under my arm. Prop myself against a stack of three pillows and wedge the fourth under my knees. *Lovely.* With the open folder on my legs I rake through the extraneous details surrounding Catriona's situation.

So – her uncle is called Kenneth Murdo MacLennan – I hadn't paid much attention to his name before, too keen to read about Catriona herself. But now my head buzzes. I see Kenneth and Margaret and their sons Finlay and Kenlish on the photo I found in the cupboard. Murdo is Finlay's son and his grandfather was Kenneth. Could Murdo's actual first name be Kenneth? Negotiating one's way through the names of the native islanders is like finding one's way out of a maze. Then there was Peggy's mention of 'the girl'... perhaps she wasn't referring to Catherine at all. Finally Catriona told me her only real home was on Lewis – it can't be... But it seems likely that it is my house she was talking about.

9 'o clock – not too late, I don't think, to ring the mobile number scribbled in pencil next to the uncle's name in the file.

# 40

I LEAVE THE Bed and Breakfast with a stomach full of toast and eggs and so much tea that I needed the loo three times (and probably will again). A text pings as I open my car door and I fumble to take out my mobile. *Oh, Neil.* I open the back door and chuck my bags onto the seat, then fold myself into the driver's seat and text a quick reply. *He'll think I'm a cold fish. But I can't do this at work!*

After breakfast I picked up a voicemail from Jessica. She asked me to check in on an unstable foster placement – a set of three difficult-to-place siblings living with an older couple and their two teenagers. The placement was set up with a view to permanency but one of the couple's own children is struggling to adapt. Jessica hinted that the teenage boy in question might have been messing around with soft drugs and it's him she suggests I speak to.

*Greg Mulligan* directs me to turn right in three hundred yards and I find myself on a smoothly tarmacked track. It slopes in a curve towards a large house nestling amongst an artful concealment of trees.

---

Despite the extra appointment (the teenage boy confessed to taking Ecstasy without me even asking – I think he was looking for attention and he got it, from his shouting father) – I make the noon ferry back to Tarbert. And by three PM I'm driving past the Co-op at the top of the hill near my home.

*An afternoon off... Sleep? Catch up on emails? Phone Neil? No. A good walk with Tatty...* Spears of light glint off the sea as I take the curve in the road. James Taylor sings about fire and rain and Neil's face wavers on the windscreen in front of me. I couldn't stay with him last Saturday night because of Tatty but we've arranged to spend the whole of the coming weekend together at my house. I fight a hot flush as I negotiate the sharp turn into the short driveway of Peggy's house and switch off the radio. *Back to the present.* My stomach turns over. Why did she not tell me about Murdo's niece?

Peggy opens her front door and a cannonball thuds into my ankles. I open my arms and Tatty scales my legs and body, claws scrabbling against my chest. 'Ouch!' She licks my face. I wipe my mouth and lower her to the ground with my other arm, where she bounces around my feet.

'She's taken to *you*, that's for sure,' Peggy says. 'I knew she would, that's why I brought her to you. Perfect for each other, you two are.'

The smug expression's back on her face. I brush curls away from mine and swallow the feeling I've been betrayed by Peggy. It's ridiculous. It probably never crossed her mind to tell me about Catriona. *Yet she knew I was a social worker...*

'Coming in for a cuppa, are you?' Peggy lifts one eyebrow. 'Aw, go on, just the one won't hurt, will it? Whatever important work you've got to do.'

I always have the slight suspicion she's having a bit of a go at me. *You're over-sensitive, Lauren.*

'Just the one, then.' Echoes of Da's infuriating "I'll just have half a cup."

Tatty clings to me like a burr as I follow Peggy through her dark sitting room – the curtains are inexplicably drawn – into the bright, small kitchen at the back of her house. The dog springs onto my lap when I take the proffered seat at the kitchen table. While arranging cups on saucers, Peggy gives me a sideways look.

'Bit tired, are you dear?'

'I suppose so. The ferry, you know, and the driving. Also, I had to mediate a family argument this morning.'

Peggy places a teapot on a trivet and carries the cups over from the worktop. I run my hand down Tatty's smooth coat from her head to the base of her whippy tail. She wriggles and gives me a grateful lick on the cheek.

'A family?' Peggy likes a bit of gossip.

'On Skye, before I caught the ferry home. It was a placement matter really but my colleague asked me to check in since I was on the island anyway.'

'You're *drugs*, aren't you dear?'

'Technically, yes,' my mouth twitches. 'But we all help each other out.' *This is my opportunity.* 'You never told me about Murdo's niece. I felt a bit of an idiot once I realised he was my client's uncle.'

'I told you about the girl, dear, I'm sure I did.' She closes the fridge door and passes me a small jug of milk. I want to protest that I thought she was talking about a younger sister, but it seems churlish. But it's odd that Murdo didn't tell me either. What *did* we talk about while I cooked him supper in my kitchen? My ailments mainly, I remember, blushing. Then there was the distraction of his heritage. On the phone last night he still wasn't keen on talking about Catriona. Perhaps he feels it compromises our professional arrangement. Maybe Peggy will tell me more. I shift on the hard wood and settle Tatty more comfortably in my lap, pressing her down with my hand. I notice Peggy's mouth is downturned at the corners when she lowers herself into her chair opposite me.

'Your client, you say?'

'Hmm, yes. A bit of trouble with some company she's keeping. Nothing serious, I don't think.'

'Such a pretty girl,' Peggy muses. 'Such a pity if she's getting into trouble. I hope she's not going the same way as her mother.' She closes her fingers around the handle of the teapot. 'That lovely long, dark hair Catherine had – then she went and shaved it into one of those mo... mo... what's the name of that punk hairstyle they used to have, you know, like the Indians in the Wild West films? Mo-something. Catherine's was bright pink.'

'Mohicans.' The scabbed sides of Catriona's head. The tangle of black hair down her back. *She needs a mother.* 'When did you last see Catriona?'

'About a year-and-a-half ago, it would be. On second thoughts maybe the time I'm thinking of was more like two-and-a-half. But Janet's funeral was after that, so I saw her then, and then again at her mother's – pathetic affair as it was. They buried Catherine here, you know, beside her parents.'

Peggy blinks rapidly, tilts her little finger as she raises the cup to her lips. After taking a sip she continues less shakily. 'The time I was first thinking of, Catherine brought the girl to see her grandmother when she was ill. Murdo had to put some pressure on her, mind. She'd left the little girl with Janet on a few occasions in the past, once for a whole summer. Catherine used to take off with that no-good boyfriend, nobody knew where. So Janet got the idea they should keep the child here on Lewis. She wanted Murdo and Ann to become the child's official guardians but of course Ann wasn't keen.' She mutters something unintelligible under her breath. 'Catherine came back eventually and snatched Catriona away. She was in an awful state. Accused her brother of betraying her and she hated Ann. Always has done. Janet got called into the school once because of a fight between the two girls, this was years ago, of course. Not surprisingly, Ann wasn't prepared to go to Skye with Murdo and help Catherine when she really needed it. Didn't even go to her funeral when he brought her back here to be buried.'

Some girlfriend Ann turned out to be. I feel a surge of empathy. Murdo must be sad and lonely, especially now his niece has turned on him as well. I stretch to ease my knot of confusion. Tatty lifts her nose from her paws and gives me a puzzled look.

'It's all right,' I murmur. 'Settle down.'

'What is it?' asks the ever-vigilant Peggy.

I take a gulp of tea, lower my cup carefully into the saucer.

'Catriona told me that her grandmother's house on the Isle of Lewis is the only place she ever thought of as home. I didn't know until I made the connection with Murdo that she meant my house. I... I feel guilty for taking away her chance of living here.'

'*Tha mi 'tuigsinn.* I understand, dear.'

Peggy purses her lips thoughtfully, gaze fixed on me. I meet her eyes. *Stop it,* I want to tell her. *Stop looking at me like that.* But I find I'm pursing my lips in a similar way. Our silence is punctuated by the clink of cups on china, and Tatty's occasional drawn-out sigh.

---

Rabbits scatter across the machair, thumping warnings from the entrances to their burrows – *quick, hide.* Tatty gallops in crazy circles, close on the white fluffy tail of one rabbit after another, covering four times as much ground as me with her tiny legs. At the top of a hill I pause to catch my breath and disentangle myself from the strap of the bag I wear across my front. The dog collapses at my feet, panting. I perch on a smooth boulder, stretching out my throbbing leg.

The scenery looks Mediterranean with the spread of white sand against the vivid green of land, the transparent sea under a cloudless sky. Turning my gaze to the left I allow my eyes to rest on the cemetery – on a hill further along. My destination. 'Come on, Tatty, help me up.'

The other side of the hill has a steeper downward slope. I half-slide and angle my feet sideways so as not to take off in an uncontrolled run. At the bottom I rub my knee and stretch my back – pause to get my bearings and locate my destination, masked by surrounding hills. I catch Tatty by the collar and slip her lead on as we walk through a narrow gully between the hills, steep sides peppered with rabbit holes. White flags and drumming accompany us as we move through the otherwise eerie quiet. Tatty breaks it, yelping in delirium at the promise of such abundance of potential dinner. At the other end we emerge into the open again. I work out that the cemetery must be over the next hill.

Up a steep slope again and down another. I breathe quickly in the unseasonable warmth. There's a final, slighter climb before the walled graveyard comes fully into view. I can feel every hummock of grass and jutting-out stone through the soles of my trainers. I cling tightly to the strap of my bag with one hand and Tatty's lead with the other. When I reach the cemetery wall I tie the lead to the gate and withdraw a plastic tub and a bottle of water from my bag. Tatty laps thirstily. I take a swig of the remaining water in the bottle. She gives me a baleful stare from the shade of the stone wall as I move through the gate but it seems disrespectful to take a dog into a graveyard.

I search amongst the Donalds, Catherines, Murdos, Peggys and Angus's of many generations. Finally I find the grave of a six-month-old baby named Mhairi. *There's always a baby.* And this one is fitting, since I gave my Barbara the middle name of Mhairi. I kneel carefully before the old stone. *Mhairi, beloved daughter of Murdo and Peggy MacLennan.* No. But yes, it must be. The dates tie in with what I learned about the current Murdo's ancestor. My chosen resting place for Barbara is all the more poignant for this connection. I lay down an arrangement of stones and shells from the beach, choosing carefully from my collection – *baby's toenails* and mother-of-pearl shards. I make a heart shape, outlining the half-curve of a second heart within the first. I scan the graveyard and the road leading down the hill. Mhairi died a hundred and sixty-five years ago so I don't imagine anyone will mind if I claim her for my own.

*Every time the grief for Barbara washes over me it's as if I step to one side and observe myself, marvelling that it's lasted so long. Maybe if I'd had another child of my own the pain would have eased...* I dry my face, get stiffly to my feet, lean on the headstone for support. Now I need to continue my search amongst the monuments and adopt a grave for Sheena.

# 41

I WATCH THE first colours of sunset bloom over the sea from my kneeling position by the grave of Anna MacLeod. This young woman died when she was about the same age as Sheena, three decades after baby Mhairi – still long enough ago to be somebody's great aunt. Perhaps Peggy's. I feel justified in claiming her. I make a tiny alteration to the arrangement of shells I've laid on her grassy bed. Leaning back, I'm struck by the similarity to Sheena's decorative pattern of buttons on my Kindle cover.

After staggering painfully to my feet I'm short of breath. A piercing whine emanates from the other end of the field, followed by a sharp bark. Tatty! *How long have I left her tied up at the gate?* The light's draining rapidly from the sky and though I'm carrying a torch this time, a flutter of fear starts up in my chest. I want to be home.

And now I feel as though I'm floating, as if I'll be blown away with the next gust of wind – a sensation of absence from my own body. I force my feet down into the uneven clumps of grass, one step at a time, avoiding the age-old humps on the earth under which sleeping bodies lie. Grasp the iron of the gate, hear it creak shut behind me after what feels like an eon, bend to untie Tatty's lead. She huddles close to the ground with a low snarl when I try to pull her towards me, lips pulled back from her tiny snout. How odd, she's never greeted me with anything but adoration before. For a moment I can't breathe. Can't feel my own skin. Air blows through me before I succeed in gulping it into my lungs, before I feel solid again. Tatty sits up now, sniffs me and then bounces to her feet, wagging her tail. *It's you!*

'Good girl.' I'm left with an aftershock and still don't feel fully present. Maybe I'm just hungry, that's it. It must be – the strange emptiness is only down to lack of food. I'll cook something nutritious for dinner. I pull in several more deep breaths, fighting off panic – all I can think about is getting home. Aiming my head through the strap of the bag I settle it against my hip, grasp Tatty's lead firmly in one hand and switch on my torch. I direct it at the ground, find the path that leads down to the track at the bottom of the hill and make my way carefully over the uneven ground.

---

The light in the kitchen hurts my eyes. Tatty stands at my feet, panting. Then she points her nose at her bowl. I feed her and wash my hands, scrubbing my nails with the brush that lives on the wooden drainer by the scullery sink. When I've finished there are still traces of soil under them. I apply hand cream to my roughened skin.

Beat some eggs in a bowl and chop an onion, a stick of celery and a red pepper. My stomach's so hollow I can't think of anything more challenging than an omelette. The omelette reminds me of Murdo. A well bursts inside me, it should have been Murdo and Catriona inhabiting this kitchen, not me. I go back into the bathroom for a handful of tissue and blow my nose – snot blocks my sinuses. It's not fair that Catriona can't come home. *The raw sides of her head, her red-rimmed eyes, the crust of blood under her nose.* Inexplicably, I recognise myself in her.

'You could take her in,' Peggy finally voiced our simultaneous thought earlier. But it's not my place to, is it? And what about Murdo? The situation would be too uncomfortable.

*I came here to start again.*

Tatty's exhausted and has settled in her basket in the kitchen. She refuses to come through to the sitting room where I've already lit the wood burner. *Margaret* consents to join me, though. I need her tonight, and as if in response to my need she seems more solid than ever before. I imagine her nodding with approval at my sitting room, casting her eyes over the throws on the sofa and armchair. I imagine that she pushes the crocheted blanket off her legs as flames begin to lick at the logs in the stove. The room can't have changed much since her day.

I doze in the comforting heat. Later I wake to the sound of a car on the road outside. The engine noise is swiftly followed by the sweep of headlights around the walls of the room. *I forgot to draw the curtains.* Now I feel vulnerable, exposed. *Who could it be?* The car stops outside my house. Maybe Peggy forgot to give me something earlier – something that couldn't wait. Butterflies in my stomach – the mad, impossible idea that she's brought Catriona home. *Don't be silly, Lauren.*

I test my stiff knee by placing my foot on the floor before bringing my weight onto it. The pain has gone, totally gone, how odd. I fairly spring over to the window, lightweight as a lamb, pulling the curtain closed after sneaking a quick glance at the figure separating itself from the shape of the car in the dark. It's not Peggy – it's a man.

The gate creaks. I ready myself by the door, take two slow breaths before opening it a moment after the knock comes. It could have been either of them – but it's Neil.

*I want to look up at his face, the face I know is there across the table from me on the ferry, but I won't. Not yet.*

He's standing in the porch. My fingertips tingle. He rubs his hands together, sounds so normal.

'Cold comes down as soon as the light's gone, doesn't it?'

My sinuses prickle as they did at the graveside. 'You'd better come in, then. It's nice and cosy in here.' I feel awkward, like a girl bringing her boyfriend home for the first time.

'Wow, it is.' Neil shrugs off his duffle jacket, tucks it under his arm and stands on the threshold of the sitting room. His mouth curves at the corners, his eyes are warm. I seem to have floated into the centre of the room. The front door's closed but I don't remember shutting it. Perhaps I'm still half-asleep.

*Have I looked up yet?*

Perhaps Neil's a dream.

'Sorry Lauren. I shouldn't have just turned up like this, but I wanted to see you so badly. I know it's only a few days since we were together and we have plans for the weekend but it seems ages until then.' Not a dream, then. Neil takes a step closer. A faint vibration in my ear. I give my head a slight shake. 'Here, let me hang this up for you.' I snatch the garment from him, struggle to pull my gaze away from his scar. Extract myself from his proximity and drape the heavy jacket over a hook in the porch, flick off the light, push the porch door closed behind me. Braving contact, I slip my arm through his, waving my spare hand at the room.

'What do you think?'

'Yes, cosy. Really nice, Lauren.'

I watch him smile in profile, squeeze his arm, interlocked with mine – press it against me. My cheeks burn from the wave of heat flooding me, nothing to do with the smouldering logs in the stove.

'I'm thinking of having one of those installed.' Neil indicates the wood burner with his free hand. 'Get rid of the gas fire. Did I tell you, I put in an offer on my house? It's convenient for work, yet still out of town. Lovely location. I must take you there at the weekend... you'd love it. I know we'd planned to spend it here, but I'm here now instead, aren't I? Seriously Lauren, you'll love my house. Especially the field at the back and the quirky path to the sea, it's lined by wild rose bushes, you know. You'd love it,' he says for the third time. He's talking too quickly, trying to convince me of something.

'I love it *here*,' I counter. 'Wait 'til you see it in daylight.' Oops, have I just invited him to stay the night? I'm not sure. I stumble on. 'I'm also close to the sea. It's so fresh and raw here. And surrounded by mountains.' *There.* However much I might like his house, I love mine more. And there are, well, other people to think about.

'But this is so far away from town.'

'That's true, but I like it this way.' *Stalemate.* My arm's no longer tucked in his, I don't know which one of us pulled away first. There's a cold space between us now my personal heat source has switched off again. Neil's face falls.

'Shall I make us a pot of tea?' I force brightness.

'I'd love one. I came straight from the surgery – I don't know what made me do it. I reached my turnoff home as usual but I just kept on driving – couldn't help it. You must be magnetic, Lauren. I should have gone back as soon as I realised what I was doing. . .'

He trails after me through the dining room, glances at the rocking chair and the table and the laptop and at my files on the shelves in the alcove. 'I feel a bit of a goon now, to be honest. Sorry.'

I glance at him and see he's got his boyish face on. A nervous habit. 'Stop apologising, it's okay. I'm happy to see you.' *Smile, smile; look away quickly.* I don't know what's wrong with me. In the kitchen Neil clears his throat. 'Sorry for, well, apologising so much, I suppose. I'm out of practice at this, you know. Going out with someone and all that.'

The hairs on the back of my neck bristle but only slightly. I sniff. 'It's okay.' I open a cupboard and get out the teabags. 'I am, too. Oh, Tatty!' she takes me by surprise, erupting from her basket practically under my feet. She lets out three sharp, belated barks. Nevertheless she wags her tail at Neil.

'Aw, I forgot you have a dog. She's cute.' He sounds more Canadian than ever. 'You're cute, aren't you?' Gets on his knees and fondles Tatty's ears. 'You're a cute doggy, yes you are.' I picture the golden, lolloping Labrador I've attributed to his picture-perfect family in Canada. His children with golden hair and skin, too: healthy and outdoorsy. Standing at the kettle, resentment nibbles me. I keep my back to man and dog, so engrossed in each other, they're both forgetting about me. I bite my lip. The kettle comes to a noisy boil and I pour water on the teabags, replace the kettle. Forget myself for a moment. Come to with a start, plant my hands on the counter ready to turn and face Neil with a smile rather than the scowl that won't seem to leave.

When I do, he's only inches away. My eyes are parallel with the cabled neckline of the fisherman's jumper I imagine he bought at the market in Stornoway. An icicle breaks inside me. Neil places his hands on my shoulders. From the corner of my eye I can't help but see the scar leering at me, livid and red, and I wonder yet again if this can work. I already wrote the ending of us, there on his skin. *Blood for Barbara.*

But I remain in place, rippling like water through his fingers. His hands move purposefully down my arms, grip me back into solidity. He kisses the top of my hair and my head tilts of its own accord until my lips have found the hollow of his throat where they press themselves. *So familiar.* Then I turn my face wholly up to his, and his mouth closes over mine, and we go back to the past.

# 42

IT WAS ABOUT love, not sex. Communion. My body's changed with age – I have stiff joints and I suffer from something that's difficult to talk about. A *woman's problem* as Granny Mary would have called it. It could have spoiled things between us but it didn't. Somehow Neil knew what to do without me having to go into details – despite our overwhelming desire, each movement necessitated a carefulness we couldn't have imagined when we were young. But Neil was so gentle, I think as I lay in my pre-dawn bed, still half-asleep. His hands understood my altered physicality. His touch was as tender as if I'd been a newborn baby. He aroused me beyond belief and I felt... holy, that's the word. From the sounds he made I think he felt the same. I wrapped my arms around him until we'd both stopped shuddering and took his hand in mine, ran my finger repeatedly over that ridge of skin, acknowledged my authorship of it. I brought the scar to my lips and pressed them onto the buckled skin. Before we fell asleep, Neil whispered that he would rest beside me for a while but that he planned to get up at first light and go home, grab a couple more hours in his own bed before he had to go to work. He said he wouldn't wake me when he left and that I shouldn't feel deserted if I woke up and found he wasn't there.

I hadn't expected to sleep at all – thought my senses were too elevated. But sleep I did.

At almost dawn I open my eyes. Before I can properly

make out the room's shapes in the half-dark, I think I see Margaret sitting on the stool. But it's not her – only Neil's thick jumper draped across the edge of the dressing table and onto the stool where he dropped it in a hurry. My eyes rove the room, I search for Tatty on her blanket by the fireplace before I remember we shut her in the kitchen. Neil promised to let her in with me when he leaves.

Neil stirs behind me in the bed and I turn over to face him. He yawns and stretches, his body taut. Relaxing, he smiles and hooks a finger under my hair, tucking a stray curl behind my ear. His voice is morning-rough. 'Perfect. You still are, just as you always were to me. *Oh, Lauren.* I can't believe we've found each other again.'

'I think it's going to be okay,' I murmur. 'I really do. We've truly opened up to each other now, haven't we? Nothing left to hide. Mmm, oh, Neil. Thank you. It's wonderful to be with you again.' I know where I belong, now – it's here, with my nose nuzzled into the hair on his chest.

He strokes my hair and pushes himself up and I feel the air on my face as we separate. He leans over to kiss me on the mouth.

'It was wonderful, and it'll keep on being that way now we're together again.' He gives me an intense look.

I sense a frown forming between his eyes, though it's too dark to see properly. I push myself up in the bed and reach over to move the curtain aside. Pale light seeps into the room. Neil's eyes are more opaque than I expected. Something off about his gaze.

'What is it?'

'Are you properly awake, love?'

'What do you mean? Of course I am.' The feeling I had in the cemetery comes back to me, an uncomfortable hollowness at my core. 'Why are you asking that?'

'Oh, nothing, don't worry. Just that I wanted to tell you something but not if you're still half-asleep, that's all.' He fits his palm reassuringly over the side of my face. I turn my nose into it. It smells of us. A sharp jolt in my lower belly.

'Yes, I'm awake.' I'm coming to life again – can feel the tell-tale huskiness creep into my voice.

'*Love*. Ah... Mmm. Love, listen.' He gives me another kiss on the mouth and grasps my roving hand gently. 'Something I wanted to tell you. I meant to mention it last night but we, you know. You were just too irresistible.' He laughs.

The ring of his laugh cuts the air. I pull my hand away from his, aware of a sense of inevitability. I don't know – yet I *know* – what he's going to say. Certainly that it's something I won't want to hear, anyway.

'Now I'm starting to feel worried.' I pull the quilt up to cover my nakedness.

*Watching the hand-of-Neil, across the table. The scar blinking a warning. I won't look up. Not yet.*

'Don't be.' Neil swings his legs over his side of the bed, bends away from me to pick up his clothes and clears his throat. I count the knobbles of his spine in the increasing light. He still doesn't speak. Instead he stands to pull up his boxers, then sits again and slips his arms into the sleeves of his shirt. He turns to me as he fastens his buttons. 'Would you like me to bring you a cup of tea in bed, while we talk? I can let Tatty in, too.'

'Not yet, Neil. Just tell me, whatever it is.'

Neil posts one foot, then the other into his trouser legs. He stands again to zip up the trousers and fasten his belt. Grabbing his socks from the floor he spits out the words he needs to say quickly, the volume of his voice diminishing as he bends forward to pull each sock on. There's a pause in the air before I hear it properly.

'My daughter's coming to live with me.'

'What?!'

My limbs go heavy.

'Helen.' He mumbles her name into his chest. 'She wants to go to school over here. She thinks she can catch up with the work – it's less than a term, after all. Also, uhm, she's not getting along with her mother. So she's asked to come and live with me.'

Neil stands again, walks around the end of the bed and kneels by my side, kisses me on the forehead, sits back on his heels, his eyebrows raised. 'I can't say no, can I?' His face is open, trusting.

*Of course. Why didn't I realise? I could never have got away with pretending his children don't exist.* As the silence ticks on, a shutter comes over his face. He licks his lips, stretches a hand out to the dressing table stool and transfers his weight on to it, regaining his feet. He turns half-away from me as he stoops again to pick up his fisherman's jumper. The garment now looks ridiculous. *Who's he kidding? He's a doctor, for Heaven's sake, not a fisherman.* His head pops out like a jack-in-the-box from the cable-stitched neck. Towering over the bed he folds his arms, studies me, reads my contained silence with infuriating attention. Heat floods my skin. Slowly, Neil's face changes again, defensiveness setting in. The frown between his eyebrows deepens. I still haven't said anything, I can't.

'I'm sorry if that *upsets* you, Lauren. But she *is* my daughter. I'm not going to say no to her. Anyway, I want her here – of course I do.'

Of course he does.

Right in front of my eyes, my newfound *Neil-from-before* retreats back into his shell. My blood comes to the boil. It's as if hot oil floods every bone and muscle in my body and they all suddenly ache. I put my hand up to my neck, feeling the glands there swelling under my fingers.

I swallow painfully. My mouth opens and closes.

'Well, it's funny you should be telling me this now, Neil,' I hear myself saying in a croaking voice. 'Because I have some news of my own. A girl is coming to live with *me*, as well. A girl probably about the same age as your daughter.' I watch his mouth fall open, just like mine. 'Her name's Catriona. This is her home as much as it is mine and I'm not going to deny her the chance to live here.'

# PART THREE

I can never hold onto this.
When January beckons,
with its nothing-to-do,
we'll frighten ourselves recluse.

**From *Love in the Cold*, By Nick Conroy**

# 43

## *On the foam of the sea*

At a time when travel for many is easy and anodyne, their voyages through the Sahara, the Balkans, or across the Mediterranean – on foot, in the holds of wooden fishing boats, on the backs of land cruisers – are almost as epic as that of classical heroes such as Aeneas and Odysseus.

*Patrick Kingsley, The New Odyssey, Guardian Books and Faber & Faber Ltd, 2016*

**Isabella MacDonald – Isle of Lewis to Nova Scotia, 1841**

Isabella saw a man being chased by a policeman. He tried to hide in the Marram but the policeman called the men with the dogs and the dogs hunted him down. The man did not want to leave his country but was forcibly brought onto the ship and he was guarded by policemen until it was time for the ship to sail. It was a long journey to Canada. People had sold most of their worldly goods to help pay for the passage but supplies on board became so low that the people felt they were starving. Not that they weren't used to that. Families crowded together in the hold and many of the children got sick. Their parents threw the little bodies overboard for burial at sea. Many services were held on board for the departed.

Isabella and Donald were lucky to survive and arrive in Nova Scotia healthy. They found that they were expecting their first baby. It was a son whom they named Angus Felix, because Isabella had learned from somewhere that *Felix* means happy.

### Phuong Nguyen – Vietnam to the UK, 1978

Phuong's family lived in fear of reprisals. Her grandfather owned a thriving general store. Piece by piece, he sold everything and bought a boat named *Tu Do*, meaning 'Freedom'. The vessel was designed to look like a fishing boat. This was to avoid suspicion – theirs wasn't the only family planning to escape. Phuong's grandfather pretended that his fishing boat's engine had broken down and he was fixing it but in reality he was replacing it with a more powerful engine. The family had to push the boat across many kilometres of tidal water at night, in silence, before Grandfather started the motor. On the journey they were chased by pirates in the Gulf of Thailand. Their engine was powerful enough to escape but it was at the expense of another vessel which they had to watch go down. One night there was a great storm. In the huge waves Phuong's grandmother and two young cousins were washed overboard. They could not find the bodies the next morning. The family were permitted to disembark as refugees in Malaysia. They were exhausted and dehydrated. After a month, Phuong's father was successful in gaining an audience with a UK Embassy official and was granted asylum in Scotland. He, his wife and children travelled to the UK. Grandfather and Phuong's aunt and uncle remained behind in Malaysia with their surviving child.

### Israa Nasri – Syria to Germany, 2015

There was silence in her head. Israa looked out to sea. Her father was in the water, struggling to hold Sami above the waves. Israa could see the bobble on Sami's hat, and his little arms splashing frantically. She saw his open mouth and willed him to close it and to stop fighting, to trust that Papa would keep him safe. Her head then filled with the sounds of panicked cries and the whoosh of air exploding from the dinghy. The boat slid away beneath them. She held onto her mother, and when the freezing water sucked them under she kept her face close to her mother's ear, telling her to stay calm, that they would be all right. They were so close to the shore. Israa kicked hard and kept her grip on her mother. They were crashed against a rock by a strong wave. Israa made her mother hold on. Then a wave took Israa by surprise and her mouth was full of seawater, she thought she was going to choke. But a strong man strode waist-deep through the churning water and lifted her mother out. Israa vomited onto the rock. With frightened eyes she watched the vomit dissolve into the seawater. The man came back for her, he carried her out and placed her next to her shivering mother on the stony beach. That was only the beginning of their journey.

# 44

## *Uig, Isle of Lewis, September 2016*

I CAN'T GET warm. I've turned the heating up and re-lit the wood burner in the sitting room – the sawdust logs were still faintly alight and the room felt cosy when I emerged from the bedroom this morning. But still I'm huddled under a quilt on the sofa, the chills deep in my bones. I have Granny's patchwork throw tucked around my feet and a hot water bottle on my stomach (not to mention Tatty), but nothing makes a difference. It started when Neil told me about his daughter coming to live with him – the pain flooded into my joints and my throat felt sore. I ache so badly now and my skin burns. I'm also sore between the legs from what Neil and I did, but that's not something I tell Jessica when I call work.

'Are you on your own?' she asks. 'Do you want me to ring your neighbour and ask her to check on you?'

I picture *she-who-was-dropped-on-her-head.* More realistically it would be Peggy and she'll no doubt be over in due time anyway. News of my rapid-onset illness will magically get to her – if not that of a mysterious car turning up in the middle of the night and driving away again in the early hours of the morning. *Oh, she'll find out.* Her probable disapproval looms large in my fevered brain.

'No, I'm fine, Jess,' I lie. 'Don't fuss. Just ensure Rab

makes alternative arrangements for my clients today. He can see one or two of them himself. I'm sure I'll be better by tomorrow...'

'You don't *sound* as though you will. Have you called a doctor?'

A painful choke of laughter sets me off coughing. There's a muffled sound, as of Jessica's hand covering the phone. 'Everyone wishes you a speedy recovery,' she comes back on. 'Check in with us tomorrow so we won't worry too much.'

'I will,' I promise. But my voice has already crumbled to dust.

It must be the fever, because throughout the day I perceive shadowy figures lurking at the edges of my blurred vision. When I first came to live here I brought Margaret to life, but only with my imagination... or so I thought. Now she seems more solid than me. Fussing over me. I swear she even refilled my bottle of water. It's much cooler to the touch the next time I reach out for it. I distinctly remember the last few dregs that had remained tasting warm. I see other figures too, ones I hadn't previously imagined. Two boys in dark clothes, playing on the floor, a different rug covering it. Even Tatty notices them. From the corner of my eye I see her tail wagging. She spends most of the day laid across my feet, which are still cold. Next I see a younger woman and a man – I guess they must be the boys' parents. Oh, that would mean the young woman is Margaret, too. She's less present than the older Margaret but I'm sure I manage to catch her eye as she bends to scoop the youngest boy up from the floor and carry him out of the room. She gives me a faint smile.

I must have slept. When I come to again Tatty's claws are digging into my chest. The quilt and the throw have ridden down my body. The dog stands over me, peering intently into my face, the tip of her tongue peeping out and withdrawing slightly each time she pants. She whimpers when I try to swallow the thicket of thorns in my throat. I reach for the water bottle but find it empty. The young Margaret must have better things to do than look after me.

'Move, then,' I croak at Tatty. She edges backwards, paws now digging in to my bladder. I *need* to get up for a pee. With small movements I manage to push away the quilt and the throw. Everything wavers in front of my eyes, as in a heat haze. Tatty slithers to the floor, widens her dark beads of eyes and keeps them fixed on me. She dances backwards. Wincing from the pain, I lift my legs one after the other and place each foot on the floor. Tatty yaps encouragingly.

'Shhhh, it hurts.' She continues her backwards trajectory. My progress across the floor towards her is precarious, I could do with something to hold on to. *Where's Margaret when you need her?* Or Peggy. Or... no. Neil's going to be busy from now on. He's put in an offer on his two-bedroomed house. 'I'm planning to have an extension built,' he'd said. 'But there won't be room for a second teenager as well. Why would you want to take in a stranger, for goodness' sake?'

*Why would I want to take in your daughter?* I make it across the room.

Fastening my hands around the back of a dining chair, I do a visual scan with careful movements of my eyes. Nobody here except me and Tatty. Margaret's rocking chair is empty. A few more steps and I'm at the kitchen door, hanging on to the frame. I was really hoping to find Peggy standing at the sink, or peeling open the wrapper of a Battenberg cake at the table. *It's Murdo who likes Battenberg, not me.* For a fraction of a second I think I see Catriona coming in at the back door – even Tatty's head jerks round with a sharp movement. *Catriona's hair has grown back at the sides, it looks kind of pretty – velvety, and she has a long ponytail down her back.*

*Silly me. She's not here. Not yet.*

Coughing, I open the scullery door and muster enough strength to lift Tatty's bag of food down. Keep hold of the counter while she gobbles until the bowl's empty. Then I feel my way across the kitchen to the porch, nudge her outside the back door with a weak foot. 'Don't you dare run away to

Mrs Her-on-her-head,' I think I say. Tatty scuttles over to the bushes on her short legs and sniffs around for a suitable place to pee, her eye still on me.

In the bathroom I lower myself creakily onto the toilet. When I've managed to get myself upright again I wash my hands and then my face, which looks swollen. Like someone who's been underwater too long. It gives me the creeps. I look at anything but that horrible reflection – at the ceramic whale on the end of the toilet chain, the stainless steel coating of the handwash-dispenser, the ornate hook on the bathroom door. In the kitchen I refill my bottle, watch water streaming over the top, over my shaking hands, and feel a deep, numbing chill. *It's the water.* Wrench the tap off, turn away. Grab a packet of biscuits from the cupboard in case I want to eat later, though I can't imagine such a thing at the moment. I wait for Tatty to take a long drink from her water bowl. Then I lock both back doors and retreat gratefully through the rooms to my sofa with its pile of covers, my little dog trotting ahead of me.

---

It must be late afternoon – still light – but the sun's low in the sky and the rays shine on a different part of the room from when my eyes were last open. Tatty's wedged between me and the back of the sofa, her eyes fixed on my face. Perhaps she's never looked away. I swallow, surprised that I no longer feel pain. Push the covers away from my face. *I feel different.* Tatty scrabbles to her feet as I push myself upright, her legs akimbo on the quilt. She growls softly and wags her tail.

*Amazing.* Perhaps I'll be back at work tomorrow after all – my illness seems to have receded as rapidly as it came. I move my legs and feel an unfamiliar chafing between my thighs. *Ah, Neil!* Then there's a slump of disappointment in my chest as I remember about Helen. The dog drags her tongue over the back of one of my hands while I stroke her wrinkled forehead with my other, gulping down sadness.

Tatty makes her squeaky-toy noise. I swallow hard and clear my throat. 'Help me up, then.' I allow her to think she's dragging me off the sofa.

I'm slightly giddy when I stand up (I have to reposition myself once or twice for balance on my way across the room) but I feel much, much better. I move on smoothly-oiled joints along the wall to the dining room door, then feel my way via the chair-backs to the bedroom corridor. On impulse I continue a few steps past my bedroom and push open the door of the other. With the curtains pulled mostly to, it's dark in here. *I wonder where Catriona slept when she stayed here with her grandmother and Murdo – did he sleep in the sitting room and let her have this room, or did she go in with Janet?* 'Catriona's room,' I say softly. Tatty tips her head sideways.

I'll begin the proceedings as soon as possible – with Catriona's approval, of course. I'm already cleared for fostering. *If I'd gone ahead with Sheena* – well, I wouldn't be standing in this cottage with Tatty now, would I?

---

I could walk indefinitely. No part of me hurts anymore, not a muscle or a joint, not even my bad knee. My head's as clear as a bell. My skin tingles where the air seems to blow through it. *This day has gone on forever.*

Tatty and I walked all the way around the loch. The otter appeared, sleekly popping its head out of the water, twitching its whiskers. Tatty sat by my heels as we watched him swim over to the far bank. Then, stepping off the marshy path onto the stony track opposite where my walk began, I looked up at the mountains and guess what? I spotted the red deer, stalking along the ridge above the road – a hunter in his attitude, not prey.

We're climbing the hill to the cemetery now. I want to say goodnight to my girls. Tatty whines as I loop her lead around the bar of the gatepost, knowing I'm about to leave her. But she flops onto her stomach resignedly. She's panting, tired from the long walk but I still feel fine. I climb to the top of the sloping field and visit Anna/Sheena first. I lay a fresh stone from the edge of the loch – sleek and black like a wet otter's head – on top of the pile I made for her yesterday. I shall try and bring a new stone every time I come.

*And now for my baby.* The need to see her is as strong as ever. But when I stand to search out Mhairi/Barbara's grave I see the dark-coated figure of a man. Standing exactly where I'm headed. *What?* Through the still bright evening – it must be evening by now, surely? I think I recognise him as Murdo, but he looks different. Why would Murdo visit the grave of his ancestral relative? *A baby.*

Perhaps he wanted to further our conversation about Catriona and decided to stop off at the cemetery on the way. Perhaps it's a thing here, that you pay your respects to your ancestors. It's not the anniversary of the baby's death, I know that much. Anyway, surely he would more fittingly lay tribute at the graves of his parents and sister, lower down the field in the newer area of the cemetery? I move carefully between the mounds towards baby Mhairi's grave in the centre of the field, but pause when I get closer. Murdo's presence feels ominous. I can feel my pulse jangling in my throat. Murdo's face is pinched, shadowed with dark stubble, his eyes glazed. Everything about his demeanour is different to when I last saw him. He wears an unusual coat, long and thick. And close against his coat, wrapped in a dirty blanket, he's clutching a baby.

# 45

A BABY.

I resist an instinct to reach out and say *give it to me*. Instead I keep my arms to myself. The dark-haired baby, a *she* I'm sure of it, swivels her eyes towards me. She wriggles in the confines of the oily wool, struggles to release her arms, fights to lever herself upright. But he holds her in that uncomfortable prone position, too tightly. The blanket's thick and roughly woven. Grubby and holed. Murdo hadn't seemed the type to let his appearance go but I see that his clothes are as stained as the baby's blanket – the collar of his shirt greyish against the lapels of the black coat. It's not just his unkemptness that sits so strangely but his cheeks are hollow, his facial structure slightly different. How can he have lost so much weight since I last saw him? Despite his thick coat his malnourished appearance is obvious.

His eyes look dangerous. Alarm bells ring but I ignore them and take another step forward

'Hello?'

He's either bitten his lip or someone's hit him. The skin round his mouth's cracked and sealed with dried blood. There's a bruise on his cheekbone, too, though it may simply be a dirty mark. He doesn't answer but his eyes flicker restlessly. Can he even see me? I think back to when he was in my kitchen and his teasing manner, the hint of flirtation. Even on the phone the other night. But there's no sign of humour now. *Something's happened.* He has the look of a madman.

'Murdo?'

His eyes are slitted now under half-closed lids.

'Aye, what's it to you?' *A voice like an old man.*

'Nothing. I, err, is there anything I can do to help?' A cold pit in my stomach – bottomless. He doesn't recognise me. 'It's Lauren, remember? I'm renting your house.'

The baby sneezes. She needs her nose wiped. I feel in my pocket for a tissue, fingers closing over several folded squares. I itch to pinch the green mucus from the baby's face, as I've done so many times for clients' children. What on earth is Murdo doing with this baby? Peggy would have told me if she was his. She – the baby – wriggles again, squawking frustration. Green snot slides down her cheek. 'Maaa,' she lets out. I move closer.

'Bá, mo leanbh.' My mouth puppets unfamiliar shapes. The baby whips her face towards me and my fingers tingle. I wedge them under my arms. Switching my gaze to Murdo I think what to do.

'I don't know what's happened, but you must let me help you with this baby.' Perhaps he's on drugs. He's got that glazed look I've seen so often. What if it was *Murdo* who supplied Catriona with Skunk and that's why she's cross with him? And where the hell did he get the baby? *Oh God, there could be a woman hurt somewhere, overdosed, and he's on the run with their child...* My training kicks in.

'I'm sure we can sort this out. Let me help you with the baby. Her nose needs wiping, and she's crying, look at her. Here, I've got some tissue.' I pull it from my pocket. He stares at it dully. 'What's happened, Murdo? You look unwell. Please, let me take the baby.'

He licks cracked lips. A stream of Gaelic pours out which I don't understand.

'I'm sorry, would you please speak English?' I use my most professional voice – he looks like a cornered animal.

'Rentin' ma hoose?' he suddenly barks. 'What are ye talking about, woman? The laird moved us all out of oor hooses and well ye know it.'

He must have tightened his grip, for the baby screams and strains in his arms. A tide of nausea rises in my throat. I swallow it down and take a firm step towards him. Whatever this madness is, my instinct is to ensure the baby's safety.

'Give her to me.'

The force of my demand makes him look at what he's holding and I see the humanity in his eyes, the effort of restraining emotion. *He's not on drugs.* I have no doubt of this. I force my voice to come out steadily and banish the racing questions in my head. Murdo coughs. The baby fights harder in his arms.

'Tell me, I might be able to help. What's the problem?'

He holds my eyes with his. Tortured, blue eyes that were laughing only a few weeks ago. Sweat coats his forehead, strands of hair plaster his skin. His brow furrows, dark eyebrows coming together.

'It's Peggy,' he gasps. 'Ma Peggy. She's sick and she willnae wake up. Ah need a wet nurse for the babe, just until ma Peggy's better.'

*He's not Murdo.* Not the Murdo I know, anyway. For a moment I claw the air to stay upright. Something's happened – I can't understand how, or what, but the sudden cessation of my fever was a clue to this mystery. I can see that much. The strength I found from nowhere for the massive walk Tatty and I have undertaken – I knew it was impossible. The way the sky's still light, though hours must have passed since I left the cottage. The way my body feels no pain, even my knee. Yet my heart does. *The baby.* The baby is all that matters.

He holds me with his pleading look. He calls me ma'am. He says it again, 'Will ye take her for me, Ma'am, for Peggy's sake? Look after her until ma Peggy's better, then I'll come and fetch her hame.' His arms, around the squirming bundle, loosen.

'I will.'

It strikes me like a hurled stone. With the agreement I'm well aware of what I'm giving up.

The earth rocks under my feet. When I feel steady again I glance at the cinnamon sky and the deepening blue of the mountains. At the grass of the hills, so vividly green. Down on the machair by the sea the rabbits play, oblivious. Their white tails flashing warnings. And I, I hold out my arms. Murdo's scent is stale as he transfers the baby into them.

I adjust her position to hold her upright, because I know she prefers it that way. Loosen the blanket so she can have her arms free – it's not cold, after all. She stops crying and tilts her face to mine, her delicate hands patting my shoulders. Her bottom lip hangs open and her eyes widen. Her hair's lighter than I'd thought it would be. I examine every detail of her face and the soft folds of her neck, while Murdo turns away without another word. From the corner of my eye I see him striding down the hill between the gravestones.

I refocus my attention on the baby. She is, of course, my very own Barbara.

## 46

'A THASGAIDH!' At last I get to wipe the snot from Barbara's nose. She splutters, then laughs and I do too. I stroke the silk of her hair. Shift her into a more comfortable position on my arm and she dives to tuck her head under my chin, her mottled arms together at the elbows. *Neil, if you could see us now...* But it's too late for that. Barbara settles into me and her small hands curl into buds on my chest. I step carefully between the gravestones. As I pass through the gate, Tatty crouches against the wall. She gives me the same frightened growl as the last time I left the cemetery. When I bend my knees she presses her body down onto the damp grass. I stretch one hand towards her, fingers extended. Studying me with her blackbird-like eyes, she finally gives an uncertain wag of the tail. I allow her time to sniff.

Dew begins to settle. *Now the day is over, night is drawing nigh. Shadows of the evening steal across the sky.* A song Granny taught us. The dog eyes the baby, unconvinced. I persuade her to sniff the edge of the blanket, and then the baby's wee foot. The baby wiggles her toes. Tatty makes an odd noise in her throat. The baby curves herself over the roundness of my tummy. I unhook Tatty's lead with my spare hand.

We walk down the trodden path to the stony track, Tatty at the utmost end of her lead and to one side of me but she doesn't pull. We cross the track and she waits, trembling, while I unhook the metal gate at the bottom of the field leading up to our house. I bend again, holding the baby securely in my arm. The baby pats my neck, laughing. Her chortle goes right through me and I'd do anything for her. I mustn't think about what could have been. When I've let Tatty off the lead she gallops up the hill ahead of me. The Highland cattle are nowhere around. Holding Barbara close, I follow Tatty with no effort at all, in fact I can barely feel my body. Except the parts that touch Barbara. The sky darkens rapidly as we go through the second gate into our garden. *Sileadh e a-nis!* – We're home and dry now.

When I turn and look behind me I notice several inky clouds descending towards the sea.

---

The night with the baby is the best of my life. Barbara doesn't cry anymore, only smiles and chortles. She burbles playfully and reaches for my hair. I take her into the dining room where I set a match to the newspaper and kindling I always keep ready in the fireplace. We sit together in the rocking chair and play pat-a-cake. She manages to grasp one of my curls in her tiny fist, pulls tighter and tighter until I wince. I gently disentangle the strands. When I open her palm to check I haven't hurt her, I see red lines left by my hair. She looks at me with the inside of her wet lower lip exposed. Her cheeks are flushed.

After a little while Tatty trots through from her basket in the kitchen. She whines and I offer soothing noises but the baby's my priority now – Tatty will just have to fit in. Barbara takes no notice of Tatty, even when she consents to lick the baby's toes. I hoist Barbara up so her cheek rests on my shoulder. I hear her snuffling breath. I only want to hold her while she sleeps. She gums my neck and I breathe her in. But she doesn't sleep.

I think I may have dozed off, whereas Barbara's still wide awake in my arms. I look for Tatty but she must have gone back to her basket. The baby's sparkling eyes have turned a darker shade of brown. I press my lips to the curve of her cheek, over and over. She thinks it's a game and I let her. My eyelids are drooping again.

Barbara peels my lips apart with tiny, probing fingers. I come to with a jolt. The room reforms itself into familiar shapes once I've wiped the sleep from my eyes. Barbara laughs and bats her hands at invisible things. The rags she has on in place of a nappy ought to be soaked through, but they're dry. Still, babies need to be bathed. I hold her against my chest and go through to the kitchen. Then an idea prompts me back towards the dining room. I see that the sitting room door's ajar – I avert my eyes from the couch where I lay so ill before. The stove in there's gone out but the chill emanating through the door is more disquieting than the mere lack of a heat source.

So I pull that door closed and move towards the corridor, the floor cold under the socked soles of my feet. I hurry into the end bedroom. Barbara's quick breaths and a trickle of dribble tickle my neck and she babbles, her fingers opening and closing like starfish. From the cupboard in the alcove I pull out a woven basket. Shield Barbara's face while I blow the dust off. From the shelf I take a clean sheet and fold it into the bottom of the basket with one hand. I cuddle Barbara with my spare arm and she grabs at my clothes and wraps her arms tightly around my neck. In my own bedroom I peel Barbara away from my neck. I place her in the basket on the bed, where she lies staring up at the ceiling. I leave her to kick her feet while I pull a suitcase out from underneath the bed. At the bottom, in a yellowed paper bag, is the cream shawl Ruth knitted. I slide the shawl from the bag, smooth the folds of it out over my knee – slip the old-new softness between my fingers. Barbara's eyes flick over my face. 'Maaa,' she says, smacking her lips.

I carry the cradle, baby and all, back to the kitchen.

There I run warm water into the sink and test it with my elbow, like Maw used to when she bathed the babies in the jawbox at our auld tenement hoose. I balance baby Barbara on my lap while I unfasten the ribbons at the back of her grubby gown. She gurgles, swivels her head on its stalk-like neck, seeming surprised at having her bare body exposed. I assess her with my social worker's eye. *Ma wee lassie.* She feels plumper than when I first took her from Murdo's arms. She lifts her arms up to me.

I cup water over her tummy and gently rub her hair. She kicks and chortles. When the water in the sink's cool I lift her out and wrap her in a towel. Carry her back to the dining room fireside. She gums my neck as I cuddle her, rocking in the chair. I think I'm weeping.

'Whit shall we put on you, ma wee barra? Your gownie's aw glabber.'

In the end I grab a t-shirt from the pulley and cut into the neck. Tie the ends together to make it fit. Fold a tea towel into a makeshift nappy.

*Thank goodness for the safety pins in my first-aid box.* With Barbara fastened into the chequered nappy and my old t-shirt a droonin' her, I swaddle her in Ruth's shawl.

Time to rock ma bairn in ma arms. '*I'll wan' a pho'ograph, mind,*' Ruth said when she presented me with the shawl. '*Right after the barra's born.*'

'I'll get the camera,' I murmur to the baby. It's only fair to Ruth.

Barbara coos in agreement, one hand poking out of the shawl. She grasps a bunch of the tassels around its edge. Holding her in the crook of my arm I move over to the sideboard for my camera. With it balanced on the table and the timer set, I move in front of it. I lift Barbara up next to my face and hold her there. We both smile.

---

I need to brave the unnatural chill of the sitting room to fetch Granny Mary's patchwork throw from the back of the sofa. Trying not to look, I shake off the used tissues and the memories of my delirium. One of those sudden Hebridean storms is raging outside the house – the spindly tree in the front garden bowing almost to the ground. Things clatter against the fence. The sea must be crashing wildly against the cliffs. I shiver. *She-who-was-dropped-on-her-head*'s lights flicker in the gap between her curtains and for a moment I miss normality. I miss Peggy and hope she's got plenty of candles in her kitchen drawer. Knowing Peggy, she will have. If things were as they should be, Peggy would have rung me to check if I needed anything. Neil would have rung me to say sorry that I became upset and to ask if I'm all right and should he come over? Even though it would be stupid in this weather. *Oh, Neil. You should be here with us. You should see our beautiful baby...* Murdo – the one I know – would have wanted to check that the house is secure in the storm.

But instead I have Barbara, waiting for me in her basket on the dining room table. *The only thing that matters.*

The lights are out but it's no longer of any consequence to me. I shore up the fire and tuck Barbara – still wrapped in her shawl – and me underneath the patchwork cover in the rocking chair. Suddenly Margaret's joined us. She sits on one of the hard-backed chairs at the table, watching. She nods approvingly. But something's wrong with Barbara. The baby's wrestling with her covers, raking her head searchingly from side to side, bumping my collarbone with her forehead. My breasts tingle. *Ah.* I know what she needs. My breasts feel swollen and sore – the milk's come back. Under Granny Margaret's tutoring gaze I lift my jumper and feed my nipple carefully into Barbara's mouth. A rush of woozy hormones reaches my head. I can see the workings of Barbara's jaw in the firelight, suckling contentedly. Her hand closes and opens on the tassels of the shawl.

# 47

I FALL ASLEEP again. When my eyes reopen I find Barbara gazing up at me, her contours soft in the dawn light. My jumper's slipped back down over the breast she'd been feeding from. Wind rages at the window. I hear the occasional crash and boom of the distant sea, audible in the gaps between gusts. It's warm and cosy in the room. At a movement on my foot I look down to find Tatty leaning against my leg, shivering.

'Hey, girl, it's all right,' I whisper. 'No need to be afraid.' Barbara opens her mouth in a gummy grin and I can't resist blowing bubbles on her cheek.

Tatty leaps up and barks shrilly. 'Don't be jealous...' I start to say. Then I too hear the knocking on the back door, insistent above the storm. Tatty's ears lay flat against her head and her tail quivers between her legs. She shivers violently.

Cold rushes through me. I check and yes, Barbara's as solid as ever. I tighten the shawl around her. The knock comes again. I stand, the patchwork throw slipping down my legs. *Soon, Granny Mary.* Tatty presses herself against my ankles, blocking my path. She makes a high-pitched noise I've never heard before, angling her head at me with a pleading glance. The whites of her eyes show. She tries growling, lips peeled back from her teeth – a warning, not a threat.

'You stay here, Tatty-girl.' Regret blocks my throat. 'I'm sorry but you can't come with me. Stay here by the fire.'

She whines but obeys me, good dog that she is. I glance behind. She's mussing up the fallen quilt, digging into it, settles with her nose tucked under her tail. My sweet dog. I swallow the lump in my throat. I knew what I was doing when I accepted the baby.

I move through into the kitchen. Manage awkwardly to open the back door with the baby in my arms. I have to reshuffle Barbara into a more secure position – babies are so wriggly and slippery! As soon as I step out into the porch the cold hits me and I see how bad the storm's been. There's broken glass on the floor, a bag of sawdust-logs has been split open – disgorged among the shards. I pull the first door to behind me, thinking even now of Tatty's dainty feet. Outside, the barn door hangs off its hinges and scattered machinery from the workshop litters the flattened grass. Whispers of fog writhe, suspended above the ground.

Murdo's there, standing on the other side of the glass door with his hands shoved into the pockets of his black coat. The light's behind him so I can't see his features properly. I take a couple of steps forward, trying to avoid the broken glass. Barbara's getting heavier, I hold her against my chest with one arm and balance with my hip against the window frame, using my free hand to hold my boots in place while I shove my feet into them. *I won't need a coat.* I push open the door to outside. As I suspected, I can't even feel the power of the wind though all the branches are bending and the broken barn door crashes to and fro. I push the porch door closed behind me.

Murdo turns away without speaking – not the Murdo I know. Beckons me to follow him through the gate onto the field. My jaw chatters. I feel butterflies in my stomach, a sudden panic – *it's all right, Barbara's safe.* She tucks her small head under my chin, curls her hands loosely on my chest – sleepy at last. Murdo indicates something moving through the faint mist. *Oh yes. His Peggy.* I cup the back of Barbara's head possessively in my hand and nip at strands of her hair with my lips. I'll breathe her in. Granny Mary's friend Aoifer used to pinch Meg's cheeks and say *I could eat you up*. And I get that. I just want to keep Barbara inside me.

The figure on the hill approaches.

*Should I look up from the table yet? Neil's hand draws closer as the sea swirls. The buckled skin of his scar reflects the white horses on the waves outside. No, not yet.*

I'll do anything, *anything* not to give Barbara up. Sweet sorrow washes through me – *you really were mine*. But then I see that the approaching woman isn't Peggy at all. She's me, when I was young. Her hair in a curly ponytail. *It's me.* I'm distraught, the young me – my cheeks blotched from crying – until I see the baby.

Then I open my arms, making a strange, animal sound. I pass Barbara over willingly to the young me. I have to turn away at how her face crumples before it smooths out into neat planes. I'm telling Barbara a story that sounds suspiciously similar to *The Sea Baby*. My baby is fast asleep now.

'Wait,' I call softly, so as not to wake her. But the young me isn't listening and she won't stop. She's off to live her life.

*Is it time, yet?*

*It's time. I look up from the scar on the back of his hand and I see his face. Neil, sitting opposite me at the table on the ferry. We look into each other's eyes. Time melts.*

Then – I'm swimming. But my head hurts from the bash it took as I lowered myself, hands slipping on the rocky edge, into the canal to save Sheena. My heart pounded impossibly hard while I hung off the ledge before letting go, my head already aching. Too late I realised I should have used the ring. But all I could think about was her panicked cries and I was desperate to help her. I didn't think properly. I do manage to get hold of Sheena though and force the ring over her head when my colleague on the bank throws it to me. Sheena's thrashing legs kick water into my face as Angel drags her away from me with the life-ring. My girl calls my name as she's whisked away to helping hands.

*Sheena's safe.*

Angel throws the ring back in for me. I see it landing on the water with a splash. It's not too far away but too far for me. I've gone under the surface by now.

Underneath the water I open my eyes. A baby swims towards me, her eyes and mouth wide open as if she can breathe in this element. I recognise her. Of course I do.

*Both my girls are safe.* I open my arms and Barbara swims into them.

# 48

*Ferry to Stornoway, September 2016*

**Neil**

THE SCAR ON the back of his right hand throbs, like it often does when he's tired or under stress. Saying goodbye to his kids has been the hardest part of the past few months but leaving Naomi, too, however impossible their marriage was – well, it was more painful than he'd imagined. Canada's so far away. Accepting the GP position in the Outer Hebrides is the final step out of his comfort zone. But he needed to do something new, some*where* new, and now there's no going back.

The ferry throbs beneath his feet. Staring through the glass display case he scrutinises the pastries on offer. His head's an absolute fucking whirl. When did he start thinking in swearwords, anyway? *Custard croissant or a pecan-and-maple Danish.* It should be simple enough but hell, he can't decide. Someone nudges into him from behind and he sees he's holding up the queue...

Neil steps aside to allow a stream of people past. Choosing between a pecan Danish and a custard-filled croissant becomes the pinnacle of all the choices he's had to make in the last year. He could have stayed in Nova Scotia to be nearer the kids but something pushed him all the way back to Scotland. His mother? Moving to her home country after she died soothed him once, as he hopes being closer to where she grew up will soothe him again now. *Balm to all his frenzied pain.* His father's ancestry could also be the influence behind his choice of the job on the islands, rather than the one he was offered in Aberdeen. He's tired of self-analysing.

Why couldn't Naomi have forgiven him. . . ? He'd only had a *tiny* affair. But Naomi lives with her new boyfriend now. And Neil's teenage children have told him they're happier in that house than they were in their parents' marital home. So many shouted arguments and the silences that were probably even worse... well, it seems best he stays out of the way. *But he'd expected Naomi to argue with him.*

His few weeks in Edinburgh prior to the ferry trip have helped him get his thoughts in order. Revisiting old haunts, reliving old memories. He'd thought he might bump into *her*; that she would have been magically transported back to Edinburgh for the benefit of his nostalgia. But rationally, he knows she left the city before he did. She probably never came back. Anyway, the Festival was on, he would never have spotted her in the crowds. His scar throbs again as he stands to one side of the queue and thinks of Lauren. He'll never forget the panic of that moment. . .

*The way she went at him with the knife! Yet all he was trying to do was put his arms around her. She always had a short temper, Lauren. She held grudges. That was why she refused to get over the thing that happened.*

*He had to explain some of it to Naomi when she told him she wanted to have a baby. He said the decision was difficult for him because of the loss of his first child. 'You had a baby before?' 'Yes – no – not exactly.' He told her Lauren had lost the baby. The scar on his hand he explained away as an accident – she'd been cutting vegetables and when he reached across her for a teaspoon from the cutlery jar, her hand had slipped. She'd been all over the place at the time because of the baby.*

*Naomi had been sympathetic, towards both him and Lauren.*

'Are you in this queue or not?' A fat, old woman's trying to get past him now.

'I, err, sorry. Yes, I am.' He reaches under the counter for the pair of tongs and dumps a custard croissant on a plate, decision made. Taking his place back in the queue he glances around the restaurant. Not as full as it was when he first popped his head in at the beginning of the ferry journey, since there's now only half an hour before they dock at Stornoway. Just enough time for a cup of tea. Outside the windows, foam builds on the sea and the sky's a flat grey. His stomach does a somersault (which coincides with the lurch of a wave crashing against the boat) at the thought of the new life he's about to begin. His mind's full of qualms.

He looks around for somewhere to sit while he waits in the queue, since it's always embarrassing to have to wander around searching for a seat when you're carrying a tray. The tables closest to the counter are full but the ones nearer the exit seem to be less crowded. Over there, in the corner. But wait...

*It can't be.*

It is. *It is!* It's Lauren. *Sweet Jesus.* After scanning the streets of Edinburgh the past few weeks and not finding her, she's bloody *here...* on the ferry. Sitting in a booth in the restaurant, engrossed in a book as if she's been waiting for him to look in the right direction all along. His legs tremble – and his hand with the scar – so much that he fears people'll notice he's shaking. He must have gone white as a sheet! Lauren looks different and yet the same – that level of similarity people you once knew always have, even after nearly thirty years. Her hair's shorter and less richly-coloured than he remembers and she looks sort of... heavier. But, oh God, it really *is* Lauren.

*What should he do?*

'Any hot drinks?' He jumps, causing the plate to slide sideways on the tray. The custard croissant launches itself into the air and he catches it just in time. 'Any hot drinks?' the impatient voice says again. He looks back over his shoulder at Lauren, still engrossed in her book. He could take her a mug of tea, place it on the table in front of her and she'd look up from her book and they'd see each other again for the first time in, what is it, about twenty-nine years? And... *we could start again.* Could they start again though, would she even want to – does he?

'Any hot drinks for you – *Sir?*' The look on the girl's face is anything but respectful. He knows he's blushing. The woman behind him, the fat one who tried to push past him, tuts and shakes her head. Maybe it was all meant to be, the breakup of his marriage, seeing Lauren again after he's been thinking of her constantly since arriving back in Scotland. Seeing the real person and not the fantasy he carried in his head for so many years. Maybe he can redeem himself? The scar prickles on the back of his hand.

'Sir, I'm going to have to take that as a no, if you're unable to make up your mind. Other people are waiting to be served.'

*One mug or two?* Should he order a cup of tea for Lauren, and just take it over to her table? *Surprise, it's me!* He sneaks one more glance at her over his shoulder, a shiver running up his spine. *No, I can't.* She might take offence at his presumptuousness, the way she was always prone to. Like the day she scarred his hand, for example. *Don't you think I've managed without you all these years?* She'd say. Not to mention she might have a husband. Could reappear at any moment – that would be awkward! And anyway, with or without a husband... In reality, despite having searched for Lauren for the past fortnight, he sees now that it'd be too painful. Never any sense in raking up the past. He's seen her, just as he wanted to. He's supposed to be moving on now, making a new start. It would be too awkward and embarrassing. That's it, his mind is made up. He's free now, perhaps he'll meet a new woman in time – someone younger, who'll look up to him. Someone without as much emotional baggage as him and Lauren. Lauren looks so... well, older.

'Tea, please,' he says to the assistant, with a pleasant smile. 'Just the one, thank you.' She utters an exasperated sigh as she serves him.

He pays at the till and then worries that Lauren might see him, now he's made his negative decision. What the hell is she doing on this ferry anyway? It was the last thing he expected. He keeps his head down and points himself towards a table in the opposite direction from Lauren. He'll be hidden from her view there, if she should happen to look up from her book. He places the tray on the table, removes a newspaper from the seat before he sits down. *Just one more glance at Lauren.* Holding the newspaper half-over his face, he glances across the room, his eyes hungry for another look at her now he knows it'll be the last. But the table he's sure she was sitting at a moment ago is empty. Even the plate that had been pushed to its furthest edge, gone.

Discombobulated, he picks up his tray again, tucks the paper under his arm and negotiates his way towards the empty table. He slides into the empty seat, as cold as though no-one has ever sat there. He slides his hand over the table's smooth surface. No traces of Lauren.

*He must have imagined it. Got all excited about nothing.*

Phew. But there's disappointment, too. Still, never mind – proceed as planned. Taking a deep breath he unloads the tray and sips the cooling mug of tea. Absently he raises the croissant to his mouth and nibbles, catching the drip of custard with his tongue just in time to save his shirt. He's obviously more stressed than he realised, thinking he actually *saw* Lauren, sitting here in this very seat. He laughs out loud. A child stares at him curiously from another table. And yet, the details of Lauren's appearance were so clear. But she couldn't have moved that quickly, gathered up her book and her bag – taken her empty plate away. She's never been here, he'll have to accept – strange as it seems – that it was stress playing tricks on him.

To take his mind off things, he opens the *Stornoway Gazette* and flicks his way slowly through the pages. His eyes are caught by a photograph staring out at him from the bottom of page four, heading a short article.

He nearly chokes on the remains of the croissant.

---

Staff of the Western Isles Family Services will be planting a tree in the garden of their headquarters today in honour of Lauren Wilson, who was due to take up a position with the team next week. Lauren drowned recently whilst rescuing a young client who had jumped into the Union Canal in Edinburgh. The girl, fourteen-year-old Sheena McGill who is safe and well, paid a tearful tribute to her rescuer at Ms Wilson's funeral, saying, 'I didn't want her to go. She was like a Mammy to me and I will never forget her.'

# 49

*Isle of Lewis, September 2016*

**Murdo and Catriona.**

MURDO CLOSES THE curtains on the last light of the evening. The woman Peggy calls *She who was dropped on her head* has been craning her neck across the field at them all day. Peggy's finally left, having served them the dinner she brought with her from the community centre and then washed all the pots and put them away despite his insistence that he and Catriona were perfectly capable of doing it themselves. 'I've left your favourite cake in a tin on the top shelf,' Peggy called out as she went. 'And there's a new packet of biscuits in the cupboard as well. *Gabh a mhath!*'

Aye. See, you, Peggy. Sooner rather than later, he expects.

Food isn't the only thing she brought with her. Catriona's in her bedroom now, playing with the dog Peggy insisted would be just the thing to bring the troubled girl out of herself. That's all he needs – another mouth to feed. But Cat was overwhelmed when she found out the dog's name is Titania. 'Like in *A Midsummer Night's Dream*, Uncle Murdo. It was Mum's favourite play.' Then she closed her mouth tightly again. But it's a start.

Murdo's sorry about the woman who was due to take up the tenancy of his mother's cottage, but glad he's now able to give his troubled niece the chance of a settled life. It's what his mother wanted, *sith dha h-anam!* He hopes she *will* now rest in peace.

He and Catriona unloaded their boxes this morning and he fitted the wood burning stove he'd made especially for the fireplace in the sitting room. When he went through to the kitchen to wash his hands, he could have sworn he caught a glimpse of his granny, rocking in her old chair by the dining room fireplace. Only a quick flash though. He shakes his head. *Too long a break from work, sorting out all this Catriona business.*

He'll be glad to get the workshop in the garden reorganised and run his business on Lewis again. It was a pain having to travel here from Skye all the time.

Catriona comes into the room with the stout little dog at her heels – a mix of several kinds of terrier, he wouldn't be surprised. Murdo blinks several times. Cat's the spit of her mother at the same age. That long black hair hanging down her back, the black clothes she always wears. The pain hits him in the chest, as always. He couldn't help his little sister and hopes it's not too late to save the girl.

'Got your room sorted?'

She nods. He sees that she's holding a photo, which she hands over to him to examine. 'Where did you find this?'

She swallows and licks her lips before speaking, only recently emerged from her months of self-imposed silence. 'It was on the shelf in my room. I found it when I was putting my box of Mum's things up there.'

He studies the photograph. A young woman with dark brown curls cuddles a baby wrapped in a cream-coloured shawl. She holds the baby against her face. Strange, she's sitting in what looks like Granny's old rocking chair, by a blazing fire, in their dining room. He stares at the image a moment longer before replacing it in Catriona's outstretched hand.

'I don't know who she is. Must be something to do with the

family who rented this house for a while. The ones who went back to London. Maybe a relative of theirs who came here for a visit, that's all I can think of.'

But it leaves him with an uncomfortable feeling in his gut, as if he somehow recognises her. He glances across the room at the mottled mirror on the wall, sees what appears to him a prematurely aged man with dark stubble on his face.

'Nope,' he says aloud, even though Catriona has already walked out of the room with the dog winding in and out of her legs, claws scuttering on the dining room lino.

'Nope, I don't know who she is.'

## Author's Note

The story of The Sea Baby as told by Granny Mary in this novel is adapted from a short story called *The Sea-Baby* by Eleanor Farjeon.

## Acknowledgements

Reading Elisabeth Gifford's *Secrets of the Sea House* inspired me to visit the Outer Hebrides (instead of our planned trip to France) in the summer of 2015. I fell in love with the landscapes of Harris and Lewis, and was moved by them to set Sea Babies there. So thank you, Elisabeth Gifford!

In Sea Babies, Lauren makes her home in a township which I've based on Ardroil in Uig, Lewis. We've stayed there several times in our campervan, at a perfect and unspoilt wild campsite, facing on to the limitless, white sands of Uig Bay. I cannot possibly describe to you how beautiful and elemental it is – you'll need to go there and find out for yourself. The honesty and friendliness of the Islanders is inspiring, and I wanted to evoke this in my novel.

The story of 'The Sea Baby' that Lauren remembers Granny Mary telling her when she was a child, is an interpretation of Eleanor Farjeon's short story of the same title, as chosen by Shirley Hughes in her wonderful edited collection *Mother & Child Treasury*.

My original title for Sea Babies was going to be 'Sixty Seconds', inspired by the 2010 MoMA Marina Abramović performance, *The Artist is Present* in which she stares into the eyes of her former lover for a whole minute, without speaking. I want to thank her for inspiring me to frame the first part of the novel in the way I did.

Thank you to Nick Conroy for the words of his poem *Love in the Cold* that I use as part headings in my book.

Thank you to Uig Museum for allowing me access to the Islands' historical census files, I was fascinated by the repetition of names throughout the generations of families. Thanks also to the Uig Community Centre for their warm welcome and good food.

In the course of my research into historical conditions in the Highlands and Islands during the Clearances and beyond, the following books – in no particular order – proved invaluable: *Go Listen to the Crofters*, A.D. Cameron (2005 Acair Ltd); *The Old Outer Hebrides*, Guthrie Hutton (2011 Stenlake Publishing); *Lewis in History and Legend*, Bill Lawson (2008 Birlinn Ltd); *Heartland* (novel), John Mackay (2015 Luath Press Ltd).

For research on refugees I read *Cast Away* by Charlotte McDonald-Gibson (2016 Portobello Books) and *The New Odyssey* by Patrick Kingsley (2016 Guardian Books). I also quoted from this book. I watched the BBC series of personal documentaries, *Refugee*.

I found the poem *The White Birds* by W.B Yeats in *Best-Loved Yeats, selected by Mairead Ashe Fitzgerald*, and quoted lines of it in my narrative.

Thank you to various readers of my books, including Sharon Booth, Bruford Low, Sarah Carby, Debra Urbacz and Ali Edgley, for their words of encouragement and for believing in me as a novelist.

Thanks to M. and to E. for help with the manuscript, and for all the useful feedback (although rejections!) I received from the plethora of agents I sent it to.

Thanks to Daniel Donson, Events Manager at Waterstones Nottingham, for his unfailing support of my work.

Thanks to Book Connectors and The Book Club (TBC) on Facebook, for knowledge, inspiration and fun conversations to do with the book world.

Thanks to Kelly Lacey of LoveBooksGroup for her help in launching this novel, to Jane Dixon-Smith for her wonderful cover design, and to Phil – in his Wild Pressed Books role – for all his technical work.

Mostly, thanks to Phil and our dogs, Luna and Pixie (and Riley, RIP) for our amazing adventures in the van and all the incredible locations we visit and the characters we meet – without which my books would have less colour and mood. (Lauren's experience with a worker at the ferryport closely reflects one that happened to us – in which we were asked to take a trailer from Leverburgh to Berneray, and leave it in a layby there.)

## Other novels by Tracey Scott-Townsend:

*The Last Time We Saw Marion*

*Inspired Quill 2014*

Meeting author Callum Wilde is the catalyst that turns Marianne Fairchild's fragile sense of identity on its head, evoking demons that will haunt two families.

*'This is a haunting read, enriched by its references to uneasy mother/daughter relationships, to uncertainties around existence... The plot is strongly and carefully crafted with one mystery layered upon another. The settings are well chosen to embody this shifting so that the storyline never lacks atmosphere.'*
Rosalind Minett, Goodreads

*'It's like no other story I've ever read. A ghost story with a living phantom; a heartbreaking tale of grief, separation, obsession, devastation; a story of spirit, family, love.'*
Sharon Booth Goodreads

*'Life. Death. Does reincarnation exist? Do memories of our past bubble under the surface of our consciousness? This novel certainly made me consider my answers to these questions.'*
Claire Hill, Goodreads.

## *Of His Bones*

(sequel to The Last Time We Saw Marion)
   *Inspired Quill 2017*

Of His Bones explores uncertainties around existence, identity and predestination. The characters must come to terms with events in the past that continue to echo in their present, and resolve unfinished issues. Eventually, two families are able to become a coherent whole through a painful progress of interactions which involves losses as well as gains for all of them.

*'Tracey Scott-Townsend crafted a haunting, emotional tale of complicated and difficult relationships within families and how much past events can mark the future.'*
Magdalena, Goodreads

*'A fabulously haunting, atmospheric tale that I couldn't put down.'*
Ange, Goodreads

*'The story kept me gripped from the start and kept me interested throughout. Highly recommended and I will be reading more from Tracey.'*
Kerry, Goodreads

## *The Eliza Doll*

*Wild Pressed Books 2016*

It can be lonely on the road. Ellie has two companions: her dog, Jack, and the mysterious Eliza who turns up in the most unexpected places. At every encounter with Eliza, Ellie feels as if she's standing again in the aching cold of a waterfall in Iceland, the sound of crashing water filling her with dread. Ellie can't change the past. But is it really too late to rectify the bad thing she did when her third child was a baby?

*'Wow. I finished this book and sat and held it for a moment, breath stopped. It was extraordinary. So many layers. So patiently building up to a devastating reveal, one that wasn't tricky or gimmicky, but beautiful, raw, painful and heart-breaking.'*
Louise, Goodreads

*'Ellie's character is both compelling and enigmatic in her earlier years and her continual strength resonates throughout. Raw emotion and traumatic events give the book gravity and presence, whilst the descriptions in Iceland and relationships between some of the characters tenderise it perfectly.'*
Debra, Goodreads

*'Vivid characters, some beautiful description particularly of Iceland, which is such a powerful presence, almost like another character, and Ellie is a wonderful creation.'*
Ali, Goodreads

## *Another Rebecca*

*Wild Pressed Books 2018*
Rebecca Grey can't shake off the hallucination she had while in hospital, but her alcoholic mother Bex is too wrapped up in the 'Great Grief' of her youth to notice her daughter's struggle to define dream from reality.

The two of them lurch from one poverty-stricken situation to another. But why does an old woman she has never met believe she is Rebecca's grandmother, and why did Bex swear to stop living when she was only nineteen?

Another Rebecca is a family story of secrets, interdependency and obsessive love.

*'This is an incredibly well written book with enough emotional suspense to make you want to read it in one sitting.'*
Joanne Cartwright, Goodreads

*'The stark narrative of this novel is coloured in with beautiful, poetic imagery.'*
Sharon Booth, Author and Book Blogger

# The Vagabond Mother

*Read on for the first chapter of Tracey Scott-Townsend's next gripping, emotional novel*

Out with Wild Pressed Books in January 2020

# Maya

*Melbourne, November 2014*

## *Identification*

Somebody brought them pale, sweet tea. Not exactly hot. Maya wondered how many corridors the tray had been carried down before reaching them. The remains of their family each held a cup between their shaking hands. 'But I don't take sugar,' said Lola. Her eyes looked enormous to Maya, bewildered. Just like when she was a toddler and the health visitor had given her a sugar cube after a vaccination. The sugar in her tea would no more take away her pain now than the cube had done then.

A woman – a nurse, perhaps – spoke to Lola in a gentle voice. 'You ought to drink the tea, darl. It'll help with the shock.'

Maya saw Daisy encouraging her twin by taking the first sip. It was always Daisy's mouth Maya had aimed for first with the feeding spoon when they were babies, as Lola would copy her sister. On Maya's other side sat a white-faced man whom she recognised as her husband. Con's hand lifted a cup to his lips in a mechanical sort of way and brown liquid leaked down his chin. Maya found that she had taken hot tea into her own mouth. She watched her hand reflecting Con's movements.

'Are you ready, Sir?' The officer reappeared in the room, directing his question at Maya's husband. 'Yes.' Con placed his cup somewhere to one side. He stood but his body immediately collapsed back onto the chair. He tried again.

'Where are you going?' Maya surprised herself with the loudness of her voice. She snapped her mouth shut.

'Madam, forgive me,' said the officer. *What the hell for, he hadn't killed her son, had he?* 'I'm taking your husband to identify the body.'

The book, Joe's precious book, fell from her lap as she jumped to her feet, the cup in her waving hand slopping liquid. She yelped at the sight of outspread pages on the floor. The nurse picked the book up, closed the covers and handed it back to Maya with practised tenderness, gently removing the half-empty cup from her trembling fingers.

'There you are, darl.'

Maya clutched Joe's journal to her chest with one hand and reached with her other towards Con. 'I'm coming with you,' she said. 'You're not going without me.'

'Madam, I...'

'Let her come.' Con spoke in a distant voice. 'She's the boy's mother. We're in this together.' He reached for her with a trembling arm.

'But Sir, it's not... the water, you know.'

'She's strong enough,' Con allowed his chin to rise. 'We both are. We're in this together, aren't we, darling?' He tugged gently on her arm and together they made a move towards the door.

After a few steps Maya stopped and took a shuddering breath. Turning back, she beckoned the nurse with a hand which wouldn't quite straighten from its former claw-like grasp of the book. When she opened her mouth to speak, words at first refused to emerge. But she tried again and eventually shuffled the words on her lips until she could get them organised. 'Will you give this to my daughters to look after, please?'

The nurse nodded and came forward. She carried Joe's journal like a crown back to the twins. Placing her cup on the chair next to her, Daisy accepted the book. Lola unravelled the scarf from her neck and offered it in her two hands to Daisy, like an open shawl for a baby. Daisy placed the book in the folds of the shawl and wrapped it tightly. With the book on Daisy's lap, both girls laid a hand on it. Maya felt her mouth practising the shape of a smile, aimed at her daughters. Turning her head stiffly back to face forward, she shuffled her feet a few more steps through the doorway. Con took her arm again.

It was cold in the pale-painted lobby. Con and Maya waited before an internal window while the officer entered the room behind it. A white-sheeted figure lay on a bed, the face covered. Maya and Con grasped each other's hands. Maya could see that Con's jaw was clenched as tightly as hers and she made an effort to loosen her muscles. They should be smiling, she and Con. When they uncovered his face, Joe would want to see his parents smiling. An attendant stood on Maya's other side, perhaps ready to catch her if she fainted.

*Pause, breathe.* She focussed on Con, who had turned to her. She delved into him with her eyes. The moment stretched. *Do you trust me? I trust you.* Their favourite line from a film back in the eighties. Then they both returned their searching gazes to the window.

'Ready?' asked the attendant at Maya's side. Maya replied yes as firmly as she could. The attendant nodded at the officer behind the glass, who folded the sheet back with touching courtesy.

He'd been right about the distortion from the water but it wasn't too bad, not really. He was still no more than a boy. Someone had brushed his lightish hair. His beard was so much thicker than when Maya had seen it on their last video call and the person must have brushed that too – it could never have come out of the water that neat. Maya considered the poignancy of the hairdresser's job – or whomever had to perform that task. The boy's eyes were closed of course. Something swayed beside Maya, while her feet had taken root in the tiled floor. The swaying thing was like a tree in a gale: indeed, a wind seemed to be blowing down the corridor towards them. She felt hair lifting from her neck. But when she looked up she saw that the swaying tree on her right – sighing along with the wind in its branches – was in fact her husband. It was only Con, the breath from his lungs rising to a musical note of pain.

## About the Author

Tracey is the author of four previous novels and is also a poet. She has performed at Hull's Freedom Festival and in many local open mic settings. She won an Apples and Snakes commission for Deranged Poetesses: 'Maidens' at ARC Stockton in March 2018.

As a Visual Artist, Tracey's narrative work utilises digital photography and moving image as a starting point. Drawings, mixed media paintings and delicate 3D work made from materials such as tissue paper and muslin, (and now the Apple Pencil) are inspired by the emotions of her own experiences and perceptions.

She has a Fine Art MA (University of Lincoln) and a BA Hons Visual Studies (Humberside Polytechnic). She has exhibited throughout the UK (as Tracey Scott) and initiated several independent artist led projects with diverse groups of people within the community, schools and residential homes.

Lightning Source UK Ltd.
Milton Keynes UK
UKHW011948290419
341806UK00001B/9/P